"You haven't heard the news then," said Susan, taking a tiny sip of coffee.

"What news?" said Jane cautiously.

Maggie looked over at Kari, who was being served her lopsided cake. Before Elliot was able to safely set the plate down in front of her, Kari stood up, knocking into his arm and sending the dish crashing to the floor. Without looking at anyone, she turned and bolted out of the room.

"What's going on here?" asked Jane. "Is someone going to tell me or is it a big secret?"

Maggie cleared her throat, trying to form just the right words in her mind. Before she could say anything, Susan answered. "It's not a secret anymore, Jane. It seems our little girl wonder was, in reality, a queer."

"What?" said Jane, involuntarily sucking in her breath. Astonishment froze on her face.

"You never knew her, Susan," said Maggie, barely controlling her rage. I for one don't appreciate your tone or the name calling."

"I'm just calling a spade a spade." Susan took another tiny sip of coffee.

Also by Ellen Hart:

VITAL LIES
STAGE FRIGHT
A KILLING CURE

HALLOWED MURDER

Ellen Hart

BALLANTINE BOOKS • NEW YORK

Copyright © 1989 by Ellen Hart

All rights reserved under International and Pan-American Copyright Conventions. Published in the United States of America by Ballantine Books, a division of Random House, Inc., New York, and simultaneously in Canada by Random House of Canada Limited, Toronto.

No part of this book may be reproduced in any form, except for the quotation of brief passages in reviews, without prior permission from The Seal Press, 3131 Western Avenue Suite 410, Seattle, Washington 98121.

This is a work of fiction and any resemblance to events or persons living or dead is unintentional and purely coincidental.

Library of Congress Catalog Card Number: 89-34275

ISBN 0-345-38140-8

This edition published by arrangement with The Seal Press

Manufactured in the United States of America

First Ballantine Books Edition: September 1993

For Kathy

Acknowledgments

Many thanks to Roseann Lloyd for her wonderful energy and support, and especially for her assistance in introducing this book to Barbara Wilson and The Seal Press. And also, my thanks to Claire Lewis for reading the manuscript at an extremely rough point and still finding those all-important positive comments. And most especially, my sincere thanks to Kathy Kruger for her critical judgment, humor, and patience. Her delight in reading each new chapter was a continual source of encouragement.

CAST OF CHARACTERS

CORDELIA THORN: Artistic Director of the Allen Grimby Theatre in St. Paul; old friend of Jane Lawless.

JANE LAWLESS: Restaurant owner; sorority alumni advisor for KAS.*

ALLISON LORD: Social chair at KAS; sister of Edwin Lord; daughter of Adam Lord.

ORVILLE TREVELYAN: Detective, Minneapolis Police Department.

MAGGIE CHRISTOPHERSON: House manager of KAS; friend of Allison Lord.

SIGRID MUNSON: House president of KAS; friend of Allison Lord.

EMILY ANDERSON: Graduate student, University of Minnesota; friend of Allison Lord.

EDITH HOLMS: House mother at KAS.

MITCHEL PAGE: University of Minnesota student; busboy at KAS.

ADOLPH MAUER: Cook at KAS.

ELLIOT KRATAGER: Busboy at KAS; University of Minnesota student; member of student government.

SUSAN JULIAN: Alumni advisor at KAS.

KARI BERGSTROM: Rituals chair at KAS; friend of Allison Lord.

CLARENCE AND BERTHA ANDERSON: Parents of Emily Anderson.

ADAM AND MURIEL LORD: Allison and Edwin's father and stepmother.

EDWIN LORD: Allison Lord's brother.

JAMIE MCGRAW: Mitchel Page's girlfriend; member of KAS.

GLADYS BAILEY: Housekeeper at KAS.

BROOK SOLOMON: New pledge at KAS.

PETER LAWLESS: Jane's younger brother; cameraman at WTWN-TV.

BETH MCGRAW: Jamie's younger sister.

*KAS—Kappa Alpha Sigma Sorority.

PART ONE

A Seed of Falsehood

Against whom do ye sport yourselves? Against whom make ye a wide mouth, and draw out the tongue? Are ye not children of transgression, a seed of falsehood . . . slaying the children in the valleys . . .

Isaiah 57:4

1

The dark figure moved quickly along the wooded path. It was unusually cold even for a November night in Minneapolis. The bitter rain that had begun falling about an hour ago had cleared the path of any who might still be hanging around. No one had seen them. And what was the difference if they had? It was only a matter of time now before the truth came out. People like her should be exposed for what they really were. What kind of world was it when someone could commit a filthy act and not be ashamed? What was it she had said? Something about not living on her knees any longer before somebody's warped image of God. What did that mean? There was no point in trying to understand her. She would get what she deserved now. Punishment was waiting.

2

"This is the worst idea you've ever had. I can't possibly see that my health is any business of yours." Cordelia Thorn was puffing up a sweat as she strained to keep up with her old and considerably thinner friend, Jane. "And if you tell me one more time that I'm a big baby, I'll stop right here in the middle of the path, sit down, and weep. Loudly."

"When did I ever call you a big baby?" asked Jane a little too politely. "It's possible I did say something about diapers. . . ."

"Very funny." Cordelia's glance could have spawned a tornado. She was not in a good mood.

"You know what I think, Cordelia?"

"Should I prepare myself for another pearl of wisdom?"

"I think you should calm down. A morning walk in the park is supposed to be exhilarating. Relaxing."

"Relaxing! My idea of relaxation does not include sweating." Cordelia slowed her pace. If Jane wanted to continue barreling ahead, fine. She could carry on her conversation with the trees.

"All right, then. It will improve your appetite. Your digestive juices."

Cordelia snorted. "In case you haven't bothered to look at me in the last fifteen years, I *have* no problem with my appetite!"

She is a big baby, thought Jane.

For the last week, Cordelia had consented to accompany her old friend on several early morning walks around a part of Lake of the Isles in south Minneapolis. It was beginning to strain their otherwise solid friendship. It had begun as a simple invitation. One evening, several weeks ago, Jane had merely mentioned that Cordelia was looking a bit pale. They had been bagging up dry leaves in a mutual friend's backyard at the time. She had suggested that Cordelia might like to join her for a brisk morning walk sometime soon. The exercise would do her good. The fresh air would invigorate her. And the beauty of nature would be an inspiration. It had been a mistake.

Cordelia Thorn was a large woman in her middle thirties. She was taller and more opinionated than most of the women she had ever dated. Her largeness was compounded by a vast manner and an even vaster voice. Jane had thought for years that the theatre was the perfect profession for her because it was one of the few environments that easily held someone with such a strong personality. Elsewhere, Cordelia was apt to seem an exaggeration. And today, she was in rare form.

The two had first met each other in high school. Cordelia had recently moved from Boston, and Jane had spent the last two years living with her aunt and uncle in England. Since both knew so few people in St. Paul, their outsider status had brought them together. The fact that they both came out to each other almost immediately only served to cement their relationship. And they found they both enjoyed many of the same things. Photography. The theatre. And of course, food. Throughout college they had remained close friends even though Jane made the hideous mistake—according to Cordelia—of joining a sorority. Cordelia hoped that it would be a temporary aberration, much as Jane's flirtation with the writings of Ayn Rand had been in high school. When it became apparent that membership in a sorority was going to become a permanent situation, Cordelia sniffed her disgust but remained steadfast in friendship.

And now, many years later, Jane was the owner of a successful restaurant in south Minneapolis, and Cordelia had recently accepted the position of artistic director at the prestigious Allen Grimby Repertory Company in St. Paul. It had been years of hard work for both of them, but through it all they still found time to remain close.

Up ahead, an old stone bridge appeared rising out of the morning fog. Had they actually walked *that* far? This was a new record.

"Unless I am allowed to sit down soon, the paramedics will have to be summoned." Cordelia leaned on Jane's shoulder.

"You'd like that, wouldn't you," said Jane. She stuck her elbow into Cordelia's ribs and laughed. "An audience to appreciate your agony."

They slowed their pace and walked off the footpath over to a bench near the shore. The bridge now stood about one hundred feet from them. Even though it was extremely narrow with treacherously low sides, it had become a landmark from which everyone enjoyed the lake. Both Jane and Cordelia had come here often during college just to relax and feed the ill-tempered geese who roamed the area. The water which flowed underneath the old bridge was deep and dark. To Jane, the bridge had always seemed like something out of a fairy tale. She could easily imagine a troll or a little old man with a long white beard guarding its entrance and exit.

On this gray November morning, Jane's two little dogs bobbed along beside them tugging at their leashes and straining to be allowed to run to the edge of the cold, foggy bank.

"You might as well let them run around by themselves for a bit," said Cordelia. "I need to rest." She unzipped her jacket and sat down. The early morning mist had settled around the base of the old bridge, making it appear to float above the water. It looked like a stage set. A perfect setting for a murder. Cordelia shuddered at her own morbidity. Get a grip. This is just an average fall day with ordinary foreboding mists.

"Say, I've got a great idea," announced Cordelia. "Why don't you come over to the theatre tonight? The show we're doing right now is admittedly awful but you never know, you might have a great time hating it. I'll get you front row seats. I'm glad," she added, "that this show was a bomb. I predicted it. I never personally considered the play worthy of attention, let alone production. It was scheduled before I took over as artistic director. The playwright is a bore. And the play is a bore. Father and child.''

Jane clapped her hands and whistled. The dogs seemed to have vanished under the bridge. ''Thanks for the invitation, but I'm afraid I'll have to take a rain check. Every Monday night I have to attend the formal dinner of Kappa Alpha Sigma. Remember? I told you that I had volunteered to be one of the alumni advisors there this year.''

Cordelia visibly stiffened. ''I had forgotten,'' she said, brushing a piece of lint off her pants with great distaste. ''Pardon my ignorance, but I *had* hoped that when we graduated, your temporary foray into the ranks of the terminally trite would end.'' She straightened her jacket with disgust.

''It seems to me that we've had this little conversation a hundred times before.'' Why did Cordelia have to become so tediously insulting every time Jane mentioned her old sorority? She took a deep breath. ''You've made your position admirably clear. One might almost say pristine. I agree that some of these young women are perhaps a bit overindulged . . .''

''A bit!'' Cordelia was turning an unbecoming shade of purple.

''Look, when I was in college, I enjoyed the community that living in a sorority offered. If there *had* been a lesbian sorority, like there is now, I would have joined that. But there wasn't. And if you must know, I now want to give my old house the benefit of some of *my* acquired wisdom.''

''Your *wisdom*?''

''So to speak, yes.''

''I see. Then this is a noble cause. A crusade of sorts. Perhaps you see yourself as a kind of Peace Corps volunteer, bringing civilization to this rather primitive enclave of right-wing ideology.''

Jane shook her head.

''I will make a prediction, Janey. You may have the best of intentions, but I'll wager if you speak your values too loudly over there in that bastion of twelfth-century thought, you won't last a month. Don't forget, *you've* changed from the eighteen-year-old who enjoyed all the fun and games but never once let any of them know who you *really* were. Just remember what I've said. Now, not to change the subject too abruptly, but wasn't I promised a large breakfast at the end of this morning's trudge?''

"Absolutely," grinned Jane, thankful for the change of subject. "See how your appetite has improved!" She glanced down at her watch. "One little problem does come to mind, however. My restaurant doesn't open for over an hour."

Cordelia teetered on the edge of another sulk. "God, is it really that early? No wonder this place is deserted. Most people have the brains they were born with. Well," she added, brightening a bit, "I vote we head back to the car. I might even be inspired to run. No, I take that back. We can clean up at your place and be ready for one of those incredible breakfasts at the stroke of eight."

They both stood up and began to clap and whistle for the dogs.

"Don't you think this is kind of strange?" said Jane, straining to see them in the brush. "They always come when they're called. Well, maybe Gulliver doesn't, but Bean always does." She bent down and grabbed the two leashes. "I'll be back in a minute," she yelled as she steamed off toward the bridge. Cordelia sat back down on the hard bench. Why don't they put cushions on these things? There was no use in both of them going. Besides, she'd had enough walking this last week to last her a lifetime. Tugging absently at her drooping auburn curls, she knew for certain that she would look like she'd spent the night in a sauna. With a roller derby queen.

She stretched her body, hands over her head, and looked up into the trees. It was that strange kind of fall day when the dampness caused the air to feel warm and cold at the same time. It was going to be mild later in the morning after the sun had burned off all the mist. And yet, in her bones, she could feel that the good weather they had been having would not last out the week.

Jane was certainly taking her time. Cordelia stood, attempting to see if anyone was stirring over near the bridge. Nothing. Sitting back down, she let her mind stray to warm scones and hot tea with lemon waiting for her at The Lyme House. Jane's restaurant was civilized. Linen and fresh flowers. Nothing trendy. And certainly not politically correct fern food. Normally, Cordelia never got up early enough to even *have* breakfast. She might as well take advantage of the occasion.

At last! Out of the corner of her eye she noticed Jane making her way slowly out from under the bridge. Both dogs raced ahead and jumped without invitation into her lap. Ugh! They were all wet! She brushed them off, not without a small comment on their general intelligence. Jane approached and sat down unsteadily on the edge of the bench.

"Something's wrong, isn't it?" asked Cordelia. "Ever since we sat down here I've felt it." She reached over and put her arm around Jane, feeling her body shiver convulsively. "What is it?"

Jane cleared her throat, not certain how her voice would sound. "We've got to call the police. I found a body under the bridge. It's a young woman. I'm afraid she's dead."

Instantly, Cordelia could feel her own body begin to quake.

"It took me a minute to find the dogs. I suppose they went under the bridge as soon as they caught the scent. She was facedown in the water by the shore. I pulled her out and laid her on the bank." Jane paused. The stillness in the air made her words sound unnaturally loud. "I know her. She belongs to the sorority. Her name is Allison Lord." For some reason she found it important to say the name out loud. A kind of benediction perhaps. Abruptly, she stood and looked around. "You stay here with the dogs. Don't let anyone go down there. I'm going to find a phone and call the police. I'll be back as soon as I can." Without another word, Jane headed back along the path they had come.

3

Detective Orville Trevelyan sat at his desk studying the file on Allison Lord. Someone from the Hennepin County Medical Examiner's office had pulled her out of Lake of the Isles earlier in the morning. Nothing certain was known as yet about the cause of death, but the time of death had been tentatively placed at between eight and ten P.M. on the night of November the ninth. Last night. The autopsy would be performed later in the day. No obvious marks were found on the body. On the face of it, it looked like a simple drowning. Trevelyan had been on the police force for over twenty years and knew things were rarely simple. It was an odd night to have been over at the lake. He recalled taking his toy schnauzer out around nine. It was not a night for a pleasant stroll.

Sergeant Meeker poked his balding head inside the chief's door and announced that the woman who had discovered the body was waiting outside. Trevelyan asked to have her shown in.

The officer at the scene had reported that a Miss Jane Lawless had found the body at approximately six forty-five A.M. She had been walking with a friend, a Miss Cordelia Thorn. Trevelyan thought he recognized the second name. It was not a pleasant memory. Curiously, Miss Lawless had said she knew the deceased.

The door opened and a tall woman with long chestnut hair and unusually deep violet eyes entered. Trevelyan thought to himself that she was a handsome woman. A little windblown perhaps, but elegant in her own way. A young man entered behind her and sat down at a small table in the back of the room. He opened his pad and nodded to the detective. Jane took a chair opposite Trevelyan.

"Thank you for coming down, Miss Lawless. I'm Detective Orville Trevelyan. I've been assigned to this case." He studied her for a moment. She looked vaguely familiar, but he couldn't place her. "First, I'd like to begin by asking you just why you were at Lake of the Isles at such an early hour this morning?"

Jane looked around at the young man taking notes. She had never been interrogated by the police before and did not like her words being cast in stone on some stenographer's pad. She had expected the first question, and responded easily. "I often go for early morning walks, and that particular lake is one of my favorite spots."

"I see," said Trevelyan, checking his notes. "It says here that you own a restaurant in Minneapolis."

"That's right," said Jane. "The Lyme House. It's on the south shore of Lake Harriet. I've owned it for the last eight years."

"I understand you knew the deceased. I wonder if you'd mind telling me what you know about her?" Trevelyan wrote something down in his notes.

As he was writing, Jane took her wire-rimmed glasses out of the old backpack she was carrying. She wanted to be able to see more clearly the man who was asking her these questions. Trevelyan seemed to be nothing like Cordelia had described. What had she called him? A wild moose? Leave it to Cordelia. Her midwestern metaphors were getting out of hand. "Yes, I knew her. She belonged to a sorority at the University of Minnesota, Kappa Alpha Sigma, of which I am an alumna. I graduated in 1974. I've recently been volunteering some time as an advisor to the executive board. Allison was also a member of that board. I'm not absolutely certain, but I believe she was the social chair. I've only attended four meetings, but Allison was at each of them. I really know little about her personally."

Trevelyan found her low voice appealing. She sounded intelligent. And Orville Trevelyan was a man who understood faces and voices. She did not have an accent exactly, though the inflection wasn't entirely Minnesotan. "I see. And do you have any reason to believe she might have had enemies?"

"No, not really."

"Did she seem depressed to you?"

"Does that mean you think this might be a suicide?"

"Do you think it was?"

"No. I mean, I don't have any particular reason to believe that. I guess I thought you might have found some kind of evidence to suggest some reason for her death."

"Actually, we haven't." Trevelyan leaned back in his chair. "Of course, there are only a few possible ways she could have ended up in that lake. It might have been an accident. And then yes, it could have been a suicide, although we found no note. Of course, there is always a third possibility."

Jane slowly nodded her head. He did not have to spell it out.

"You haven't answered my question, Miss Lawless. Did you think she was depressed in any way?"

All morning Jane had been thinking back over the few conversations she'd had with Allison. Nothing seemed to suggest anything unusual. "On the contrary, she seemed unusually happy. She'd just come back from a summer in England. I recall we talked about that quite a bit since I've also spent a good deal of my life there. Allison had apparently had a wonderful time."

Of course, thought Trevelyan, England. That's the slight inflection I'm hearing in her voice. "Yes, I understand she'd been over there. Do you know someone named Emily Anderson?"

Jane thought for a moment. She ran quickly through the names of the young women she had met at the sorority. It didn't sound familiar. "No, not that I recall. Who is she?"

Trevelyan closed the file on his desk. "We found Miss Lord's purse just off the footpath a few yards from the bridge.

There was a letter inside from Emily to Allison. She had apparently accompanied Miss Lord on her trip to England last summer. The letter was written after they had returned. About two months ago. Miss Lord was visiting her father in Philadelphia at the time."

"And?" said Jane. "Did the letter indicate any problem?"

"I suppose it's all in how you want to look at it." Trevelyan stood up. "Thank you for your time. If you think of anything else, even if it doesn't seem all that important, please give me a call. I'll be going over to the sorority later in the day to inform them personally about what has happened. Your statement will be typed and we'll need you to come down and sign it later today."

Jane assumed she was being dismissed. Trevelyan's response to her last question was irritating. Perhaps it was his style, but half answers always annoyed her. "May I call you later to find out the results of the autopsy?" She took off her glasses and carefully put them in the case before rising and meeting his eyes straight on. "I didn't know Allison well, but I did like her. After finding her this morning, I feel I need to understand what really happened last night."

It finally dawned on Trevelyan who this woman resembled so closely. Ignoring her question, he walked around the desk and sat down on the edge. "I wonder if you'd mind answering just one more question. It's personal. Off the record." He paused, studying her a moment longer. "Are you any relation to Raymond Lawless, the defense attorney?"

Jane narrowed her eyes with growing impatience. "Yes," she admitted finally. "He's my father."

"I thought so," said Trevelyan, smiling ever so slightly. "You look quite a lot like him. I've known your father professionally for many years. We haven't always been on the same side, but I've always respected him. He's a fine man."

"Thanks," said Jane. "I agree with you. Now, will you answer *my* question?"

"Of course," said Trevelyan calmly. "Please feel free to call me whenever you like. I'll give you any information that I can."

4

In a room strewn with clothes, books and an inordinate amount of dirty dishes and assorted junk, Maggie Christopherson searched desperately for a paper on personality disorders she had written last week for her psychology class. She was almost positive she'd seen it underneath an empty bag of caramel corn next to her wastebasket. Thankfully, the report did not have the capacity to crawl somewhere on its own and hide. Perhaps she'd taken it with her to the library last Saturday morning, in which case it would be in her geography notes. Now where were they?

"Hey Christopherson! You got a phone call." Sigrid Munson's voice bellowed from the hall outside her room.

Maggie opened the door and reluctantly peered out. It was going to be another dreary Monday morning. Her hair was a mess and her best jeans were smashed underneath the typewriter. Even though Maggie was a third year psychology major and the new house manager at Kappa Alpha Sigma, she had more than a slight problem with organization. "Just a minute," she yelled as she rummaged through the pillows and blankets in a heap on her bed, looking for her robe. Too bad she couldn't wear a sleeping bag. She knew where *that* was. "Who's calling, Siggy? Did they say?" This was going to be a lousy time for a phone conversation. She had to keep it short. Her first class would be starting in less than an hour. Unfortunately, it was on West Bank. That meant a twenty minute walk unless she could bum a ride.

"I think she said her name was Emily," yelled Sigrid, the newly elected chapter president, who also had the misfortune to room right next to the second floor phone. Normally, someone was assigned to phone duty. This morning, however, everyone was still in bed after last night's homecoming party at Sigma Nu. Just as the slogan suggested, everyone had partied till they puked. Sigrid had no particular interest in tiptoeing around so that the rest of the house could sleep. If *she* could get up, *they* could get up. She burst out of her door singing a country-western song in a high hiccup, headed for the bathroom. "Hey Maggs, if you're going over to West Bank, meet me downstairs in twenty minutes. I'm driving." She disappeared into the doorway.

Maggie raced down the hall. Do I know someone named Emily? She squeezed into the phone closet and closed the door slightly. "Hi, can I help you?"

"Maggie! I'm so glad you're there." The voice was unfamiliar. "You may not remember me. We've only met once. Ally Lord introduced us a couple of weeks ago. Do you recall? She and I were having dinner at the Campus Grill and you came over to talk to her about something. Please say you remember! It's terribly important." The breathy voice spoke quickly, almost as if she feared Maggie might hang up on her.

Maggie did remember that night. She recalled a pale young woman. Blonde. Large soulful eyes, and terribly shy. She had not said very much when they were introduced. "Yes, I remember you. I think Ally said you were a graduate student. English lit I believe."

"Yes! That's right. You have a good memory!" Emily's reactions seemed excessive. It was obvious something was wrong. "I was wondering. Have you seen Ally this morning? She had an appointment last night and was supposed to call me afterward. I haven't heard from her, and I'm getting a little worried." There was an almost hysterical edge to her voice.

Maggie was certain that Emily was overreacting. Yet it *was* strange that she hadn't seen Allison at the homecoming party last night. Allison said she would be there no later than nine. "Hold on a minute. I'll check her room." She laid down the phone and ran to the opposite end of the house. Allison's room was in the old north wing. She knocked on the door. No answer. She tried to open it and found it unlocked. Inside, the room was empty. Neat as usual. The bed was made and a single red rose rested in a thin vase on her desk. Either Ally hadn't slept here last night or she had already left for morning classes. Maggie closed the door gently and ran back to the phone. "No, she's not in her room. I know she doesn't have a nine-fifteen on Monday. My guess is she stayed elsewhere last night. She's been doing that a lot lately. I'm afraid I don't know where she goes when she's not here, but I don't think there's anything to worry about. Do you want to leave a message?"

There was silence on the other end.

"Are you still there?" asked Maggie.

"Yes," said Emily almost inaudibly. Another uneasy silence. "Maggie, did you know that Ally was going to talk with Mitchel Page last night? She was supposed to meet him at Ernie's Bar at seven."

"Yes, I knew that. I talked to her yesterday afternoon just after she made the date. How did you know about that?"

"I spent several hours with her yesterday. She left from my apartment to go see him. I didn't want her to go. I don't trust him! We had kind of a fight about it."

Maggie could tell Emily was on the verge of tears. Maybe even a breakdown. Her voice was thick with worry.

"I don't know where to look for her. I don't know what to do! Why hasn't she called!"

"Really Emily, I don't think you should worry. I know Mitch. He's been a busboy here for a couple of years. He's not one of my favorite people, but he isn't a bad guy. You probably know he and Allison were dating last year. Maybe they went back to his room at Selby Hall."

"No! She wouldn't do that!"

Before Maggie could respond, the receiver clicked on the other end. Emily had hung up. Isn't that charming, she thought coldly. How on earth was *she* supposed to know where Ally was every minute? Obviously, there were a lot of

things Ally wasn't telling her anymore. And anyway, there
was no time to think about it now. She had to get back to her
room and find that psychology report. Emily would just have
to wait until Ally called her. I mean really, thought Maggie,
she's acting like a jilted lover.

Ten minutes later, having ignored the frayed reflection in
her mirror, Maggie entered the dining room hoping to have
just enough time to grab a glass of orange juice before Sigrid
was ready to leave. Maybe a little vitamin C would help her
headache.

As she approached the juice machine, she spied Edith
Holms, the housemother, talking to a policeman in the back
of the room. Not again, she thought, shaking her head in
amazement. Not another theft.

Since the beginning of fall term, two thefts had occurred
in the house. The first had been during the second week of
classes. Someone had taken a very expensive camera and
gadget bag out of the coatroom. The young woman who had
recently received them as gifts from her parents had threatened to quit the sorority unless everything was returned to
her immediately. The executive board had voted to handle it
within the house. No police would be called. Then, two
weeks later, during dinner this time, someone had taken an
emerald pendant out of one of the bedrooms on the second
floor. Mrs. Holms had insisted on calling the police. But
once again, the executive board overruled the idea. There
would be *no* police. The board members themselves would
see to it that the thief was found and punished.

Maggie poured herself a glass of juice and leaned against
the counter, watching Edith talk quietly to the policeman.
There would be hell to pay if she had called in the police
without first talking to Sigrid. Any kind of decision, especially one that affected the entire house, had to be cleared
with the president before any action could be taken. This was
not Edith's usual style. Normally, she would huff around and
pout openly, but rarely did she take any direct action.

Maggie was surprised to see Edith motioning for her.

Thankfully, the dining room was empty. No one would be around to witness Edith's folly. Maggie laid her books down next to the juice machine and wove her way through the tables until she reached the back of the room.

"Maggie," said Mrs. Holms, drawing her close, "this is Sergeant Ramsey of the Minneapolis Police Department." Was it just her imagination, or did Mrs. Holms look like she'd been crying? It was hard to tell since she often looked teary. Edith was the kind of woman who continually talked of being hurt by things other people said and did. It was an odd way to define anger, thought Maggie. "Sergeant Ramsey, this is our house manager, Maggie Christopherson."

She shook his hand.

The sergeant was a tall man with cottony gray hair and deeply set red-rimmed eyes. It never ceased to amaze Maggie how large men grew. Kind of like a succulent little summer squash that had been allowed to grow wild into a ten-pound monster and then ended up by being used as a door stop in the garage. Ramsey's uniform was tight around his body, making him look neglected and lumpy.

"The sergeant arrived just a few minutes ago," said Edith, her voice quavering. She fluttered her eyes at him, desperately hoping he would take over the conversation.

He nodded to Maggie and rested his hand over his gun. "I'm sorry, Miss Christopherson. I've come with some bad news."

He doesn't look sorry, thought Maggie.

"We pulled one of your members out of Lake of the Isles earlier this morning."

"What?" said Maggie. "What does that mean?"

"I believe her name was," he checked his pad, "Allison Lord. It looks like she died sometime last evening."

"Died?" Maggie struggled to make sense of the man's words. Her mind suddenly felt like it was swimming in thick syrup. "Ally? Dead? I don't believe you!"

"Sergeant, Maggie was very close to Allison." Edith rested a heavy hand on Maggie's shoulder. "I feel like we all were."

Maggie clenched her teeth and looked up at the officer. "How did it happen?"

"We don't know that yet, miss. It looks like a drowning. It's impossible to say more than that right now." He paused. "You don't suppose she could have gone in there for a swim, do you? I mean, as some kind of lark? Or maybe a dare? I know these sororities and fraternities do some crazy things now and then." He glanced at Mrs. Holms for support.

"No," said Maggie. "Not possible."

"Why is that, miss?"

"Because she couldn't swim. She was terrified of water." Maggie's voice was flat. Her mouth felt stiff.

"I see," scowled the sergeant, looking at his watch. "We'll probably have more specific information for you later. In the meantime, we've got to notify her parents. I wonder if one of you could find their address and phone number for me. It would save us some time."

"Yes, certainly," said Mrs. Holms, glad to have something to do. "I'll get it for you immediately." She walked off, dabbing at her eyes with a linen handkerchief.

Maggie and the sergeant stood waiting, each silently examining the other. The policeman spoke first. "So, you and Miss Lord were good friends."

"Yes," said Maggie, folding her arms protectively in front of her. "We both started at the university three years ago." This was ridiculous. Her best friend had just died, and she had to stand here and make small talk with Mr. Sensitivity. "We roomed together last year."

"Did you!" He looked her up and down.

Was that a particularly fascinating fact? thought Maggie. A clue of some kind?

Sergeant Ramsey looked appraisingly around the dining room. "Must be kind of a swinging place."

"What the hell do you mean by that!" She caught the slur, she just wasn't sure what he meant by it. Before he could answer, Mrs. Holms returned with the information.

"Thank you," said the sergeant. "Someone will be coming out later today from the department to ask all of you a few questions.'' He nodded to Mrs. Holms and then smirked ever so slightly at Maggie. Before he left, he took one last look around the room.

"Obnoxious man," said Maggie watching the door close behind him.

"Oh, did you think so, dear? Under the circumstances, I thought he was rather nice.''

You could always count on Edith Holms for an accurate character appraisal.

5

Emily sat rigidly in her chair, the air sour with her own fear.

"So, Miss Anderson, you say that you knew Allison Lord for almost a year?" Detective Trevelyan sat thumping a pencil against the top of his desk.

Emily wondered if this was an attempt to rattle her. If it was, it was working. "Yes, we met at a mutual friend's house last Thanksgiving." Why the overly polite manner? Was it her imagination, or did he seem to be enjoying this? Don't tell him any more than he asks for. Don't give him any reason to suspect.

"Would you say you were close friends during the past year?"

"Not at first. But later I guess you could say we became close." Her mouth twitched.

Trevelyan wrote something down in his notes. "You say that she left your apartment last night around six-thirty. Do you know where she was going?" Trevelyan had learned long ago to recognize fear. And he knew how to use it.

"Yes. She went to talk to Mitchel Page. He's also a student over at the university, and a busboy at Kappa Alpha Sigma. Allison was a member there. If you want, I can get his address for you."

Trevelyan shook his head. "Go on."

"Well, she was supposed to meet him at Ernie's Bar at seven. She had dated him last year, but they broke up in the spring." Emily hesitated. "I have no idea what happened after that."

Trevelyan paged through his notes. "Yes. Mitchel Page. Do you know him personally?"

"I've met him a couple of times." Emily looked at her pale hands. The fluorescent lights made her skin look ill. Just how much did she dare say about what she knew? "As I think about it, I guess there is something you should know about him. I realize this may sound kind of strong, but I think he could be a dangerous person. I mean, I'm not saying he had anything to do with her death, but then, he did have a violent temper."

"And have you seen him express this temper?"

"No. Not exactly. That is, not personally. But Allison told me about several incidents."

"Do you have any reason to believe Mr. Page had anything to do with Miss Lord's death?"

"I said that I didn't know."

"But you suspect it?"

"I'm not sure. I have no actual proof. I thought Allison had mentioned something about his being angry with her, but maybe not. I guess I don't really remember." She lied. She was sounding like she knew too much.

"I should tell you," said Trevelyan searching again through the papers in front of him, "that I have already spoken with Mr. Page at some length."

Emily could feel the muscles in her neck tighten.

"Just so that you will know we are doing our jobs, we've also checked out his story. He said that he and Miss Lord talked for about half an hour. He left her sitting in the bar and went over to a party at Sigma Nu fraternity. It was a homecoming event, I believe. We have several witnesses that say they saw him there. He left some time between eight-thirty and nine with a girl named Jamie McGraw. I believe she belongs to the same sorority as Miss Lord. She is apparently his current girlfriend. They drove to her apartment, and he spent the rest of the night, last night, at her place. She confirms his story."

Emily was desolate. With that kind of alibi, nobody was going to believe he had anything to do with Allison's death.

If Allison had died between eight and ten, as she'd been told, couldn't they see how easily he might have done it? It was obvious that he'd found some bimbo to lie for him.

"Miss Anderson?" Trevelyan was staring at her. "Are you all right? Can we proceed?"

"Of course. I'm sorry. It's just that I was thinking. Mitch has only his girlfriend's word that they were together for the whole evening."

"Yes, that's true. You know, Miss Anderson, one might think you *wanted* to pin your friend's death on Mitchel Page. Why is that, I wonder?"

He *was* playing with her! She could feel it. Cat and mouse. "I'm sorry it sounded that way. I didn't mean it like that."

"You didn't?" Trevelyan pulled a memo from the file and studied it. "You say that last night you spent the entire evening at home. You didn't go out and you received no phone calls. This is all in your statement. Is that correct?"

"Yes."

"And the first you heard about Miss Lord's death was this afternoon when the officer we sent over to your apartment informed you?"

Emily nodded.

"I see." Trevelyan took off his glasses and laid them on top of his desk. He reached inside the top drawer and pulled out a small thin envelope.

Emily recognized it at once. It was the frail, light blue air mail paper she had bought at Marks and Spencer in London. "What's that?" she said, straining to sound casual. Her voice was an octave too high. She reached to take it from his outstretched hand but changed her mind. "I know what it is. How did you get it?"

Trevelyan let it drop onto the desk. The fragile, almost weightless envelope made no sound as it landed. She knew the thoughts inside were too clearly stated to ever be denied. She didn't *want* to deny them. "What is it you want to know?" Her voice sounded lifeless. Only now did she realize how tired she was. He knew everything. Why go on pretending? No, she smiled inwardly. That's not quite true. He didn't know everything.

Trevelyan put the letter back into his desk drawer. He closed the file and folded his hands over it. "We know that you and Miss Lord had been lovers at least since the summer. That in itself means very little. But after talking with Mitchel Page, it became quite clear to me that Miss Lord was what you might call a very confused young woman."

Emily looked up, aghast. "On the basis of that vile, muscle-bound idiot's word, you feel you *understand* Allison? Is that it? This is a spectacular investigation, Detective Trevelyan. If I may contradict your star witness, Allison had never been less confused. She had finally managed to lift herself out of the confusion she'd been in all her life."

"Yes. I don't doubt that you would believe that. But it doesn't change the facts. It is clear to me that she *was* ambivalent about her feelings. According to Mr. Page, she wanted to renew their old relationship. In the absence of Allison's own words on the matter, I will say that I am inclined to believe Mr. Page. He said that this was the reason she had asked to meet with him last night. He was supposed to give her his decision."

"That's a lie!" Emily stood up and slammed her fist down hard on the center of Trevelyan's desk. "Did he tell you that? It was nothing like that! He's lying!"

"Sit down, Miss Anderson." Trevelyan looked at her calmly. His reasonable manner only served to infuriate her all the more. It tacitly said that she had no reason to be so upset. She was a child, a *woman*, who was unable to control her own emotions. She did not move.

"I want you to sit down now, Miss Anderson. This will not take much more of your time."

Emily heard the sarcasm. It was no use. He had all the power, and she knew it. She realized she'd bitten her lip when she stood up. The salty taste of blood filled her mouth. Trevelyan had apparently noticed it, too. He pulled a box of tissues out of his desk drawer and offered them to her. That simple act seemed to deflate her completely. She took one and sat back down. What was the use?

"Were you aware that Miss Lord had attempted suicide in high school?"

Emily looked at the bloody tissue in her hand. "Yes. I knew."

"I received the autopsy report several hours ago. Your friend's death was ruled a drowning. No foreign substances were found in her body and the only unusual marks that were visible were some old scars on each of her wrists. We checked on it and found out that she had attempted suicide when she was sixteen. It seems some girl she thought she was in love with had been sent away to a private school by her parents. I imagine it was an attempt to separate them. Shortly after the girl left town, Allison's father found her in one of the bathrooms. She'd slit her wrists. I suppose you already know the whole story." He studied her for a reaction.

"So, what are you trying to say?" she said angrily. "All gays and lesbians are innately suicidal? Depressed? Ambivalent about their sexuality? Is that it? Except that Allison was nothing like that. When she was sixteen she fell in love. It happens all the time. Poets write about the joys of young love. The problem was, she happened to fall in love with another young woman. Everyone in her family told her she was either sick or sinful. It's quite a dilemma for a sixteen-year-old. She knew she was neither of those things, but it's terrifying to be different. Especially when you're sixteen. You probably wouldn't know what any of that felt like because I doubt you've ever had an original emotion in your entire life."

Trevelyan smiled. Character abuse from someone like her was like an ant attacking an oak. "Let me tell you what I believe happened, Miss Anderson." He leaned back in his chair and folded his arms over his thick stomach. "Miss Lord was confused. She'd had a good relationship last winter with Mitchel Page. She'd found it satisfying." He made the word sound lewd. "Then her old ambivalence came back when she met you. The two of you spent a happy summer in England indulging your, how shall we say, whims? But when Allison got back and bumped into Mitchel one afternoon, the old feelings for him came back.''

He's describing a yo-yo, thought Emily.

"Now she has a problem. What should she do? She decides to make a date with Mitchel to see what her chances would be for a reconciliation. He refuses her and leaves her sitting in the bar. She drinks, and as she does, she becomes more despondent. Eventually, she leaves. She drives around thinking about what a mess she's made of her life. On an impulse she decides to drive over to Lake of the Isles. Maybe it was actually a plan. Who can say? She parks the car and walks over to that old bridge, which by now is completely deserted because of the rain. I think we know the rest.''

Emily wrapped her arms around herself and rocked slowly. "None of that is true. She didn't love Mitch, and she didn't want him back. If he told you that, he lied. She would never have killed herself. I know you could never understand how a woman might prefer another woman. But Allison did.''

"You're right, Emily. I don't understand that.'' He stood up. "If we're going to talk about who had the best motive, I think your name would be at the top of the list. But in the absence of any evidence to the contrary, we will probably rule this a suicide. I wish I had the manpower to spend more time on every case that comes across my desk, but the city fathers seem to think we're already spending too much of the taxpayer's money. I think you should consider yourself lucky. And one more thing. Don't leave town just in case we'd need to talk to you again before the formal ruling. Thank you for coming down.'' He smiled his wonderful smile and lifted his arm, pointing toward the door.

6

Maggie spent most of the rest of the day in her room up in the east wing. She needed to be alone to sort things out. Except, things were not really getting sorted out. A while ago she had wandered downstairs and was now sitting, staring absently into a mug of lukewarm coffee. It had tasted so bitter she could not bring herself to drink it. And more to the point, she was sick of thinking. Sick of feeling things she did not know how to handle. No one in her life had ever died before. How was someone supposed to understand death? She had never really thought about it much. If she was going to be honest, what she felt right now was not sadness, but anger.

Mrs. Holms had knocked on her door shortly after the sergeant left to let her know that a Detective Trevelyan had called to say he would be coming by later in the day. He said he wanted to speak with any of Allison's close friends who might be around.

Her close friends. That was an easy request. Sigrid, Maggie, Kari, and Ally. Someone had once been trite enough to refer to them as the four musketeers. They had all entered the university the same year and pledged Kappa Alpha Sigma together. They had roomed together, taken trips together, agonized over each other's problems together, and dreamed their innocent futures together.

Ally had always been the most philosophical. She tried to see all sides of an issue. And Sigrid was the pragmatist. The one who really got things done, and the most logical choice for house president. And then there was Kari. She had the strongest moral sense of any of them. She tended to look at things flat on, often thinking only in terms of right and wrong. And Maggie. How would she describe herself? She hoped she was the most psychologically sensitive of the four. She liked to think about motivations and intents. Most behavior she felt was not intrinsically good or bad, just something to be understood. Among the four of them some heated debates had taken place. They hadn't always seen eye to eye, but each in her own way had helped the others. They had moved through the sorority as a block, always loyal. That had been their strength. At the beginning of this year, they had been elected to the four highest offices in the sorority. This was going to be *their* year. Sigrid would be president. Maggie the house manager. Allison the social chair. And Kari the rituals chair. Everything they found wrong with the house could now be worked on and eventually changed. They had ascended to power as a group, just as they had known they always would.

And now, Ally was gone. Dead. And for the simple reason that Maggie couldn't imagine living at Kappa Alpha Sigma without her, she felt that for the rest of the year she would just be going through the motions. Looking like she was doing her job. Attending meetings. Acting interested. But everything would be halfhearted. The meaning they had found as a group had somehow evaporated with Allison. She was sure Sigrid and Kari would feel the same.

Maggie turned around, hearing someone come through the kitchen doorway. "Oh, Mrs. Holms. I thought you had left." Maggie's smile was a little crumpled.

"I'm sorry to have to break into your reverie, dear." Edith was out of breath and had to sit down.

"Is there something wrong?" Almost before she said the words, she knew the question was inane. "I mean, is there something *else* wrong?" Maggie pushed the coffee cup away from her. Would this day never end?

"I'm afraid so. Could you come downstairs with me for a moment? There's something you need to see in the rituals room."

* * *

The Kappa Alpha Sigma rituals room was located in the finished part of the old basement. It was hardly a room at all, no bigger than a large walk-in closet. The food-storage room was next to it. And directly across the hall was the small but cozy apartment of Gladys Bailey, the sorority's housekeeper.

All the private items sacred to the initiation rights of the sorority were stored in the rituals room. Only three people had keys. As house manager, Maggie had access to all the rooms in the house. The same was true for Sigrid. And Kari, who was directly responsible for the security of the room, had the third key. The door was kept locked at all times.

Maggie was shocked to find the door standing open, the light on inside. Mrs. Holms swept her hand toward the unlocked door.

"When did you find this?" asked Maggie. She opened the door still further. Inside, the floor was completely littered with rituals mementos. Two old steamship trunks stood open and empty.

"I found it just as you see it a few minutes ago."

"Look down there!" Maggie pointed to the strongbox which held the chapter's rituals dues. She reached over one of the trunks and picked it up. Someone had broken off the padlock. "Damn! Oh, sorry, Mrs. Holms. It just slipped out." Generally, Edith took a rather dim view of girls using any kind of profanity.

Maggie opened the box.

"Is the money all gone?" asked Edith in a tone that suggested she was sure it was.

Maggie said nothing but held it out for her inspection.

"I don't understand! The box is still full of money. What's going on? Why would someone go to all the trouble to get into this room, make a terrible mess obviously looking for the money, break open the strongbox, and then take nothing?" Edith stared at it in disbelief. "I have to sit down." She brushed some robes off an old bench by the door and eased herself onto it.

"I don't get it either." Maggie jammed her hands deep into the pockets of her badly wrinkled jeans. "It doesn't look like any money was taken. It's still clipped the same way Kari and I did it two weeks ago." She stared bleakly at the mess all around her.

"Well," said Mrs. Holms confidentially, "someone must have had a key to get into the room. The lock on the door hasn't been tampered with. I think the first thing we need to do is find out where all the keys are. Maybe Sigrid and Kari were down here last night. You girls sometimes do some odd things, you know."

"They would never have made this mess!" She kicked closed the smaller of the two trunks. "Besides, everyone was at the party at Sigma Nu last night. Nobody was even here!" She picked one of the robes up off the floor and laid it down on top of the trunk. "It should be easy enough to find out if someone has stolen a key." She glanced quickly at Mrs. Holms, glad that her nervous expression went unnoticed.

"Well, all I can say is this is very upsetting." Edith slapped her hands on her knees and stood up. "I guess there's nothing more we can do right now. I should tell you that I came down here last night around six-thirty. I remember because my son was going to pick me up at seven and I wanted to say goodbye to Mrs. Bailey before she left for her *Doctor Who* convention in Des Moines. Her daughter was going to pick her up later in the evening and take her to the train depot. I don't know how we'll take care of all her duties while she's gone. I told the board that it was going to be a big problem if she left, but they overruled my objections. I suppose I'll just end up having to do it all myself."

Maggie could feel she was entering the twilight zone of one of Mrs. Holm's long, pathetic martyr speeches. "What was it you said about coming down here last evening?"

"What? Oh yes. Well, I always check the food-storage-room door and the rituals-room door when I come down to talk to Mrs. Bailey. Once in a while Adolph forgets to lock the food-storage room. We can't have that. He complains because you girls go in and take all the chocolate chips.

That's stealing too, you know. Anyway, never in my twelve years here have I found that rituals door left unlocked.''

"And you're saying you checked it around six-thirty last night and it was locked, but a few minutes ago you found it open?''

"That is correct.'' Mrs. Holms leaned closer to Maggie. The cloying smell of her floral perfume was overwhelming. "I don't mind telling you that I find the goings on around here a little scary. Two nights ago Kari came into my room to tell me she thought she had seen someone outside her window. You know yourself how many of the girls have said they felt they were being watched. And always at night. Isn't that eerie? At first I thought it was just some fraternity prank. Those young men don't always show the best judgment when it comes to their little games with you girls. But it has gone on too long for that. I don't mind saying I'm a little frightened. I close and lock my door now every night. I've never done that in all the years I've been here. And when you consider that we have had two thefts and now *this*,'' she pointed at the strongbox, "I say something must be done about it. The police should be notified.''

"I agree with you. Something will have to be done. But I think everyone agrees we should try to handle it within the house. We don't want any bad publicity. Something odd is going on around here, I'm certain of it. And I'll make a point of discussing it at tonight's executive board meeting.'' Maggie was itching to get back up to her room. There was something she had to take care of immediately.

"All right,'' said Mrs. Holms with a note of officiousness. "Let me know how you progress.'' She turned and marched up the stairs. Even the back of her permed blue-gray hair looked determined.

She is a strange woman, thought Maggie. Possibly from another planet.

7

It was nearly six-thirty before Jane finally walked up the dark tree-lined path to Kappa Alpha Sigma. All afternoon things at the restaurant had conspired against her. She knew she would never make it on time for the formal dinner at the house. Standing outside in the darkness, she could clearly see Sigrid up in front of the assembled group giving the general announcements. Dessert would follow. The most important part of the evening, the executive board meeting, would come after the general meeting. She was glad she had at least made it for that.

Jane noticed the front door standing slightly ajar as she climbed the crumbling concrete steps. She made a mental note to speak to someone on the house corporation board about having them repaired. Two stone gargoyles rested on either side of the beautifully carved wooden door. She pushed it open, grateful that she didn't have to announce her lateness by ringing the doorbell. She could hear Sigrid in the dining room talking about the funeral arrangements that had been made by Allison's father. Jane moved nearer to the French doors to hear more clearly. Allison's father and stepmother would be flying into the Twin Cities on Wednesday. The memorial service would be in Minneapolis at Good Shepherd Presbyterian on Thursday afternoon. And the burial would take place later in Philadelphia.

Jane peeked carefully around the corner. She wondered just how many people had made it to tonight's dinner. It looked like just about everyone. The short announcement period would be over soon. She didn't want to interrupt things by entering and taking her seat directly in front of Sigrid. Instead, she walked back through the front foyer and entered the kitchen from the side door. She would be able to hide in there until the announcements were over. She might even be able to grab a bite to eat. The side door squeaked as she pushed it open and stepped into the back of the room. One of the busboys who was sitting on a stool a few feet from her looked up over his evening paper as she entered. She remembered meeting him several weeks ago. His first name was Mitch. The last name escaped her. She did remember that after less than a two-minute conversation with him she had wondered if the art of conversation had indeed died. He wasn't bad looking. Straight white teeth. Thick, curly, black hair. A tall, well-muscled body. But his demeanor had put her off. He held his mouth petulantly, and his eyes were deeply set and sly. He fairly oozed sarcastic detachment. And his voice! It was a ridiculously studied attempt at blue-collar cool. It might have been funny had he not also seemed so threatening. She didn't like him and probably didn't hide that very well. She wondered what was underneath all the veneer. Tonight he was wearing a T-shirt that said VICTIMIZED.

Jane approached the center island where the cook, Adolph Mauer, was cutting up chocolate sheet cake. The other busboy, Elliot Kratager, was helping by taking completed trays away and replacing them with empty ones. Adolph had his back to her but turned stiffly as she approached. His large round eyes squinted through thick, old-fashioned spectacles. He seemed to be somewhat ill at ease tonight. Perhaps he didn't appreciate strangers in his kitchen.

Adolph reminded Jane of a squirrel. His cheeks looked like little pouches. He was a small man, though she had recently seen him lift a hundred-pound sack of flour as if it had been filled with cotton balls. His head was bald except for tufts of wispy salt-and-pepper hair that circled his head in a kind of halo.

"I'm sorry to have to come through your kitchen like this, Adolph. You probably don't remember me. I'm one of the two new alumni advisors this year. My name is Jane Lawless."

Adolph went back to cutting cake. "I remember you," he said in a low, almost sweet voice. He motioned for Elliot to bring over another tray.

Jane moved around the front of the island. The cake smelled wonderful. She *must* be hungry since she rarely found anything he made even edible.

"The cake looks good," said Jane. She turned toward the door and heard Sigrid's voice still speaking in the other room.

"Thank you," said Adolph nodding formally. "It's a standard cake mix."

Was there ever any doubt?

"I hear you were the one to find Ally this morning," said Adolph quietly. "That must have been awful for you." He wiped his knife on a towel. While he wasn't looking, Elliot snatched a piece of cake, flashing Jane his famous full thirty-two tooth smile.

"Yes. It was awful. I still can't believe it happened." She shivered as she recalled the sight of Allison's body lying so still in the water. She hadn't been able to get that image out of her mind all day.

"What, if I might ask, caused her to die?" Adolph didn't look up but kept dishing out the cake.

"I talked with the police this afternoon and I guess they think it was a suicide. She couldn't swim. I don't feel entirely confident about it myself. The investigation seemed kind of fast, but the detective on the case said in the absence of any concrete evidence, there wasn't much more they could do. The official ruling will come in a week or so. I'd like to find out more about her myself. See if I can't find some evidence that might point in a different direction."

"I see," Adolph said, looking over at Elliot who had backed away while Jane was talking and nearly toppled a bus pan full of dirty dishes. Elliot looked momentarily nervous.

The trays were completed. Adolph handed the empty cake pans to Elliot and then carefully wiped his hands on his apron before turning to Mitch. "Mitchel, start the coffee. Now."

Slowly, Mitch got up, grunting and stretching his long body. As he walked past Jane he brushed his hand lightly along her thigh. She waited until he was almost to the door before saying, "Mitch, if you ever do that again, you and your little hand will be working someplace else." Mitch just smirked and kept on walking out the door.

"I don't like him either," said Adolph quietly.

Jane could hear the sound of applause coming from the dining room. It had coincided perfectly with Mitch's entrance, and she was sure it had not been lost on him. Sigrid was done with the announcements. The break for dessert and coffee would last around twenty minutes. Long enough to find out if anyone had heard any more about Allison.

The head table was reserved for the officers, the house mother, and any alumni or visitors who might be present. Tonight only the regulars were in attendance. Maggie got up to greet Jane as soon as she came through the kitchen door.

"Hi! We're glad you made it!" Jane found Maggie's cheerfulness extreme under the circumstances. She glanced over toward the French doors in time to see Sigrid and Mrs. Holms disappear into the foyer. Only Maggie, Kari, and Susan Julian, the other alumni advisor, were still seated at the table.

"Jane, we thought you weren't coming," chirped Susan in her high, slightly childish voice. "Everyone would have understood if today's events had been a little too much for you."

"I'm fine," said Jane pulling out her chair and sitting down. "But it was pretty awful. I understand that a Detective Trevelyan was supposed to come over this afternoon. Did he have anything new to report?"

No one seemed to want to speak. Jane looked inquiringly from face to face. "Trevelyan told me if any more evidence was found, they would reexamine the probable suicide determination. Is that what he told all of you?" She waited. The silence was disconcerting. "Why do I feel like I'm doing all the talking?"

"That's what we were told, too," said Maggie finally. She glanced furtively at Kari, who had remained very close-mouthed all evening.

"You haven't heard the news then," said Susan, taking a tiny sip of coffee.

"What news?" said Jane cautiously.

Maggie looked over at Kari, who was being served her lopsided cake. Before Elliot was able to safely set the plate down in front of her, Kari stood up, knocking into his arm and sending the dish crashing to the floor. Without looking at anyone, she turned and bolted out of the room.

"What's going on here?" asked Jane. "Is someone going to tell me or is it a big secret?"

Maggie cleared her throat, trying to form just the right words in her mind. Before she could say anything, Susan answered. "It's not a secret anymore, Jane. It seems our little girl wonder was, in reality, a queer."

"What?" said Jane, involuntarily sucking in her breath. Astonishment froze on her face.

"You never knew her, Susan," said Maggie, barely controlling her rage. "I, for one, don't appreciate your tone or the name calling."

"I'm just calling a spade a spade." Susan took another tiny sip of coffee.

Maggie couldn't let it drop. "Is that what you're doing? You know, I've heard that same snide little voice around here all afternoon, and I'm getting pretty sick of it. Christ, you all must think you're so perfect. Ever since that detective came over here with his big news flash, everyone has been acting like they were raised in a convent! All this breast-beating. It's disgusting." She glanced back at Jane for a moment and lowered her eyes. "I guess it's true. Although, I never knew anything about it. Kari and Sigrid and I were very close to her, and she never told any of us."

"If I were you," said Susan dryly, "I'd stop telling everyone how *close* you all were. You wouldn't want people to get the wrong idea." Susan watched Maggie shift uncomfortably in her seat. She knew she'd hit a nerve.

"I thought older people were supposed to be smarter," said Maggie, pushing the cake away. Nothing had tasted right all day.

Jane was beginning to recover from her momentary shock. "I think both of you can probably appreciate that it's not the kind of information you might always want to give all your straight friends." She chose her words carefully. "People have been known to use information like that to hurt other people."

Susan snorted. "You're right about that. If something like this were to get out into the rest of the Greek community, we could be ruined! Having allowed a—I even hate to say the word—*lesbian* in our midst would destroy our reputation. We can only hope it doesn't make the papers. I mean, no one would feel safe joining. I don't suppose any of you thought of that. We have to protect this house! We should have thrown her out long ago."

"How could we do that when we didn't even know," said Maggie angrily. "And even then, I doubt it would be grounds for expulsion." Maggie tried, but clearly did not feel comfortable with the entire subject.

"Don't be too sure about that, Maggie. After all, homosexuality is a sin against God and nature. And in many places it's against the law." Susan finished her coffee, dabbing the napkin at the sides of her mouth. "I think this is one subject we should try to cover in our next Bible study down in the green room. I'd like to see *you* there for a change, Maggie." Susan had the odd habit of bulging out her eyes to emphasize specific words.

"Our what?" said Jane, sitting up straight. Had she heard correctly?

"It's a little Bible study I started here two weeks ago. It was my idea," she added warily, knowing Jane might not think it the same stroke of genius Edith Holms had. "These girls have so many spiritual questions that it's a shame not to try to answer some of them. If I can help anyone find their way to Jesus, I'd consider it a privilege." She picked up her coffee cup and then realized it was empty. "Every Tuesday from three to four, if you're interested in attending."

Was Jane hearing right? Susan Julian talking about Jesus? It must be some kind of joke. Jane had known Susan since college. They had both lived in the house the same year. Jane had been a sophomore and Susan a senior. If she recalled correctly, Susan's reputation for drinking and general hell-raising was legendary. She had been Susan Bergemeyer then. Her father owned a brewery in Milwaukee and had sent his only daughter to the University of Minnesota because he didn't know what else to do with her, and he didn't want her any closer to home than was absolutely necessary.

Jane looked back and forth between Susan and Maggie. "This is a joke, right?" A slow smile trickled onto her face. "Come on."

Susan was clearly offended. "It most certainly is not! I would never joke about something so important. I gave my life to Jesus three years ago and was born again. It was right after my husband Bob died. As I recall, you and that rather large friend of yours, what's her name . . ."

"Cordelia." Jane knew Susan remembered Cordelia's name. Those two had always rubbed each other the wrong way. Old feelings died hard.

"Yes, Cordelia. You and Cordelia came to the funeral, I believe. I was a basket case back then, I'm sure you could tell. I don't hide things well. I was on pills, drinking too much, the whole nine yards as they say. But I finally asked the Lord Jesus to come into my life and show me the truth. And He has! He's shown me the truth about so many things since then, and *one* of them is *homosexuality*." She puffed her eyes out wildly. Jane was afraid one might land on her cake plate. "It's a vile, horrible act in the eyes of Almighty God. And at the risk of sounding cruel, Allison's punishment was just what she deserved."

"Her punishment," said Jane, unable to let that pass. "You mean you think God was punishing her?"

"Most certainly," said Susan.

Jane hesitated. Maybe Susan knew something she wasn't telling. "Do you think it's possible God might have used some *person* to punish her?"

Susan looked confused. "What? Oh, I get it. You always were like that weren't you, Jane? Picking apart everything someone said in order to make them appear to say something else. You should have been in the media!'' She glared across the table. "God knows what I meant. He sometimes works in strange ways, yes. However she died, it was a fitting reward for her actions. God was her judge, not me.''

Jane couldn't believe what she was hearing. "Do you think, then, that all gays should be punished?''

"They *will* be punished. That is a certainty.''

"And you think they deserve to die?''

Susan folded her hands calmly around her coffee cup. "Look. I don't know if you can understand this, but let me try to explain. The sin of homosexuality is a lot like leprosy. At first you don't really notice much is wrong. A tiny little speck on your skin doesn't seem like it could hurt you much. But then it starts to ooze pus, and by then it's too late. The wages of sin is *death* according to the Bible. I didn't write that, but I believe it. Homosexuality is a sin, and therefore punishable by death, unless repented of. Sexual intercourse between a man and a woman, on the other hand, is an acknowledgment of the plan of God. It's a picture of how the church works. A homosexual act is like slapping God right in the face! And of course, it leads to other things. Bestiality. Bondage. Prostitution. Rape. Drugs. It's all just around the corner. This country is going to have to pay for its sins, just like Allison did. She told me that nothing—'' A loud bell announced the end of dinner. Susan had been cut off midsentence. Everyone now had five minutes in which to get downstairs to the chapter room for evening meeting.

"I'm sorry,'' said Susan, checking her watch. She pushed her chair back and got up. "I get carried away sometimes. Too carried away for my own good.'' She tapped over her heart. "It's just that I hold these truths very strongly. I know it's not a great tactic to preach at people, but someday you'll see that I'm right. Now, I'd better get downstairs.'' She nodded to Maggie and Jane and then joined a group of girls headed for the French doors.

After she had gone Jane said, "I think we need to talk.''

Maggie looked up. "Yeah. It's so hard to figure all this. Susan's so sure of herself. And yet, I can't believe God wouldn't allow for people who were different. Except, you know, I'm so angry at Ally myself. Why couldn't she trust me? I would never have done anything to hurt her.'' She paused to organize her thoughts. "Today has been one of the worst days of my entire life. I don't know what to think. And there are some odd things going on in the house that have me worried.'' She looked around as people continued to exit the dining room. "We've discussed some of these problems during the executive board meetings, but always after you and Susan had left. We voted in a closed meeting to keep everything quiet until we could decide what to do. But I think we made a mistake.'' She paused, making sure everyone had left before continuing. "I've got some information about what happened last night that nobody else knows. I feel like I've got to tell someone, but I just don't know who I can trust.'' She seemed terribly agitated. Almost on the verge of tears.

"I would hope you feel you could trust me,'' said Jane. "I understand how you might feel betrayed by Allison, but I want you to know that it's not a simple decision to tell someone you're gay. You also should know that Susan's views aren't shared by everyone. I need to know what's going on in this house if I'm ever going to find out what really happened to Ally last night. Do you think we could get together and talk about this sometime soon?'' She looked at her watch. "I know you have to start the meeting downstairs in a few minutes, but maybe some night this week you'd be free?''

Maggie thought for a moment. "I probably won't have any free time until after the memorial service on Thursday. How would Friday night be? Right now I'm behind in all my classes because I missed them all today. And I'll probably miss a bunch tomorrow since I've been asked to arrange the food for the gathering in the church basement after the memorial service. It's going to take me most of tomorrow to figure all that out.''

"Consider it done,'' said Jane.

"You're kidding!''

"No, I'll have my restaurant take care of everything. Just

tell me where and when. I'll need to know by this Wednesday at the latest.''

"I can't thank you enough! I've never done anything like that before, and I didn't even know where to begin.''

"What would you think of asking Kari and Sigrid to join us on Friday night?''

"Well, I guess I could ask them, although their reactions to this latest news about Allison have me confused. Sigrid didn't even act surprised and Kari refuses to talk about any of it.''

"I see,'' said Jane. "Well, bring them if you like, but if not, we can still get together, just the two of us.'' She pulled a card out of her purse. "This is the address. I'll write down the date and time. How about nine down in the pub? Just come downstairs and order what you like. It's on the house. I'll meet you as close to nine as I can.''

"I'll be there,'' said Maggie, feeling for the first time today that some sense might be made out of all of this chaos. "Jane, maybe I shouldn't say anything, but I've been wondering all day if Ally's death was really a suicide. She would never have chosen to die like that, I'm sure of it. And even if she was the greatest actress in the world, she couldn't have hidden that deep a depression from me. As a matter of fact, she had never seemed happier. Ever since she came back from England, she was on top of the world.'' She looked at the time. "I'm late. We'll have to talk more later.'' She picked up her notebook and ran out through the French doors.

Mitchel Page, who had been standing silently in the shadows at the back of the room, now began to shut off the overhead lights. Jane whirled around as soon as the room began to darken and found him staring directly at her. She wondered how long he'd been listening and what he'd heard. Without taking his eyes from her for a moment, he shut off the lights one by one until the room was in total darkness. A moment later the back door creaked open and then closed softly.

PART TWO

Voices From
the Whirlwind

*For they have sown the wind, and they shall reap
the whirlwind.*

Hosea 8:7

8

Jane stood motionless in the bay of her dining room window. It was a gray, chilly northern morning. Frost covered the ground. During the night a cold wind had begun blowing, rattling the storm windows and awakening her from a fitful sleep. In the creaking of the old house she thought she could hear a faint whisper, warning of the north wind. One had best be prepared. Winters in Minnesota could be dangerous.

Earlier the wind had switched around to the west. Low, heavy clouds, the color of steel, appeared in the western sky, bringing with them the smell of snow. It was a smell Jane always found exhilarating. After breakfast she had gone out to the woodpile to fetch an armload of dry logs and kindling. Perhaps a fire would take the gloom out of the old house.

She turned and looked into the living room at the two little dogs who shared her house. They snuggled up next to each other in front of the fireplace like perfect little sausages. The snapping of the fire seemed to make the room feel even more silent. Jane was all too familiar with the bleakness of a space that had once been so filled with life and warmth. She had found little pleasure these past few years in the privacy of her home. She scrubbed and dusted, but she was never quite able to sweep the smell of loss from out of the corners.

A cream-colored BMW pulling into the driveway brought her attention back to the window. She watched as the driver sat motionless in the front seat, smoking a cigarette. A few seconds later the car door opened and a small woman in a gray fur coat and hat got out. It was Susan Julian. She walked unsteadily across the lawn and up the front steps. The bell had still not rung when Jane opened the door and found Susan already on her way back down the steps. She looked as if she had been caught doing something illegal.

"Jane. Hello. I thought maybe this was kind of early to come calling. I didn't want to wake you."

Even with her face partially obscured by the fur hat, Jane could see how tired and pale she looked. "As you can see, you haven't. You look cold standing out there. Why don't you come in and sit by the fire? I'll fix us some coffee if you like."

Susan acknowledged Jane's offer with a weak smile. "Thanks, I've had kind of a bad night." She walked into the front hall holding herself tightly, as if her entire body hurt. "A cup of coffee sounds good. I haven't had much sleep." Her eyes moved quickly around the room. Bean and Gulliver had already begun their professional examination. She nearly tripped over them as she walked into the living room.

"If you aren't comfortable with the dogs, I can put them in the other room. Sometimes they can be kind of a pain." Jane dragged Bean away from Susan's purse.

"Oh no," she said, patting Gulliver tentatively on his ear. "I love animals." Both dogs had already determined that this rather cold human had no interest in them whatsoever. With one last mighty snort, Bean followed Gulliver back into the living room and both resumed their positions in front of the fire. Some people just weren't worth further sniffing.

"You have a lovely home, Jane. It's so big, so open. Some of the newer houses seem like little boxes, don't you think? Though I must admit a preference for the modern. Who did your decorating?" She moved around the room nervously, picking up an object here and there. Jane had never seen Susan look so disheveled. Her normally pink skin was ashen.

"I've owned the house for many years," said Jane. "Most everything I've done myself. Cordelia helped with the wallpapering and painting, and another woman, someone you've never met, helped me do the rest."

Susan came closer to the fire and held out her hands. "One

forgets how wonderful the smell of burning wood is. I have a fireplace at my condo, but it has a gas log. It looks pretty, but then it's really kind of a fake, isn't it?''

Jane glanced over at the clock on the mantel. Cordelia would be arriving in a few minutes. They had made plans to drive to Stillwater this morning to try to find Emily Anderson. Jane had gotten her name from Maggie and found her address by contacting the English department. The manager of the apartment building said she had given a month's notice and moved out the day before. She had left her parents' home in Stillwater as a forwarding address.

"The cold seems to be coming early this year," said Susan, sitting down in one of the wing chairs near the fireplace. Jane wondered why she had come. She doubted it was merely a social call.

"I'll go get us that coffee." The dogs, sensing Jane was headed for the kitchen, got up and trotted behind her wagging their tails. They never allowed a possible food opportunity to be wasted.

"Do you take cream or sugar?" shouted Jane.

"Just sugar please," said Susan from the doorway.

"Oh," said Jane, turning around. "I didn't hear you come in." She handed Susan a coffee mug.

Susan began spooning sugar into her cup. After the fourth spoonful she hesitated. Jane wondered if she was perhaps calculating the lethal dosage. To her surprise, Susan added two more spoonfuls before stirring the sludge. Her hand shook as she lifted the mug to her mouth.

"Let's go back and sit down by the fire," said Jane, picking up her own mug. Once seated in the living room, Susan seemed to lose focus.

"Was there a particular reason you stopped by this morning?" Jane could tell her words broke roughly into Susan's private thoughts.

"Yes, of course." Her voice sounded strained. "Actually, Maggie wanted me to give you the instructions for the food tomorrow. For after the service."

Jane was confused. "Maybe I'm wrong, but I thought

Maggie and I had already gone over that. Do you want me to go over the menu with you?''

Watching Jane drink her coffee seemed to remind Susan of the mug in her own hand. She lifted it jerkily to her mouth and took several gulps. ''No, I'm sure what you decided is fine. I must have gotten mixed up.'' She took another swallow.

This conversation is going nowhere, thought Jane, looking up at the clock. Cordelia would be arriving any time.

''It's hard being single, isn't it?'' said Susan. ''If Bob were here, he'd know what to do. After he died, I didn't know where to turn, but then I found this wonderful church out in Crystal. I've been kept so busy with church services, Bible studies, and other church events, that I haven't really thought about it much.'' Her childish voice was almost a parody of itself this morning. Again, she changed the subject abruptly. ''The memorial service tomorrow must be done tastefully. I've insisted on that. Adam Lord is a very wealthy and powerful man in Philadelphia. There is a younger daughter coming along in a few years. If we could get her to pledge Kappa Alpha Sigma we would no doubt receive another generous endowment. We have to look at our finances, you know. It's too easily overlooked, don't you think?''

Jane didn't know what to think.

Susan's eyes continued to bounce around the room. ''I suppose I should be going then. I shouldn't take up any more of your time.'' She continued to sit quietly. ''Actually Jane, if you've got a minute, there is one question I'd like to get your opinion on.''

At last, thought Jane. We're getting closer to the point.

Susan finished her coffee and set the mug down on the mahogany table next to her chair. ''I'm not sure where to begin, really. I found out something terrible last night. Something really horrible.'' She stood up and walked over to the mantel. With her back to Jane she continued. ''I'm not sure why I came here really. You can't change anything. This was probably a mistake.'' She turned around. ''You know, I hardly know you. We haven't talked for more than ten minutes in the last fifteen years.''

Just say it, thought Jane.

''All right,'' she said finally. ''One question. Please be patient with me. I know you probably feel we said enough about this on Monday night, but let me ask this clearly, one more time. You do think homosexuality is a sin, don't you?''

Jane was surprised. Since Susan's little sermon the other evening, it had seemed clear that this was one subject on which she had no ambivalence. And Jane was not willing to sit through another diatribe on Allison's aberrant sexuality. ''Susan, I guess I don't think in terms of *sin*. If you were to ask me if I thought it was wrong, or evil, or even unnatural, I'd also have to say no. It's a view you don't share, I'm sure of that. So I don't see any point in arguing about Allison anymore.''

At the mention of Allison's name, Susan looked up quickly. ''No, I don't want to argue. But, I want to understand how you can live with what you believe. The Bible does say it's unnatural. And a sin. Doesn't that bother you?''

''I think arguing about what the Bible says or doesn't say is a bog, and not one I'm willing to crawl into.''

If Susan had looked awful when she first came in, she now looked even worse. It was as if some internal string holding her body together had suddenly snapped.

''Jane, I think I've done something terrible.'' Her eyes looked genuinely horrified. At the same moment, the doorbell rang, sending the dogs flying into the front hall. Susan jumped back as they scrambled past her. Cordelia's timing could not have been worse. Jane excused herself and walked over to the front door, silently cursing her bad luck. She knew Susan was about to say something important.

''I'm sorry I'm late,'' said Cordelia, bursting through the front door, her entire presence a conflagration. ''It was that miserable neighbor of mine. For some reason he has decided he can park in *my* driveway. The cretin! I had to get him out of bed, and *then* his car wouldn't start.'' She leaned down to tickle the dogs. As she looked up she spied Susan in the

living room. "Susan," she said sourly. "What a surprise."
It was exactly the same tone she would have used at finding
a grease stain on her best blouse.

"Cordelia Thorn," said Susan, with some of the old edge
back in her voice. "What a rare treat. Jane told me that you
two were still friends after *all* these years."

"Yes," said Cordelia snidely. "It has been a long time,
hasn't it? Next Christmas we're getting each other matching
geriatric chairs. I imagine you already have yours." She
walked regally into the room and removed her coat. "Seems
like the last time I saw you was at Bob's funeral."

"That's right. I forgot you *knew* Bob."

"Be careful how you inflect your verbs, Susan. This is a
Christian nation."

Susan seemed confused.

Jane knew she had to put a stop to this before one of them
took a swing at the other. "Susan dropped by to give me
some last-minute instructions on the food tomorrow." She
flashed her eyes at Cordelia, telling her to knock it off.

"Right," said Cordelia, marching over to the most comfortable armchair and plunking herself down heavily. Both
dogs immediately jumped into her lap.

"I hope we can talk again soon," said Jane, glancing back
at Susan. "Perhaps we can finish our conversation."

Susan smiled briefly before returning to Cordelia. "I suppose you like working in the theatre." She bulged out her
eyes ever so slightly. "So many other odd people."

"Love it," said Cordelia. Jane could hear the faint sound
of teeth grinding.

"Yes, I thought you would say that." She put on her coat,
pulling it tightly around her thin body. "Thank you so much,
Jane. I'll see you tomorrow at the service." With one last
sideways glance at Cordelia, she walked out the door into a
cold gust of wind. Jane shut the door behind her.

"How on earth did I get so lucky," said Cordelia, pulling
on Bean's tail. "She's the last person I would ever have expected to find in your living room! I should have consulted
my horoscope and stayed in bed."

"Try to cope," said Jane, picking up the empty mugs and carrying them into the kitchen. She was still a little angry at Cordelia for interrupting their conversation.

Cordelia followed, carrying a dog under each arm. "Your pups tell me they're hungry. You don't feed them enough."

Jane walked over and scratched Bean on top of his nose. "They're exaggerating."

"Oh, give them each a rawhide stick. Don't be such an ogre. It'll give them something to do while we're gone. If they're busy maybe they won't make any long-distance phone calls."

Jane's old green Saab pulled into a gas and food station on Highway 95, about ten miles outside Stillwater. Cordelia had not allowed herself any time for breakfast and had insisted that they stop to buy a quart of chocolate milk. She came back to the car carrying the milk and a large bag of taco chips.

"It warms my heart to see how well nourished you are," said Jane as they pulled back onto the highway. "I'll never worry again now that I see what good care you take of yourself."

"Thank you," said Cordelia between gulps. "You want some?"

Jane shook her head.

"I suppose you know where we're going."

"I think so. I looked at a map last night."

"What do you expect to learn from Emily? That is, if we find her, and if she's willing to talk to you."

"It's funny," said Jane. "I feel like I need to get to know Allison better. It's hard to do after someone has died, I grant you, but not impossible. If I only knew more about what was happening in her life, perhaps I'd have a better chance of understanding what happened on that bridge last Sunday night."

"Ah ha! You *don't* think it was a suicide." Cordelia nearly spilled the quart of milk. "I knew it."

"No, I don't. I haven't got any proof yet, but unlike Trevelyan, I don't think all lesbians are innately suicidal. I talked to him yesterday and he almost said that, word for word.''

"You think someone murdered her?''

"I think it's possible. Maybe it was an accident. I just need to know more. I doubt she was alone on that bridge. This is as good a place to start a little snooping as any.''

Cordelia finished the chocolate milk and stifled a small burp. "When you find Emily, are you going to tell her about you?''

Jane slowed down to look at the road sign. "I think if we take that cutoff, it will take us closer to where we want to go. And no, I don't think I'm going to tell her about me. What would be the point? I doubt she'd even believe it. She'd think it was some sort of ploy to get information out of her. That's what I'd think. I mean, picture it. Hi there, you can trust me. You can tell me everything because I'm one, too. It sounds patronizing. And besides, I've always been very careful who I give that information to. I'm not so sure I would want her to know. I don't really know anything about her.''

"Good thinking,'' said Cordelia. "A bit of healthy paranoia. For all you know, she could be an ax murderer. And if that information ever got back to Kappa Alpha Peyton Place, you'd be a marked woman. What did I mean by that? It just slipped out.''

"I think there's some reason to believe Allison's relationship with Emily might have had something to do with her death. That's why I want to begin my investigation with Emily. To hear Susan Julian tell it, Ally should have been cast out into the valley of the lepers long ago. Oh, I forgot to tell you. Susan has become a Born Again Christian.''

"Why doesn't that surprise me?'' said Cordelia. "I don't trust her. If you have any sense, you won't either. That obnoxious little girl voice of hers. It makes me sick. Always wanting other people to rescue her. She may be a Christian, but I doubt she's given up manipulation. It comes too naturally. You know, I knew her husband Bob in college. We were both on the varsity debate team. He was a nice guy. But the way she kept jerking him around was nothing short of cruel." Cordelia looked around the car to be sure no one else was listening. "I've never told a soul this before, but I never believed Bob died of natural causes. I'm probably the only one who suspected. He may have been making a lot of money while they were married, but she'd never be living in the style she's living in today if it hadn't been for that little life insurance policy."

"And how do you think he died?" asked Jane.

"She poisoned him, of course. Probably over a period of years."

"Cordelia, be careful. You can get sued for saying things like that."

"The woman is a snake, Jane. Don't take your eyes off her. Don't ever put yourself in a position where you have to trust her."

"Actually, she did say some pretty nasty things about Allison the other night. I guess a lot of the members were upset by the news."

"Ah," said Cordelia gleefully. "I can just see it. All the little princesses in a tither about having harbored a pervert. Although it wasn't the first time, was it?" She crunched down on a particularly large taco chip for effect.

"I think we're lost," said Jane. "Get that map out of the glove compartment. Let's have a look." She pulled the car off the road under a barren elm.

Cordelia handed over the folded map.

"People seemed more open-minded back in the early seventies." Jane found the spot where she should have turned.

"Right," said Cordelia. "That's why you never came out to any of them during the entire time you lived there."

Jane clenched her teeth. She was annoyed at getting lost and even more irritated at the accuracy of Cordelia's comments. She hated it when Cordelia was right. "I see what I did wrong." She folded up the map and handed it back. "We need to go back about a half a mile and take that blind turnoff." She pulled the car back onto the road.

"So," said Cordelia, "you were going to tell me what

happened last Monday night at your meeting. Who said what to whom. All the bloody details. Did anyone hit anyone?"

"It wasn't anything like that. A lot of the girls just seemed confused. Susan wants someone from her church to come and talk to everyone. I suggested Marian Svenberg from the human sexuality department at the university."

"Bet that went over well."

"Actually, it did. The president, her name is Sigrid, thought it was a good idea. I don't know her well, but I was impressed by the way she handled the meeting."

Jane found the proper turn and pulled onto Pickett Avenue. "There it is. 912 Pickett. The house is smaller than I expected." She drove into the driveway and stopped the car.

"Now remember, I'm just along for the ride," said Cordelia firmly. "I expect you to do all the talking. And if anything gets unpleasant, I hope you're a fast runner, because that's what I intend to do."

For almost forty years, Clarence and Bertha Anderson had lived in a small brick two-story on a hill overlooking the St. Croix River. Clarence worked for a storm-door manufacturer in Bayport, and Bertha, when she did work, took in sewing. Both were considered quiet, well-respected members of old Stillwater. The newer members of Stillwater had fled the dreary grind of big-city life in the Twin Cities, searching for the quiet of a small town. It seemed to Clarence that ever since these young folks had started to move in, an awful lot of building had been going on. It wouldn't be long before the whole town would seem just like the city they had tried to escape. Most of the time, Bertha and Clarence kept to themselves. They regularly attended St. John's Lutheran Church where every Sunday, Clarence was an usher. And for years, Bertha had been active in a small community theatre at the local park.

Jane opened the wooden gate and headed up the walk. The serenity of the neighborhood impressed her.

"I wonder if anybody's home," whispered Cordelia as they got to the front door. Jane rang the bell. A moment later the door opened, and a short, busty older woman with tightly permed brown hair appeared. She was wearing a particularly bright green dress and a black sweater buttoned to the neck.

"Can I help you?" she asked tentatively, blinking several times as she looked from face to face. Her eyes came to rest on Cordelia. "Don't I know you?" she said, looking more carefully over her bifocals.

"I don't think we've ever met," said Cordelia politely.

Bertha continued to stare. "Sure. You're that woman I read about in the paper last Sunday. In the magazine section. They did a big feature on you. You're that new artistic director. I don't forget things that concern acting. It's my hobby!" Her enthusiasm was growing by the minute. "You're at that big theatre down near the cathedral in St. Paul. I've been there once!"

Cordelia was new at trying to remain modest in the presence of fan adoration. She explained her lack of modesty by telling herself that it did not come naturally to some people. It was certainly *not* a character flaw. "Yes. You're quite right. I'm Cordelia Thorn. It's nice of you to remember me." I suppose this woman will want an autograph, thought Cordelia with a certain studied ennui.

"Oh, I *love* the theatre. I've been in several productions here in Stillwater. Maybe you've seen some of them."

Cordelia's mind flashed to a picture of this woman as Blanche in *A Streetcar Named Desire*. She closed her eyes momentarily trying to rid herself of the ridiculous image. It was quickly replaced by Bertha storming the halls of Dunsinane Castle as Lady Macbeth. She wondered if someone had slipped something funny into the chocolate milk. "How exciting for you." She knew her voice sounded a little too thrilled. "I wonder if my friend and I might have a brief word with you?"

"Yes," said Bertha excitedly. "Of course. What am I thinking to make you stand out on the stoop in this weather. Come in!" She stepped back, allowing them to enter. The small hallway led into a garishly decorated living room. Cordelia wondered how on earth someone could possibly have assembled such a hideous collection of plaid furniture without being arrested. She must have ruthlessly canvassed every cheap furniture showroom in the state to achieve this personal vision. Everything was either gold, orange, or avocado green. They took their seats on the couch and Bertha sat down opposite them on the edge of her recliner-rocker. She looked expectantly at Cordelia, waiting for something memorable to dribble from her lips. Cordelia, in turn, glared at Jane.

"Mrs. Anderson?" Bertha turned to look at Jane. Her rapturous expression did not change. "You're probably wondering why my friend and I came to your home this morning."

"Yes, I guess I am," said Bertha sweetly.

Jane cleared her throat. "Actually, I was wondering. Could you possibly tell me where I could find your daughter Emily? I'd like to talk to her."

Bertha's beatific expression dissolved into wariness. It finally dawned on her that she had invited two complete strangers into her home. And now, one of them was asking questions that made her nervous. "Why do you want to know? Are you friends of hers?" Her mouth closed tightly, pulling her lips into a thin straight line.

"Well, not exactly," said Jane, trying to sound friendly. "I just want to ask her a few questions."

"It's about that Lord woman, isn't it? Are you from the police?" She shot Cordelia a look that said *you have betrayed me*.

"No, Mrs. Anderson. I should have introduced myself. My name is Jane Lawless. I own a restaurant in Minneapolis, and I was a friend of Allison Lord's before her death. Is your daughter living here right now? I know she moved out of her apartment near the university."

Bertha looked back and forth between Cordelia and Jane, trying to make up her mind about something. Finally she said, "No. She's not living here. I don't know where she is, but she'll be calling me soon. I could get a message to her if I wanted."

Jane wondered what it would take to get her to want to. She pulled a card out of her jacket and handed it across to her. "That's my work number. If she calls, maybe you could give it to her and ask her to call me. I'd really appreciate your help. Next time you're in town, come on over to the restaurant for dinner on the house."

Bertha looked at the card. "There's two of us that live here."

"Of course," said Jane. "Bring your husband. I think you'd both enjoy it."

Bertha put the card into her pocket. A moment later the front door opened and a tall, thin man with watery red eyes walked into the living room and tossed his hat on the chair by the door. Bertha jumped to her feet. "I think you'd both better go now," she said softly.

Clarence Anderson brushed his hand through his slicked-back gray hair. "What's going on here, Bertha?" His tone was cold.

"Clarence, this is Cordelia Thorn. You know. I showed you the article about her in last weekend's newspaper. She's the same person who works for that theatre in St. Paul. The one we went to last Christmas."

Jane stood up. "We were hoping to be able to talk to your daughter Emily, Mr. Anderson. But your wife tells us she's not living here right now."

Bertha looked over at Jane as if she were the dimmest person she'd ever met.

"I didn't catch the name," said Clarence.

"Oh, I'm sorry. My name is Jane Lawless."

"And you want to talk to our Emily? Why?" He clenched his fists. "You want to talk to her about the Lord woman, isn't that right? Don't bother answering. I can see it in your face. You won't get any help from us. We're decent people. Godfearing! We believe in the morals we've been taught in church. What Emily has done has brought us nothing but shame. I know my daughter. She was a good girl before she met that woman. Christ, when I think of her. She deserved to die! I hope to God that Emily realizes now what she's done

to her family. We gave her everything, and she has repaid us
with this.'' His voice was thick with anger. Bertha moved
closer to Cordelia and said again softly, ''I think you better
leave.''

''I'm sorry you're in such pain, Mr. Anderson.'' Jane
backed up a step. ''I know Emily is probably suffering, too.''

Clarence looked as if she had slapped him. ''Emily?'' he
said, dumbfounded by her ignorance. ''Emily could care less
about us. She so much as told me that last weekend.''

Bertha jerked her head toward her husband. ''Last weekend? When did you talk to her last weekend?''

Clarence reached down and tucked in his already tucked-
in shirt. ''I said I *saw* her last weekend. Don't ask so many
questions.''

Bertha was not going to be put off. ''When, Clarence?''

''Last Sunday night, okay? While you were out at your
bridge club. You and all your hobbies. You know I don't like
it when I'm home and you go out. A woman belongs at home
fixing supper for her husband, not running off to some club
and leaving him nothing but a cold sandwich for dinner.''
He took out a handkerchief and wiped his neck. ''I drove
into Minneapolis. Is that okay with you? I thought maybe
Emily would have some time for her dad. I tried to talk to
her again. Talk some sense into her. But I was wasting my
time. She nearly threw me out. Said she didn't want to talk
about it anymore. Said she'd made up her mind months ago
and nothing I could possibly say would change anything. I
told her that she'd never get another penny from me for school
as long as this business continued. She said she didn't care.
Said the Lord woman had plenty of money. My God, but she
was jumpy. Kept looking at the phone the whole time we
were talking. I asked if all the years of church training we'd
given her meant nothing. She said she wanted me to leave.
God Almighty, that woman got what she deserved for doing
this to our daughter.''

''Clarence! Shut up!'' Bertha stepped in front of him. ''We
have guests. Get hold of yourself.''

''Guests?'' He spit the word back at her. ''Tell our *guests* to get out. I'm going into the kitchen, and I don't want to see them when I come back." He lumbered off without a backward glance.

"Charming," whispered Cordelia as they watched his back disappear into the dim kitchen.

"What?" said Bertha.

"I said, I'm sorry we bothered you, Mrs. Anderson. We'll be going now." Cordelia grabbed Jane's arm and pulled her toward the front door.

"I'm sorry you had to see that," said Bertha. "He's been like that ever since he found out about what Emily's been up to. He's really a good man. Maybe he's what you young folks call a chauvinist, but I love him. He has a kind heart, and he's been good to me. Right now he's just confused and angry. We both are. I don't know what's happening to this family." She took out a handkerchief and wiped her eyes.

"I'm very sorry, Mrs. Anderson. We never meant to cause trouble for you. But I really need to talk to your daughter. If you feel like you could, would you pass along my name and number to her? It could mean a great deal."

Bertha took the card out of her pocket and looked toward the kitchen door. She put it back again and held her hand over it. "You better go now," she said. "Before he comes back. He may be a good man, but he has a terrible temper."

Jane and Cordelia thanked her and walked quickly down the backyard path. Jane stopped at the gate to make sure it was latched properly. As she turned to go, she glanced up and found Clarence Anderson grimly watching them from the kitchen window.

9

Adam Lord stood casually in front of a long mirror in the bedroom of his hotel suite. He was examining himself for imperfections. "Muriel, come in here for a minute, will you? I think this button is too low for the buttonhole."

Muriel Lord entered the room, stuffing the last bit of a croissant quickly into her small mouth. She was an attractive woman, somewhat taller than her husband, and much younger. She made a point never to wear high heels in his presence. The morning they had been married, almost ten years to the day Adam's first wife had died, she knew the bargain she was making. Adam wanted a hostess and a bed partner, in that order, and he was willing to pay very well. His two children, Edwin, who was then sixteen, and Allison, who had just turned thirteen, had long ago learned to take care of themselves. Becoming their stepmother was not part of the deal. Adam Lord was rarely at home long enough to begin, let alone finish, a conversation with either of his children. He did keep a close eye on their progress in school. It was important to him that they meet certain standards, in education as well as conduct. Their behavior was monitored by the staff at his estate. For Adam, business came first, last, and in-between, and those around him had better get used to it. It was a lesson Edwin and Allison had learned long ago.

By the time Muriel arrived on the scene, it had begun to dawn on Adam that his children were growing up and would always remain a disappointment to him. Neither wanted any of the things he wanted for them. They fought him at every turn. After Edwin moved out, Allison had continued to betray him with, as he put it, some irritating sexual nonsense. Something easily remedied. Yet, somehow, this had been the last straw. The time had finally come to quit involving himself with his children's lives. They would always be his flesh and blood, and he would never let them starve, but if they continued to thumb their noses at him, so be it. He washed his hands of them. Muriel knew the exact night on which he made his momentous decision. He came into their bedroom and informed her that he wanted another child. Boy or girl, it didn't matter, but by God he was going to have one last try at molding someone into *his* idea of a successful human being. And of course, Muriel understood the threat. Cooperate or get out. Another, more cooperative hostess could easily be found. Unfortunately for Muriel, by this time she had fallen in love with him. And so, ten months later, she presented him with a little baby girl. They called her Ann, after his mother. Adam was elated. From the roof of their Philadelphia estate he had shouted that a queen had been born!

Muriel felt more and more sorry for Allison and Edwin as the years passed. After little Annie's birth, Adam rarely acknowledged that he had other children. That is, until one Christmas when Allison came home with a handsome young man riding next to her in the front seat of her car. Adam and Mitchel Page hit it off immediately. This was the first time Muriel had ever seen Adam warm to his daughter. Sitting in their formal dining room over dinner, Adam had been positively glowing with fatherly affection. He even offered Mitchel a good position in one of his corporations after the wedding. Muriel remembered how uneasy Allison had seemed after the word marriage was mentioned. She was almost positive Mitchel had been discussing it with Adam, but doubted Allison had been let in on their little secret. To Adam, Mitchel must have represented the son he wanted, and an opportunity to build his family empire. He wouldn't need to wait for Ann to grow up. He could start right away!

Muriel could see how impressed Mitchel was by Adam's money. Toward the end of their stay, she had caught him alone one evening, sitting in Adam's leather armchair in the study. By that point in the visit, he didn't even bother to stand when she entered, but merely pointed at a chair opposite him and offered her some of Adam's most expensive brandy. She wasn't sure he was bright enough to realize how much she disliked him.

Before Christmas break was over, Adam invited them both out to his estate on Long Island for Easter. Mitchel accepted immediately. Muriel had noticed that Allison had become more and more quiet as the last few days of their visit dragged on. She could only guess at the pressure Mitchel was putting on her to marry him. After they left, Adam talked continually about the future he was planning for them both. He said he knew that Mitchel was rough around the edges, but somehow, to Adam, his physical appearance seemed to make up for everything that was lacking in his personality. He told her that people should give him more credit. He was smarter than most people thought. Muriel remained unconvinced.

Then, before Easter, Allison wrote to say that she and Mitchel had broken up and would not be coming out for spring break. Instantly, Muriel could feel the change in Adam. During the winter she had watched him blossom. He seemed more content than she had ever seen him. He had even become a more loving and considerate husband. Now, all of that changed. From the day he received Allison's letter, he never spoke her name again. That is, until late one night when Allison walked unannounced into the downstairs library. She had just come back from a summer in England and had written to say she would be stopping in Philadelphia. Adam wouldn't let Muriel see any of her recent letters. She found this odd since he had never before cared whether she read his personal correspondence or not. When Allison walked calmly into the room, Adam told Muriel to go upstairs to her room and close the door. This was going to be a private conversation. Muriel did as she was told, but before long the shouting became so loud that she put on her robe and came back down the central stairway and stood outside the library door. Listening, she could tell Adam was furious.

He was threatening to cut Allison off financially. She remembered the scene all too clearly:

"Why couldn't you have stayed with Mitchel? It's the only normal thing you've ever done. Was he *so* bad? You don't know the plans I'd made for you!"

"You're an old fool, Daddy. You may have made some plans, but they were nothing compared with the plans *he* was making. I guarantee you wouldn't have liked his."

"He has ambition! I admire that in a man."

"You wouldn't have admired what he was planning, trust me."

"I can't believe he let you go that easily."

Allison laughed coldly. "I don't call a broken rib easy. We must have different standards."

Both were momentarily silent.

"I don't believe you. You're making that up. The man I met would never do something like that. I'll give you a choice, since you're always so hot on being allowed to make your own decisions. You go back to him, and you'll never have to worry about money for the rest of your life. Don't think I can't read that look on your face. You may toss all this off pretty easily right now. You still have my credit cards in your pocket. And that bank account I fill up for you every month. But a few months on your own may change your mind. You go home and think about it. You've never lived one single day without all the things money can buy. It's not easy, Allison. It's hell to make a living out there. What are you going to do with half a degree in *Communications*, whatever the hell that is? I mean, do you want to be a waitress? How about a check-out girl at a local discount store. Fine. Live with your girlfriend, and I guarantee you'll be seeing the world like you've never seen it before. I hope you've developed a fondness for cheap wine and spaghetti sauce because you're going to be living on it. No more fancy restaurants. Think about it, Ally. No more trips to Europe. No more large donations to all your crazy charities. No more expensive clothes. And do you think you're going to keep all your fine friends at that sorority when they know what you're up to? No money, no friends, no nothing. And for what?''

Allison shot out of the door without looking back. Adam continued to yell. "You go home and think about it, Ally! This is your last chance. I'm not changing my mind! Think about it hard!''

That was the last time Muriel had ever seen Allison.

"Muriel," said Adam again, "don't just stand there! Come over and look at this button! It looks too low doesn't it? It makes that suit wrinkle across my stomach.''

"You're putting on weight, dear," said Muriel absently. She walked around the front of him. "That's all. It's not the suit.''

Adam tugged at the pockets. "Yeah, maybe you're right. But a *good* tailor could hide that.''

"Arnold is the best tailor in New York City. Why don't you wear the blue suit?''

"No," said Adam, turning sideways and pressing a hand over his stomach. "No time. We've got to get over to the church.''

"Of course, darling," said Muriel softly. He's got to be more upset than he's letting on, thought Muriel. She wondered what would happen today if Edwin appeared. She knew Adam hadn't seen his son in years, but supposedly he lived somewhere in northern Minnesota. She wished, just for one day, that there could be some peace.

Sigrid and Maggie stood on either side of the wide double doors that led into the sanctuary of Good Shepherd Presbyterian Church. Each had been asked to stand in front of a large potted fern and hand out memorial programs. So far, very few people had arrived for the service that was to begin in less than fifteen minutes. Sigrid leaned casually against the edge of the door and looked through one of the programs. It contained brief details of Allison's life as well as a list of those who would be speaking during the service. Down at the bottom of the last page, one of the deceased's favorite

Bible verses had been inserted under a poorly drawn picture of Jesus holding a lamb. Sigrid shook her head, wondering whose idea it had been to include that little fabrication.

A gust of cold air blew a small group into the vestibule. After they had passed, Sigrid moved over to Maggie's side of the aisle and grabbed another handful of programs from a box behind the fern. "I bet there aren't going to be as many people here today as we all thought." She looked around the huge sanctuary, awash in colored light from the stained-glass windows. "There are a lot of people pretty angry with Ally for giving the sorority a black eye."

Maggie nodded her agreement. "Do you know if Kari was planning to come? I've hardly seen her since last Monday night." She stepped momentarily out of her right shoe and leaned down to rub her foot. "Did I tell you how strange she acted during dinner? She bolted out of the room just as dessert was being served. I mean, I didn't know what to say."

Sigrid handed the stack of programs she was holding to Maggie and tried to pin back some wisps of hair that had fallen out of her tight bun. With her blonde hair done up like the Farmer's Daughter, she looked even more the full-blooded Norwegian that she was. "Before we left, I went up to Kari's room to tell her she could ride over with us if she wanted. She wasn't there." Sigrid retrieved the programs and moved back to her side of the aisle.

"I wish," whispered Maggie, "that she'd talk to us. With Ally gone, I feel like the three of us need to stick together. I guess maybe I'm being naive."

"Maybe," said Sigrid.

Several large groups began filtering into the vestibule. Edith Holms and another longtime housemother entered looking composed but grim under their sensible hats. It had been a hard week for Edith. She had taken Allison's death very personally. For the last twelve years she had considered herself the responsible adult in the midst of reckless youth. Until now she had never considered the impossibility of such a task. People nodded politely as Edith and friend walked slowly down the center aisle, taking seats near the front.

Sigrid noticed Adolph Mauer sitting alone in the back of the church. She pointed him out to Maggie.

"That's odd. Did you see him come in?" asked Sigrid, nodding toward him.

"No. He probably slipped in one of the side doors. I've always thought he was a little weird."

Sigrid watched him carefully. He *was* an odd man. She wondered where he had learned to cook. Even his lasagna tasted like sauerbraten. She had kidded him about it once, but he seemed to be a man totally devoid of humor.

"Who's that with Elliot Kratager?" whispered Maggie.

"*Put on your glasses*, meatball. It's Brook Solomon. She's that new pledge living in the house this quarter. Maybe she's got a thing for busboys, like some other people I know." She winked at Maggie, who had briefly dated a busboy from another house last year.

"Right," said Maggie knowingly. "Isn't Brook the one that has crying fits all the time? I can't figure her out."

"I really haven't tried to talk to her," shrugged Sigrid. "I suppose I should make a point to be more friendly. The first few days of fall quarter she was a ball of fire! I thought she'd be the perfect candidate for pledge class president. Lately, I don't know. She seems so distracted. I know something's wrong, but I don't have a clue. Maybe Elliot can cheer her up. I'm told they've renewed an old friendship. Seems they knew each other in high school, though I gather not well."

Maggie watched as a blurry Elliot put his indistinct arm protectively around Brook's blurry shoulder. She liked his newly grown blond beard, even though she couldn't see it well without her glasses. It made him look older.

"Brook seems to be taking Ally's death kind of hard," said Sigrid. She smiled politely and handed programs to two older women she'd never seen before. "I think they were pretty close. Remember, Ally sponsored her for membership."

Maggie turned just in time to see a group of house corporation board members stride authoritatively into the vestibule with Susan Julian in the lead. They moved single file into the sanctuary without so much as an acknowledgment to either Maggie or Sigrid.

"What do you think of Elliot?" whispered Maggie as she watched all the fur coats bobbing purposefully down the aisle.

"I suppose he's quite a catch if you like the Young Republicans. He's out to save the world through morality and rightwing politics. To hear him talk, all we need are more businessmen, Bibles, and intercontinental ballistic missiles. Seems like a winning combination to me." She walked over to get another stack of programs and continued to stand on Maggie's side of the aisle. "You knew he was elected to a seat in student government, didn't you? I believe he will be representing the neo-Nazis on campus. I'm sure it will look great on a future résumé. And once he gets his law degree, there'll be no stopping him. I heard a rumor that he already has the word SENATOR tattooed on his chest. Or did I start that rumor? I forget. Anyway, I think he's ruthless enough to make it big."

"And I suppose you'd vote for him," said Maggie a little too loudly.

"Shhh! Yeah, maybe I would. I don't mind ruthless people. What *is* wrong with your foot, Maggie? You keep fidgeting with it."

"I had to borrow a pair of black heels. I couldn't find mine. These are a little too small. I was sure mine were under a pile of blankets in my closet. When I couldn't find them, I thought I remembered seeing them in my laundry basket. But I think that was several weeks ago. And anyway, I couldn't find it either. You haven't seen them, have you? You know what they look like?" Sigrid slowly rolled her eyes as she walked back to her side of the aisle.

At the front of the sanctuary Mr. and Mrs. Adam Lord were just entering and being shown their seats. Maggie wished now that she *had* worn her new glasses. "Who's that man who just came in and sat down by Mr. Lord?"

"Can't you guess?" Sigrid's whisper was more like a hiss. "It's Mitchel Page. Wonder Boy himself. Don't you remember? Ally brought him home to meet the family last Christ-

mas. It was just a whim on her part but I guess Daddy almost
put him on the board of directors. They really hit it off. I still
can't believe she dated that moron.''

Maggie had never really disliked Mitch. She thought he
was terribly good looking and could easily understand someone's attraction to him. The only trouble was, he *was* kind
of boring. Maybe you just needed to get to know him better.

A pipe organ began quietly playing a Bach fugue as a man
in black robes came through the side door at the front of the
sanctuary and sat down. It was Maggie and Sigrid's cue to
close the back doors and take their seats. Sigrid wondered if
anyone here knew Allison well enough to realize how absurd
all this was. She also knew that as long as she stayed angry,
she wouldn't cry.

The minister stood up and climbed into the pulpit. In a
deeply resonant voice he asked everyone to please rise and
turn in their hymnals to page twenty-three. The congregation
was invited to join with him in singing "Onward, Christian
Soldiers." Sigrid closed her hymnal and remained seated.

"They're on the last hymn," called Jane to her staff who
were just putting the finishing touches on the buffet table.
She stood on an open stairway leading up to the sanctuary.
She hoped there would be enough of everything to accom-
modate all the people who would soon be filtering down after
the service. The church had not looked as crowded as she
had expected. Still, she estimated the number at well over a
hundred.

· Jane walked back down the stairway and into the kitchen
where the silver tea and coffee services were being filled.
Trays of warm scones with jam and clotted cream and others
of finger sandwiches had already been placed on the buffet
table. Two large crystal bowls of fresh strawberries and kiwi
rested on either end. The fragrant aroma of freshly brewed
coffee filled the hall with a smell Jane remembered vividly
from her childhood. She wondered if all church basements
smelled alike.

A slow trickle of people began to come down the stairs

into the hall. Jane walked out of the doorway and leaned against a pillar to watch people arrange themselves around the room. She recognized a few faces from the sorority, but almost no one else. She wondered if Mr. and Mrs. Lord would put in an appearance.

Once the organ music stopped upstairs, the hall began to fill more quickly. Jane could see Maggie and Sigrid wading through the crowd on the opposite side of the room heading over to her. With some difficulty Sigrid broke through a wall of people lined up in front of the buffet. A moment later Maggie appeared.

"That coffee smells wonderful," said Sigrid, closing her eyes and sniffing the air. "What did you do to make it smell so good?"

Jane was sorry to see Kari wasn't with them. "It's the same coffee we use at the restaurant. I have it privately blended. I'll give you a couple of packets to take back to the house when I see you two tomorrow night."

"See us tomorrow night?" said Sigrid, raising her eyebrow at Maggie.

Maggie smiled weakly. "I'm sorry, Siggy. With all the commotion and everything, I forgot to tell you that Jane wanted to get together with us to discuss some of the problems we're having at the house. You know. The stealing and other stuff. We don't seem to be getting anywhere with it ourselves, and I thought maybe it would be a good idea to talk to someone about it." She knew Sigrid would be upset that she hadn't discussed it with her first. But she was resolute. She felt certain it was the right decision, no matter what Sigrid thought. Things were simply getting out of hand.

Sigrid turned an appraising eye on Jane. "Is that *all* you want to talk about?"

Jane was surprised by Sigrid's response. "Look," she said, not wanting to create a rift between them, "I want to be absolutely clear about this. I was asked to be an advisor to the executive board this year, but I can't do my job if you're not going to let me in on what the actual problems *are* at the house. My hands are tied. What Maggie mentioned to me was serious, and I'm not so sure you shouldn't have reported it to the police right away. But laying that aside for now, I'm wondering if all this doesn't fit into some larger pattern." She looked carefully around the room and spoke more quietly. "The more I think about it, the more I'm convinced Allison's death wasn't a suicide. It just doesn't make any sense. I've no proof as yet, but I think we need to consider at least the possibility that there's some connection between the problems at the house and her death. I *will* get to the bottom of all this, I promise you. You two could help if you want, or drag your feet and make it a lot more difficult for me. Either way, I'm not going to give up until I've found the truth." She hesitated, trying to read some meaning into Sigrid's blank expression. Before anyone could answer, an older woman inched in between Maggie and Sigrid and began to thank Jane profusely for the lovely food. Two others standing behind her smiled and nodded. After they had moved on, she continued: "Maggie and I made a date for nine tomorrow evening at my restaurant. I'd like you both to come if that's possible. What do you say?"

Maggie looked anxiously over at Sigrid. She would go without her but hoped she wouldn't need to.

Sigrid examined Jane as if she were trying to make up her mind about something. Maggie began to fidget again with her shoes. The uncomfortable silence had reminded her of how much her feet hurt. Finally Sigrid said, "You surprise me, Jane. You're not the airhead I thought you were."

"Siggy!" said Maggie.

Again Sigrid was silent for a moment. "I work until nine-thirty. I suppose I could come by after that."

Jane was delighted, though she had the sense not to let Sigrid know just *how* delighted. "Maggie, what *is* wrong with your feet?" asked Jane, looking down at the floor. Maggie had stepped completely out of her shoes.

"Don't ask," said Sigrid. "Let's just say her room was buried under an avalanche of crap, and she had to borrow those. They don't fit."

Maggie was annoyed. "You're not the most organized person I've ever met either, Siggy."

"No, but I can find my bed."

Edith Holms walked up behind Sigrid and put her hand lightly on Maggie's shoulder. "Wasn't that a lovely service," she said wistfully. "The minister had such a wonderful way with words. You should make a point to go over and thank him."

Sigrid turned to look directly at her. How could someone possibly listen to a woman whose hair was getting bluer by the day? "It was a farce, Edith." Sigrid's voice was calm.

"What did you say, dear?" Edith's ability to hear in a crowded room was less than perfect. Sigrid couldn't possibly have said what she thought she heard.

"I said, *this whole thing was a farce!*" Sigrid almost shouted the words, causing several people to cease chewing their cream scones.

Edith was clearly embarrassed, as much for Sigrid as for herself. "Yes, dear. Of course. I think I see Paula Stevens over there. She's on the house corporation board this year. I really should thank her for coming. Will you all excuse me?" She turned and marched off quickly, with as much grace as she could muster under the circumstances.

"Look over there," said Sigrid, nodding toward the front table. In a beautifully tailored dark blue suit stood Mitchel Page looking unusually appropriate. An older man was next to him, his arm around Mitch's shoulder. They were both talking to a group of older men.

"Who's that with Mitch?" asked Jane.

"That's the famous Adam Lord," said Sigrid angrily. "He's been parading that oaf around the room like the bereaved son-in-law ever since they came downstairs. You may not have noticed, but Mitch sat with the Lords during the service. And if all that doesn't put you off your afternoon snack, you're a better man than I am."

Jane watched as Adam pulled Mitch away from one group and maneuvered him over to another. She wondered how on earth Mitch had been able to afford such a suit.

"We've got to get going," said Maggie, checking her watch. "Sigrid and I promised to help move the flowers out of the sanctuary." She looked hungrily at the table of food. "Maybe I'll just grab a few things to eat in the car on the way back." She reached for a paper plate and began piling it high with fruit and sandwiches. "Well, see you tomorrow night." She popped a small strawberry into her mouth. "Come on, Siggy. We're already late." Sigrid gave Jane an enigmatic little smile and followed Maggie out of the hall.

The knot of people near the food table was beginning to thin out just a bit. Jane could see Edith's blue-gray hair across the room; she was talking animatedly to Adam Lord. Incredibly, he still had his arm around Mitch's shoulder. The buffet table was well stocked, so she decided to check the backup coffee in the kitchen. No sooner had she come through the door when the sight of a figure standing in the back of the room startled her into a complete stop. The young man looked so much like Allison that, at first, she thought it was. He was helping himself to a cup of coffee and did not seem to notice her entrance. She took the opportunity to examine him more closely. He was tall, thin, and had Allison's aquiline features. The hair color was even the same rich brown. She walked a few steps closer. What seemed most strikingly similar were the eyes. They had the same ironic expression.

The young man looked up and found Jane staring at him. He gave her a questioning smile. "Are you waiting for some coffee?" He picked up a clean cup and held it out to her.

"Sure," she said. "Why not. My name is Jane Lawless."

The man looked surprised. "Oh! I guess I'm in luck then. You're just the woman I came back here to find." He poured her a cup and handed it across to her. "I wonder if perhaps we could sit down somewhere? I'd like to talk with you if you have a few moments."

"Of course," said Jane. She was entirely too curious about what he might want to say to her to refuse. She led the way out of the kitchen into one of the empty back tables. Awkwardly, they perched on two uncomfortable folding chairs.

"I wanted to thank you," he said, smiling a little sadly.

"Someone told me you were responsible for the food here today. My sister spent many summers in England, and even though I don't understand how you could possibly have known, a cream tea was something she loved dearly. Actually, the food was the only thing here today that would have given her any pleasure."

"Of course," said Jane. "You're her brother! I should have realized that immediately."

"It's my fault," said Edwin. "I should have introduced myself right away. I saw the way you were looking at me. A great many people don't seem to find any resemblance at all. My name is Edwin Lord."

Jane gazed across the room to where Adam Lord was standing. "You don't look anything like your father." She couldn't believe they were even related.

"No, I would agree with you. And the woman with him is not my mother. She's his second wife. Our mother died when we were both quite young. Muriel married Father when my sister and I were in our teens. I think we both take after our mother, in more ways than we ever realized."

Jane liked his voice. It was deep, and yet he didn't use it the way some men *used* their deep voices. He didn't try to sound authoritative or give the impression that he was *in charge*. His manner was educated but had none of the arrogance often associated with wealth. "Do you live here?" she asked.

"In Minneapolis? No. I live in northern Minnesota. Actually, it's near the Canadian border. The closest town of any size is Thunder Bay. I live with a community of brothers."

"You're a priest?"

"No," laughed Edwin. "Nothing like that. But we are a spiritual community."

"I see," said Jane, trying to imagine what that meant.

"I can see you're wondering what Adam Lord's son is doing living a monastic life in northern Minnesota. If you have a few minutes, I'd like to explain it to you."

Jane nodded and settled a little more comfortably into her chair.

"You must have known my sister, is that right?"

"Not well. But we had talked a few times."

"How did you know about the food? I mean, was it just a coincidence?"

"No," said Jane. "I'm an alumna of Kappa Alpha Sigma. I've been donating some of my time there as an advisor this year. I sat in on a few of the executive board meetings, and since Ally was on that same board, we did get to talking a couple of times afterward. We discovered we'd both spent a good deal of time in England. In fact, I think she told me how much she loved a cream tea the first time we ever spoke. It's funny, isn't it?" Jane looked down into her coffee cup. "When she told me about that I never dreamed . . ."

"No," said Edwin kindly. "There's no way any of us could have known. But when I came downstairs after the service and actually found a piece of my sister in this otherwise empty charade, it made me feel less alone. Thank you for that, Jane."

The simplicity of his words moved her deeply. "You're the second person today to call this a farce."

"Ally had a few close friends who would have understood. But not many. In her entire life she invited very few people into her soul." Edwin sipped his coffee. His hands looked rough, as if he had recently done a great deal of physical labor. "Ally and I didn't really have much parenting after my mother died. Father was rarely around. Business always came first. But I can tell you that we both knew clearly what was expected of us. Adam Lord is a very controlling man. Our futures had been completely planned. A good college. Marriage to another wealthy family to bring more money into the business. Always the business. I know Father thought we never made any attempt to please him, but that wasn't true. I left when I was seventeen, though I came back briefly three years later after Ally had tried to commit suicide. Father had found out about Allison's relationship with another young woman and convinced the other girl's father to send her away. It was too much for Ally. She thought Father would be controlling everything in her life until the day she died. She was almost seventeen at the time. I'd been traveling around trying to make some sense out of my life. Two weeks before I got word about her suicide attempt, I found St. Victor's. I flew back immediately and sat with her for many days until she was stronger. Father was furious. It was just one more proof that she didn't love him. And you can't imagine the guilt I felt, leaving her there alone for those three years.

"We both knew the only way she would survive, literally, was to get her out of that house. Since I was living in Minnesota, I convinced her to apply that next spring to the University of Minnesota. I wanted her to live in Duluth and attend UMD, but she chose the Minneapolis campus. Even so, we could still see each other without too much trouble. I usually came down or she came up one weekend a month. My sister and I are"—he caught himself and grimaced— "were, close. We're very different people, and yet we were about as close as I expect two people could ever be.

"Living at St. Victor's was helping me to focus. I don't know if you've ever thought about it much, but it's terribly difficult to have an extended conversation with yourself. People stop trying because they get interrupted. There's simply too much noise. At St. Victor's I was finally able to cut through all that. I found out how easily people can hide what they're thinking and feeling even from themselves. I certainly had. Lately, I've begun to see myself more clearly. I've been able to actually find the love and energy inside me that I was sure didn't exist. I mean, I had always thought of myself as a hopeless cynic." He loosened his tie. "Ally and I talked endlessly. We always have. In the past few years our lives had, in some strange way, paralleled. She needed to come to terms with her personal life before she could get on with her future. And my life had stopped almost completely because I couldn't get a grip on something essentially spiritual. Do you know the kind of restlessness I mean? The kind that manifests itself in stillness? I think we both felt like we were holding our breath. These past few years, I can tell you truthfully, have been hard ones for both of us. We knew we didn't want what Father offered, but what *did* we want?

"Ally was totally nonreligious. She just could never see things that way. And I've discovered that, at heart, I'm probably a mystic. And yet amazingly, we could always talk. There were no barriers. I think it was because we were both seeking the truth of our lives. I would describe that as a spiritual search, though I know Ally would have put it some other way. Yet it was the same thing. No one can bear to live a meaningless life and that's what we felt Father was offering us. I know she would have found her life perverse without being able to live at peace in her own body." Edwin looked carefully at Jane. "Yes, I knew she was a lesbian. And I could tell last summer that she had crossed some inner threshold. Something was different. We talked about it some when she got back from England, though she apparently stopped off at home first, which was a mistake. Father can apply a tremendous amount of pressure when he wants something. He's a master at finding just the right nerve. She brought Emily up to see me as soon as she got back to Minnesota. I liked her enormously."

Jane was fascinated. "You don't have any problems with a lesbian sister?"

Edwin smiled. "How can I explain it? There are two views one can take of nature. One is that it is corrupt. It has to be corrected, must never be yielded to. Some people say nature has fallen. Like mankind, it's sinful. It has to be controlled. And most importantly, if you want to find *God*, you have to look elsewhere. God and nature are divided. Some religions believe that. The other view is that all nature is a manifestation of divinity. God cannot be separated from His creation. He is to be found *in* it. Nature is therefore to be *understood*, to be cooperated with and cherished. Some religions believe this. And so do I. Depending on which you believe, you get a very different kind of society. You can see it in the way various societies treat the earth. The ethic is totally different. In the woods that surround St. Victor's I've been learning how to experience that divinity. I know this may sound kind of wafty, but I can finally say that I've found God." He leaned back in his chair. "I know that's a pretty big statement, but what I've learned is that what we call eternal is simply the experience of life. It's very hard to express all this in words. The best things are the hardest to talk about, at least for me. But that's what I believe, however ineptly phrased. And so, no, I have no problem with Allison's sexual preference. I should say, with the truth of her own body. How could I?''

Just as he was finishing this thought, Muriel Lord walked up nervously and stood next to him. Edwin looked up.

"Muriel! How are you?" His tone was warm.

"Hello, Edwin. I wondered if we wouldn't see you today." Her eyes darted back to Adam, trying to see if he had noticed where she had gone.

"I've already seen Father," said Edwin simply. "He didn't have much to say to me. I don't think he wanted to hear anything I had to say to him. So our conversation was somewhat abbreviated. You look well."

Muriel did not seem to know what to do with her hands. The tension surrounding her was almost visible. "I guess I just wanted to tell you how sorry I was about your sister. I've never been much of a friend to either of you, I know that." Her eyes filled with tears, and her mouth trembled. Edwin stood up and offered her his handkerchief.

"Father would never have let you be our friend, Muriel. We never held it against you." He put his arms around her and let her cry against his shoulder. "How is Annie?" he said softly.

Muriel stood back and wiped her eyes roughly. "Annie is wonderful. She's the best thing in my life. She didn't come with us. Adam thought it was better if she stayed in school." She said the words nervously, looking around as she spoke.

"I'd love to see her again," smiled Edwin.

"Oh, do you think you could?" Muriel jumped on the idea. "I know Annie would love to see her big brother again. It's been years. I don't mean this in a wrong way, but I think she needs another man in her life besides Adam. Sometimes I wonder what he's trying to do. The things he asks of her. It's like she has to continually prove, over and over again, how much she loves him.'' She hesitated. "Maybe you could come for Thanksgiving. Say, that's an idea!"

From across the room a deep voice bellowed, "Muriel! We're leaving.'' Adam had at last taken his arm from around Mitch's shoulder. "Hurry up.''

"I'll ask him, Edwin. As soon as we get back to Philadelphia. And then I'll write you. It's meant so much to see you today. You have no idea. Goodbye.''

Jane stared as Muriel walked across the nearly empty hall. Before she reached the front of the room, Adam and Mitch had left.

"She has a lonely life,'' said Edwin, sitting back down. He watched as she silently put on her fur coat. "I don't begin to understand it, but for some reason, I think she really does love my father. He'll never let her invite me for Thanksgiving. I think maybe I better make a point of visiting my little sister soon.'' They both continued to look as Muriel walked wearily up the stairs, pausing just as she reached the top to turn around and give a small wave goodbye.

They both sat in silence for a few moments after she had gone.

"I hope I haven't bored you,'' said Edwin finally.

"No. Certainly not. I think you've helped me a great deal.''

Edwin turned the coffee cup around in his hand. "You don't believe it was a suicide either, do you?'' The words were spoken matter-of-factly. He did not elaborate.

"No, I don't. I'm trying to find out what really happened. That may be impossible, but I have to try.''

"You *have* to try?'' It was Edwin's face but with Allison's ironic expression. "I see.'' He reached over and took hold of her hand. "I'll think of you, Jane. If there's anything I can do to help, you can send me a letter care of St. Victor's.'' He squeezed her hand. "I wish you luck.''

10

Sniffing out the best restaurants in town was a particular specialty of Adam Lord's. The new northern Italian restaurant at the top of the Hogarth Tower in downtown St. Paul fit the bill perfectly. It was just the sort of atmosphere he'd envisioned when he had invited Arthur Manning and his wife to join him for dinner. The evening had been planned in order to introduce Mitchel Page to one of the wealthiest entrepreneurs in the Twin Cities.

It wasn't that Mitchel had pulled the wool over Adam's eyes. That wasn't it at all. Adam saw Mitch for the blatant opportunist that he was. Even Mitch's attempts to appear grief-stricken had impressed Adam as little more than a pathetic act. Still, he felt he owed the boy something. To be sure, not as much as Mitch probably wanted, but at least a push in the right direction. At the same time, he knew his momentary altruism was limited. It didn't even extend as far as offering him a job in one of his own corporations. That would be going too far. Last Christmas's little episode was best forgotten. He needed no reminder of his daughter's inability to form normal relationships. As far as he was concerned, this one push was more than enough. After that, he washed his hands of him.

The elevator doors opened, and Arthur Manning and his wife drifted casually out into the lobby. Adam, who was sitting with Muriel in the lounge, rose instantly and walked toward them with his hand thrust out.

"Artie! Good to see you again!" He pumped Arthur's arm

vigorously "And this must be your lovely wife." He turned
to Mrs. Manning who looked barely awake. She had the
glazed expression of someone who had been dragged along
on entirely too many business dinners. Adam recognized the
look. He had seen it often on Muriel's face. "It's nice to
meet you. Gloria, is it?"

"You have a good memory, Adam," said Arthur, smiling
lavishly. Gloria managed to momentarily focus her eyes.
Adam wondered if she was *on* anything in particular. Her
pupils were a bit too dilated for mere boredom.

"Where is the young man in question?" smiled Arthur
knowingly. He rocked back and forth on the tips of his toes.
Adam had always thought Arthur was a nerd.

"I expect he'll be here momentarily. I told him seven."
He looked at his watch and found it was nearly seven-thirty.
"What do you say I buy you and your lovely wife a drink
before dinner? Muriel and I already have a table. Why don't
you follow me." Adam led the way into the bar, noticing
that Muriel was now on her second drink. That wouldn't be
so bad if she hadn't already downed a double earlier at the
hotel. Muriel didn't take pills, thank God, but she did like
bourbon in ever-increasing quantities.

The waiter came and took their drink order. Muriel asked
for another double bourbon and water. Adam glared at her
while Arthur ordered an imported beer and Gloria asked for
a Mai Tai. Muriel, obviously emboldened by the alcohol,
glared back. Just as she was about to plant her right heel
squarely over Adam's left black loafer, she noticed Mitchel
step out of the elevator.

Adam excused himself and walked quickly out into the
lobby. "You're late, Mitchel," he said gruffly.

Mitch turned around and grinned boyishly. "Sorry, Adam.
Something came up."

"Straighten your tie. We'll say it was unavoidable. For
Chrissake, be positive tonight. Personable. Pretend you're
me." He gave Mitch a quick smirk and then watched for his
response.

Mitch smiled nervously.

"Come on," said Adam, leading the way to the table. He made introductions and offered a toast to Arthur and Gloria. Then he sat back to watch. The ball was, as they say, in Mitchel's court.

"So," said Arthur, playing with the parasol his wife had found nearly submerged by a pineapple slice in her drink, "you're the young man Adam has told me so much about."

Mitch looked back and forth between Adam and Arthur, grinning stupidly.

The waiter arrived, and Mitchel ordered the same imported beer as Arthur.

"Where do you see yourself in five years, Mitchel?"

"Well," said Mitch, glancing furtively at Adam, "I guess I see myself as having an important job in Manning Enterprises, sir."

Arthur smiled. "Let me tell you a little bit about my company."

As Arthur talked animatedly about himself, Mitch became aware of a familiar voice somewhere behind him. Slowly, he turned. There, talking loudly to a waiter at the front of the dining room, stood his girlfriend, Jamie. "Holy shit," he said under his breath. The waiter arrived with his beer. "Will you all excuse me for a moment," he said, interrupting Arthur mid-sentence. Adam stiffened in his seat.

Even Mitch knew things were not going well. He walked slowly into the other room, trying to get a grip on his growing frustration. Losing his temper tonight would be a big mistake. Jamie had obviously been making a scene trying to locate him. If she wanted to see him so badly, then she would get what she wanted. The waiter followed as she walked around the room. She managed to ignore him as he tried to convince her to leave quietly. Mitch inched in front of him and put his hand on her shoulder, spinning her around. "Go back to the lobby," he ordered coldly.

Jamie's eyes flashed. "You miserable sonofabitch."

"I'm going to have to ask you two to leave," said the waiter impatiently.

Mitch grabbed Jamie's hand and pulled her roughly back out into the lobby. She struggled to break away from his grip, but he held her firmly.

"Calm down, Jamie! I know what you're mad about. I *did* try to call you after the memorial service. You weren't home. I saw you leave alone, and I'm sorry."

"Let go of me, you shithead. You never tried to call me."

He moved closer and pinned her against a mirrored wall next to the elevator. A second later, the elevator doors opened and a couple stepped out. Mitch smiled at them and continued what he hoped would look like his intimate conversation. "Not unless you quiet down." He squeezed her hand.

"That hurts! I'll scream that you're hurting me unless you let go." She wriggled free of his grip and rubbed her fingers.

Again Mitch smiled at the couple who were now waiting to be seated. "Listen to me for a minute, will you! I had no idea Adam was going to want to introduce me to this bigwig tonight. For the first time in my life, someone actually is giving me a break! I think Adam really likes me. Kind of like a son." Mitch smoothed out his new suit. "He thinks of himself as my father. I can tell. And he's going to help me. Us! Can't you understand that? I know he's eventually going to offer me a job himself. He just wants me to prove myself first."

"You promised to call, and you didn't. Then you lie about it. I'm not Allison. I'm not so easily manipulated. And I don't like this runaround. I know I don't come from a rich family. Maybe that's it! My dad *works* for the phone company, he doesn't *own* it. It's all beginning to get through to me now. I'm just temporary, right? All that stuff you promised about our future is just a big lie. I'm a convenience. A convenient alibi!"

"Have you been drinking?" snarled Mitch.

"No! I told you I wouldn't after homecoming weekend. I promised. *I* don't break my promises." A threatening quality crept into her voice. "You better be careful, Mitch. I know where you were that night, or I should say where you weren't.

And I'm sure Adam Lord would love to hear everything I know about what you and Allison were up to."

Mitch grabbed her by the shoulders and pinned her against the wall. "You better watch your mouth, bitch. You don't know *nothing*!"

Jamie snarled back. "You've been lying to me, you bastard. You don't love me! You just want to keep me quiet. Promise the little girl a happy future and keep her in your pocket. Get your goofy girlfriend to lie to the police for you. A piece of cake."

Mitch pressed his thumbs around her neck and brought his face very close to hers. "Shut up, you slut. You wreck this for me tonight, and I'll make you wish you'd never been born. You think I killed Allison? Don't think I can't do the same to you."

Jamie brought her knee up hard into his groin, sending him howling in agony to the floor.

"Let me say it again," she said, standing over him. A few people came out of the bar to see what was causing all the commotion. "I'm not Allison. So don't expect me to be afraid of you. Think about what I said." She stepped over him and punched the elevator button. No one stopped her as she walked into the elevator and disappeared behind the closing doors.

Mitch dissolved into his own pain. When he finally looked up, Adam was standing over him, shaking his head. Mitchel could see Arthur and the two wives coming out of the bar, still holding their drinks. He knew he was not making a good impression. Muriel moved closer to Adam and stared down at him. Through his pain he thought he saw a glimmer of compassion on her face. He tried to smile, but it was no use.

Muriel fished around in her glass until she found the cherry. She examined it briefly before popping it into her small mouth. "I don't know about the rest of you, but I'm starving."

11

"What, pray tell, are chanterelles?" Cordelia sat with her feet propped up on Jane's desk, casually reading through the new late fall menu. The Lyme House was known for changing its food with the seasons. "It sounds like a French cathedral, although I doubt even you would have that on the menu."

Jane had given up trying to finish a report she had been working on all week. She had hoped to complete it before Maggie and Sigrid arrived at nine. However, a few minutes ago, Cordelia had grandly swept into the room wearing her immense black cape and cossack hat. It had proved to be the death of any further work. "It's a type of mushroom," said Jane as she sat back in her chair, tossing her pencil on top of the last monthly financial report.

"Uhm," said Cordelia. "Grilled chicken with garlic pesto. Braised pork with carmelized chestnuts and Calvados. Lamb pastitsio. Steamed plum pudding with Armagnac sauce. And what's this Lyme House gateau Grand Marnier?"

"How come you aren't at the theatre?" asked Jane curiously. "It's Friday night."

Cordelia yawned. "Rest for the weary. A well-deserved night off. Actually, we've got this blues ensemble from the East Coast performing there tonight. You didn't answer my question. What's the gateau?"

Jane took off her wire-rimmed glasses and laid them down on the desk. She rubbed her sore eyes and then sat looking at Cordelia, enjoying the moment of anticipation. "Just a little thing Adrienne whipped up."

"Jane," said Cordelia, elongating her name in a slight whine. "Stop teasing. Just tell me." Cordelia knew that Adrienne Vee, the pastry chef, rarely did anything *little*.

"Okay. Prepare yourself. It's a toasted hazelnut cake with apricots and orange butter cream. It's covered in white chocolate and creme fraiche flavored with Grand Marnier, and then more ground toasted hazelnuts."

"Ahhh," said Cordelia, her eyes rolling back into her head. "Isn't hedonism wonderful?"

"We've got some new breads and soups, too. One of them, a scallop and Jerusalem artichoke chowder, I think you'll want to try right away." Jane was always amused at Cordelia's very real ecstasy over food. It was something they had always shared. Cordelia also happened to like junk food, which Jane could never quite seem to understand. But then, to each her own.

Cordelia relaxed her tensed body and sighed. "As long as I have your food, I'm not sure I'll ever need a healthy, satisfying relationship."

Jane laughed. "That's good, because you haven't had much luck finding one."

"No," said Cordelia seriously. "You're quite right. But remember that woman Andromeda I lived with the first two years out of college?"

"The one who looked like Golda Meir and wanted to be a rock star?"

"That's the one." Cordelia brought her hand up to her head and pretended it was a gun. "She called me last night." She pulled the trigger.

"And?" said Jane, trying to stifle a laugh.

"And, she wants to get together. Just for old times."

"And what did you say?"

Cordelia played irresolutely with the buttons on her blouse. "I said maybe."

"Maybe?"

"Well, maybe yes."

Jane's face split into a grin.

"Don't laugh. It suggests bad breeding. I really liked that

woman. She's selling exercise equipment now in Spring Lake Park, and she said she'd really like to see me again.''

A marriage made in heaven, thought Jane. ''When are you going to get together and reminisce?''

''Next weekend. I invited her to my annual Richard III party. I explained to her about my triumphant production four years ago. She seemed to be familiar with Richard III. I explained briefly that, at the time, I was sick of the good press Richard was getting and I, for one, was going to do the play as written.''

''You mean as a blatant burlesque.''

''Shakespeare didn't write a burlesque.'' She dismissed the idea with a small wave of her hand.

''You know, about once every century somebody writes a vindication of Richard III, but it never seems to stick. I think the main reason is that play. It's such great theatre nobody wants to consider that it's all based on political make-believe.''

''And who would you be accusing of making up the story?''

''The Tudors,'' said Jane. ''Remember, I told you, any-time you want to read about it, just say the word. English history is a speciality of mine.''

Cordelia adjusted her blouse. ''Well, whatever the truth was, *my* production was a critical success. And Andromeda is definitely coming to the fifth annual Big Dick Three party. She said she'd even buy a hump.''

''Richard III didn't have a hump either.''

Cordelia was trying to keep her growing exasperation in check. ''I expect you to be nice to her.''

''I'm always nice to women wearing humps.''

''I suppose *you'll* be coming with Ingrid Bergman,'' said Cordelia with more than a hint of snottiness.

Jane stopped laughing and looked away.

In less time than it had taken to say it, Cordelia realized what she'd done. ''God, I'm sorry, Jane. I didn't mean to say that. I know how much you still miss Christine.''

Jane leaned back. ''It's okay, really. It's just that sometimes I still can't get used to the fact that she's gone. Dead. Do you realize it's almost three years? We were together for nearly ten, so I guess it just takes time.''

"I loved her, too, Janey,'' said Cordelia softly. "And I miss her. I can just see her in that outfit she came to the party in a few years back. All fringe and feathers.''

"She understood it was a burlesque,'' said Jane with a weak smile.

They sat silently for a few moments. "How about doing something together tonight. Maybe a movie? You don't have to finish that stupid report right now, do you? You need to have some fun for a change.''

"I can't tonight,'' said Jane. "Two people from the sorority are meeting me here in a little while. We have to talk.''

Cordelia picked up a blown-glass paperweight sitting on Jane's desk and examined it. "How are you coming with your investigation?''

"Well, before you came in, I was just going over in my mind the various people who might have had a motive.''

"Don't forget to include that snake Susan Julian.''

"Come on, Cordelia. Be realistic. What reason would she have?''

"She hates gays. Didn't you say that? She wanted to protect the sorority from a scandal.''

"But she didn't even know Allison *was* a lesbian until after her death.''

"If that's really true, then maybe she's psychotic. She hears voices. She wears an old Nazi uniform around her bedroom and salutes a cheap reproduction of the Last Supper. Maybe Allison had snapshots. How should I know?''

Jane shook her head.

"I do know you're going to regret it if you don't keep your eye on that woman.''

"Look, Cordelia,'' said Jane, narrowing her eyes, "I asked her yesterday at the memorial service what she'd been doing last Sunday night. I mean, I didn't interrogate her, but I mentioned what *I* was doing, and she volunteered that she'd been home all night with a terrible headache. She hadn't gone out.''

"I don't believe her," said Cordelia flatly.

Jane could almost see the wheels turning inside Cordelia's head. "What are you plotting in that little mind of yours?"

"I'll find out for you," said Cordelia. "She wasn't home that night, I can feel it."

"How are you going to prove that?"

She shook her head. "I don't know. I might have a way. Let's just leave it for now. Who are your other suspects?"

Jane pulled a small notebook out of her top desk drawer. She carefully put on her glasses and flipped open the cover. "Well, there's Mitchel Page. He's an obvious choice. He had a strong motive, whether it was love or hate. I've met him a few times, and I can say from first-hand experience that he's a strange one."

"You forgot money. Maybe this Mitch was blackmailing her about Emily. Or maybe he thought Allison was his ticket to fame and fortune."

"Yes, I thought of that. If she dumped him for someone else, his chance at the easy life was all washed up. And if the person he was being dumped *for* was a woman! Well, I expect his ego might have had more than a little problem with that."

"Maybe he and Susan Julian were in it together!"

Jane shot Cordelia an exasperated glance. "You're like a pit bull sometimes, Cordelia. Has anyone ever told you that?"

Cordelia shrugged philosophically.

"Okay, then there's Mitch's girlfriend, Jamie McGraw. She could have been jealous. Or wanted revenge. Particularly if she thought there really was a chance they were getting back together. Or maybe *she* thought she could make some easy money by blackmailing Allison. Who knows? Maggie told me Jamie has a problem with alcohol. She doesn't drink all the time, but when she does, she really loses it. She has a terrible temper. Actually, before fall term began this year, Maggie was having dinner with Allison at the Campus Grill. I guess Jamie was there, and she came up to Allison—

obviously blitzed—and threatened her. She told Allison to leave Mitch alone *or else*."

"I see," said Cordelia shuddering. "I don't think I'd mess with a belligerent drunk. Sometimes they can be pretty scary." She thought of her father.

"I'm not going to *mess* with anybody. But I might want to ask her a few questions. She's Mitchel's alibi for that night. She told the police they both were at her apartment for the entire night."

"Any other suspects?"

Jane nodded. She paused, turning the page of her book. "Emily Anderson for one."

"Really? You suspect her?"

"I think I have to include her, don't you? From what she told the police, she and Allison had had a fight before Allison went out to see Mitch. Since I've never met her, it's hard for me to get a handle on what she's like. But she was certainly involved emotionally. Intense emotion can make people do some pretty bizarre things. I hope her mother can pass along my message. I really need to talk to her."

"And," said Cordelia. "Any others?"

"Yes, one other." She looked down at her notes. "Clarence Anderson. I think Emily's father had a strong motive, and we both know he was in town that night visiting his daughter."

Cordelia sat up straight and looked hard at Jane. "It sounds like you think most people are capable of murder. I mean, it's awful sitting here accusing these people of something like that."

"If I have been listening to my father correctly for lo, these many years, *anyone* is capable of murder. A criminal defense attorney should know. But in this case, I'm not even sure it *was* intentional murder. Maybe it began as an argument. Allison could have accidentally fallen off the bridge into the water. Or she could have been pushed. Either way it is possible that the person didn't know she was unable to swim. Maybe after she was in the water they saw an opportunity. Or if it was premeditated murder and they *did* know she couldn't swim, then it would have to be someone who knew her pretty well. Someone who would know that about her. I doubt it was common knowledge. The water is deep there, and the sides of the bridge are low. It could have been easy enough for a man or a woman to push someone over.''

"What motive would a close friend have?"

"Love, hate, money. Maybe there was something she knew that someone else wanted kept secret. The more I'm able to find out about Allison's life, the more I think it will point me to the other person on that bridge with her." Jane pushed an unruly lock away from her forehead. "I had a long talk with her brother yesterday. He's living up north at a place called St. Victor's. I feel like I learned a good deal about her from what he said. He's an interesting young man."

"I've heard of St. Victor's," said Cordelia thoughtfully. "Is he some kind of monk?"

"I don't think so," laughed Jane. "Although he seemed quite religious. My gut reaction about him was positive. But you know, the more I think about it, the more something seemed kind of odd. He and Allison were very close, or so he said. He mentioned that he didn't believe she had committed suicide and then asked if I agreed. I said I did and that I wanted to find out what really happened. After that, he wished me luck, offered his help if I wanted to write, but made no attempt to actually stick around town for a while. If something like that had happened to me, I know my brother wouldn't just walk away. It doesn't make any sense."

The phone rang, breaking into Jane's thought. She answered and listened for a moment before saying that she'd be right down.

Cordelia opened the new menu again and examined it lustfully. Lemon scones. Nutmeg-scented apple pumpkin soup.

"Come over here next Friday night," said Jane. "That will be the first night for the new late fall menu. We'll try out whatever you like."

Cordelia could feel her stomach rumble. "I can't on Friday. We're in repertory again that night. *Lady Windemere's*

Fan. And remember, next Saturday is the big party at my place.''

''How could I forget?''

''So, how about next *Sunday* night! We can try out everything on the right side of the menu. The following week we can do the left.'' She opened her large purse and stared bleakly at the candy bar and can of orange pop she'd bought several hours ago. She pulled them out and set them on top of the desk. ''How about if I buy dinner tonight?''

For some inexplicable reason, Maggie was unable to find her watch. The bus would be arriving at her stop in a few minutes, so there was simply no more time to look. She was pretty certain she had dropped it into one of her loafers before taking a shower earlier in the evening. On the other hand, maybe she had rolled it into one of her socks. She did that sometimes. Now where had she put those socks? She decided they were probably still on the bathroom floor. If, for some reason she had dropped the watch on her bedroom floor, then trying to find it amidst all the crumpled clothing and dirty dishes would be almost impossible. Maybe she should clean her room. Except that seemed like a lot of work just to find a watch. She could always buy a new one. And anyway, she knew it would turn up eventually in some odd place, like between the pages of a book or in her makeup drawer. It was only a matter of time.

The bus dropped her off about half a block from where she thought The Lyme House was located. As she got down to the lake she realized she had misjudged the distance. Halfway across she could see the lights from the second-story dining room glowing in the darkness. Even without her watch, she knew she was going to be late. Hopefully, they wouldn't all be sitting around some big table waiting for her. A huge crowd of people ready to point and snicker that here, finally, was that disorganized idiot who had kept them waiting for so long. And worse yet, they would all know she had *lost her watch.* She could almost hear the collective sneer. With her hands bunched deeply into the pockets of her new winter coat, she headed toward the lights. The evening had not begun well.

Maggie entered the door on the Penn Avenue side and walked directly into a richly lit English style pub. The sign above the door read, *The Lyme Public House*. The room she found herself standing in glowed with the luster of burnished copper. The light seemed to be coming from a group of rose and amethyst stained-glass windows and a large open hearth against the back wall. An old mahogany bar ran the entire length of the room. She was certain it was antique. It looked as if it had been polished for centuries by fine furniture wax and firelight. Behind the bar was a long stained-glass panel. If her art history served correctly, it was an Art Nouveau piece. She walked over to examine it more closely.

"Can I help you?" asked a young man standing behind the bar. He was wearing a white apron and polishing glasses with a soft cloth. There appeared to be no waiters in the room itself.

"Sure," said Maggie, looking around. "I was supposed to meet someone here, but I don't see her." She could tell he was having difficulty hearing above the laughter and loud conversations, so she spoke more loudly. "I'm looking for Jane Lawless. We were supposed to meet here at nine, but I guess I'm a little late."

"You must be either Maggie or Sigrid," he said with a big smile. "Don't worry. Jane's often a bit late herself. She asked me to look out for you. Even reserved a table in the other room." He nodded toward the back. "Follow me." Maggie watched as he lifted a section of the bar top and slipped out into the room. He led the way to a table in a second room, this one darker and more intimate, and seated her next to another fireplace. Before she sat down, she warmed her hands for a moment.

"I'll give her a quick call. Take a look at the menu. If you see something you want, come on up to the bar and I'll take your order." He walked over to an old-fashioned popcorn machine just on the other side of the doorway and came back with a large basket of freshly popped corn. "Enjoy," he said cheerfully.

Maggie sat back in her seat and looked around the room for a moment. The smell of the wood fire was intoxicating. She let her eyes wander over the brick walls up to the exposed beams in the ceiling. In the other room she had noticed several older men sitting in one of the raised booths playing what looked like cribbage. She wasn't certain since she had never actually played the game herself. Another group seemed seriously engaged in a game of darts. She wondered what it would be like to own a place like this. Last summer she had eaten dinner in the main dining room upstairs. A graduate student had invited her. She hadn't been too sure of *him*, but the food had been wonderful. The dining room struck her as rustic and yet elegant. She remembered sitting out on the balcony sipping some iced tea before dinner. Across the lake she remembered seeing an old bandstand. Music drifted over the water and made it an irresistibly pleasant place to sit and talk.

A large log fell further into the fire, drawing her attention back to the present. She noticed a menu sticking out from behind a small lamp on the table. She pulled it out and saw that under the heading PUB GRUB, several unusual sounding foods were listed. There was a plowman's lunch—cheeses, bread, York ham and pickled onions—and a Cornish pasty. Several meat pies were listed as well as a fresh fruit cup with homemade scones. After four, Irish stew and fish and chips were offered. The back of the menu listed imported beers and various domestic beers from microbreweries in the Midwest and Northwest. Maggie had never heard of any of them. Wine was tolerable, but she thought beer tasted somewhat similar to the way gasoline smelled. She turned the menu back to the food and munched thoughtfully on her popcorn.

"Are you feeling adventuresome?" asked Jane, who had come up quietly and now stood looking down at her.

Maggie turned around. "Hi," she said, putting the menu down. "What do you mean, adventuresome?"

"Try the steak and kidney pie if you are. It's delicious.

The kidney part puts Americans off sometimes. Otherwise, I recommend the shepherd's pie. Do you like English mustard or horseradish sauce?''

At the mention of horseradish, Maggie scrunched up her nose. "I think I'll try the shepherd's pie, as long as it doesn't have an actual shepherd in it."

Jane laughed. "Very good." The same young man who had shown Maggie to her table appeared in the doorway. "Johnny, make it a shepherd's pie and . . ." She looked back to Maggie. "What would you like to drink?"

"A Coke," said Maggie, more as a question than a request.

"And a Coke. And bring me a lager and lime."

"Right away," said the young man, wiping his hands on his apron.

"This place is terrific," said Maggie as Jane pulled out a chair and sat down. "You even let people play games in there." She pointed to the other room.

"You mean the cribbage?" She smiled and pulled out a tall, glass salt shaker, examining a small crack near the bottom. "I wanted this pub to be part of the neighborhood. Not a pickup place. We've got lots of regulars who like to come here for darts or a game of chess or cribbage. The music is kind of special, too. In a few minutes the woman who is playing the fiddle will be back from her break. We've also got someone who comes in with a Celtic harp and another who accompanies her on the dulcimer. And I've got an old friend who is wonderful on the penny whistle. He shows up whenever he feels like it and plays with whoever else is around. It's a lot of fun. Are you a fan of cribbage?"

"No," said Maggie, rather seriously. "But I'd love to learn."

"All right," said Jane. "We'll make it a date. You come by some evening when you're not busy, and I'll teach you."

Maggie was delighted. Johnny reappeared carrying the food and drinks on a small tray. After setting everything down in front of them, Jane thanked him and added, "If anybody needs me, I'll be talking to Maggie in here for a while.''

"Right," he said, grinning shamelessly at Maggie for a moment before leaving.

"He's really cute," said Maggie watching him walk away. Jane nodded. "I imagine."

"Must be fun working around all these cute bartenders." Maggie was clearly envious.

"It must be," said Jane, taking a sip of lager.

Maggie picked up her fork and played with it for a moment. She wondered just who *was* Jane's type. She knew Jane had never married. The aroma of the shepherd's pie would not let her consider the question even one moment longer. She took a bite and chewed slowly. "It's wonderful," she said, not caring that her mouth was full. "I had no idea what to expect." She took another big bite. "What made you decide on an English pub?"

Jane leaned back in her chair and folded her arms. "There's no actual prototype for a pub. There are thousands in London alone, and they're all quite different." She watched Maggie devouring her pie and wondered if she shouldn't order something herself. "My mother was English. Dad took a vacation in England just after he finished law school. He met my mother while he was there, and they fell in love. It's kind of a long story."

"Please," said Maggie. "I'm interested. I've never even been out of the United States, so it all sounds very romantic and exciting to me."

Jane shook her head and smiled. "It's not exciting, but if you're really interested, I'll make it short." She took another sip of lager. "Dad was vacationing in a small seaport town in southwest England. Lyme Regis. It's a beautiful little coastal village, right on the sea. My mother lived in Dorchester, about ten miles away. She was working in a bank that summer, and I guess that's where they met. They were married before the summer was over. She came back with him to St. Paul, and about a month later he passed the bar. I was born the next year. I guess my mother was terribly homesick because when I was a year old, we went back to Dorchester. Dad was offered a job in Southampton and for the next seven years we lived in England. My brother was born there. When I was eight my grandfather, who worked for the Dorset police, was shot and killed by a man who had broken out of a prison near there. My grandmother died about six months later. After that, I remember Dad saying he wanted to come back to St. Paul. I imagine he was itching to finally practice law. So we came back.

"My mother died when I was thirteen. We were very close and when it happened, I just couldn't accept it. I had a very hard time in school that year. The next summer Dad sent me back to England to spend a few weeks with my favorite aunt and uncle. Uncle Jimmy had a restaurant in Poole. And, more to the point, he had three dogs and four cats and lived in an old cottage near the sea. Very close to Lyme Regis. He took me fossil hunting in the cliffs near town. I can still remember those cliffs. The green Dorset hills tumbling down into the sea near Abbotsbury. I wrote to Dad and asked him if I could stay on a while and he agreed. I stayed for almost two years. Peter, my brother, came over during the summers, and we both worked in Uncle Jimmy's restaurant. Actually, it wasn't much of a restaurant, but I loved it. I used to get the cooks to show me how they made different things. I came back home to St. Paul when I was sixteen and finished my junior and senior year here. But it was hard. Before Mom died, we were a very close family and yet, after she was gone, I would have preferred to stay in England."

Maggie was fascinated. "You make England sound wonderful."

"It was. For a child. Dad never wanted to come back over, even while I was staying with Uncle Jimmy and Aunt Beryl. He said everything was either too low or too small or too cold."

"He doesn't think Minnesota's too cold?"

Jane smiled. "Crazy, isn't it? At the time, I didn't understand. But I imagine the real reason was that there were too many memories for him. And then, I guess I hurt him a lot when I didn't come back after a couple of weeks. We've spent many years trying to repair our relationship." Jane looked away into the fire. "My father is a defense attorney in St. Paul."

"I know," said Maggie. "I read about him all the time in the papers."

"Of course, you probably would have."

Maggie could not read Jane's expression.

"He doesn't believe in a low profile." She leaned forward and took a handful of popcorn. "Is Sigrid coming? Now that I've told you my life story I think we should probably get down to business."

"She told me she was coming after work." Maggie looked at her naked wrist.

For the next few minutes Maggie explained to Jane about the thefts in the house, ending with the rituals-room incident. Jane listened with growing apprehension.

"The problem is," said Maggie, pushing away her empty plate, "only three people had keys to that room. Me, Siggy, and Kari." She leaned closer to Jane and lowered her voice. "I'm going to go crazy if I don't tell you something I've been keeping a secret all week." She took her last sip of Coke and stared down into the empty mug. "First, I have to preface it by telling you something you're not going to like. Something I'm ashamed of, but nothing I can do anything about now." She looked around the room as if it might provide her with an answer. "Maybe you've gotten the impression that I'm a little disorganized. To tell the truth, I am. I've always had a problem with losing things. Like my keys. So, I had a second set made. Just in case. I know it's forbidden, but I did it."

Jane winced. "It's all right. Just tell me what happened."

"I feel terrible about all this," said Maggie. She began to shred her napkin. "After the rituals room was ransacked I looked around immediately for both sets but could only find one. I figured either I'd mislaid one somewhere in my room, or maybe the worst had happened and someone had stolen them. If that was the case, then whoever had them had access to every room in the house." Maggie could almost feel Jane's body tense with each new revelation. She bunched up the shredded napkin into a ball and tossed it into her empty mug. "We know that someone got into the rituals room the night Allison died. And we know it wasn't Kari, Sigrid, or me. Before formal dinner on Monday night, I went to Ally's room just to sit on her bed. To kind of feel her presence and talk to her. It had been an awful day. I'd found out that morning that she was dead and the entire day was like a nightmare. I don't know why, but I happened to open her desk drawer and—I couldn't believe my eyes—there was my other set of keys! Either she took them or found them, but in any case, there they were. It made me wonder if *she* wasn't the one who made all the mess downstairs the night before. Maybe she was also the one to steal that emerald pendant and the camera equipment. But I asked myself, why would she need to do either? She had tons of money. The thing that drives me crazy is that rituals-room thing. I mean, they got into the room, broke open the strongbox lock and then didn't take any of the money. Why?"

Jane was silent for a few moments, trying to digest everything Maggie had said. She was right. Nothing made any sense. "There's something wrong in all of this," she said finally. "It doesn't add up. I don't think we can accuse Allison of anything until we have all the facts."

The fiddler began playing in the other room to the claps and cheers of everyone standing around the bar. Maggie bent her head to see into the other room. Instead of the fiddler she was surprised to find Sigrid head to head with one of the young bartenders. He handed her a drink and leaned over to give her a kiss. Wasn't that just like Sigrid, thought Maggie. She probably knew every guy behind the bar. Maggie sat back in her seat, vaguely disgusted. Jane, noticing her look, turned around just in time to see Sigrid coming through the door carrying a pint of stout. She motioned for her to come over to the table.

"You seem to have been here before," said Maggie nodding toward the next room.

Sigrid looked puzzled. She pulled out a chair and sat down.

"Do you mean Barnaby? The guy I was talking to out there? I've told you about him." Sigrid kicked off her shoes. Maggie could feel one hit her ankle. "He's that engineering student I dated last year. You remember. *The Lumberjack.*"

"Ah," said Maggie, remembering him now. "He was the one you really liked, right? I thought you'd be moving in with him for sure."

It was Sigrid's turn to be annoyed. "I've told you. I have no interest in a major relationship while I'm in college. It's like taking an extra six credit course every quarter. I don't need it."

Jane stifled a smile. Maggie and Sigrid were so different. Physically, Maggie was tall and thin. Pretty, but not in an obvious way. Sigrid, on the other hand, was shorter and less angular, lovely in a classic Scandinavian way. She looked like the girl next door, but Jane suspected she wasn't. Maggie seemed years younger though they were both the same age. Perhaps it was her innocence. It was a quality Sigrid entirely lacked.

"I think we need to get down to business," said Jane. "I'm glad you could both come. I hope this meeting can be clarifying for all of us. I've got a question I'd like to put to both of you." She paused, looking somewhat over long at Sigrid. "Did anyone in the sorority know of Allison's lesbianism before her death?"

Maggie squirmed uncomfortably in her seat. She knew Jane was going to ask that question and hoped it could be handled quickly. "I don't think so," she said. "She never said anything to me." She nodded toward Sigrid, waiting for a quick confirmation.

Sigrid sipped her beer.

"Did you know about it?" asked Jane.

Sigrid leaned back casually in her chair. Too casually, thought Jane. "Sure, I knew."

Maggie's face looked like a windshield that had been hit by a large rock. Tiny cracks rapidly formed and expanded.

"Did anyone else know?" asked Jane.

"I don't think anyone knew last year except me. She was

too paranoid about everything. But about a month ago I overheard her talking to one of the alums about it.''

''Who?'' asked Jane with a shiver of apprehension.

''Susan Julian.''

So, Susan did know *before* Allison's death! ''How is it that you know that for sure?''

Sigrid took a sip of stout before answering. ''One evening, about a month ago, she and Ally were having this major discussion out by the pine tree in the front yard. It was after formal dinner. They were shouting, so I figured it wasn't exactly a private conversation. I walked up behind them and heard Allison say something about Susan not being able to do anything about 'it.' She said she had 'made up her mind.' She told Susan to try to throw her out of the house if she thought she could, but she was not going to leave of her own accord. I believe the last thing Ally said was, 'Piss off.' I trust,'' she added with obvious enjoyment, ''that I am quoting her correctly.'' Maggie's mouth was still open. Sigrid continued, ''When Susan saw me she turned around and marched off. As I think about it now, it was more of a goose step.'' She took another sip of beer.

Maggie was in shock. Any attempt at humor was completely wasted.

''Are you certain they were speaking about Allison's lesbianism?'' asked Jane.

''They were talking about Allison and Emily moving in together and—what is the legal term—cohabiting? Yes. I'm positive.''

Maggie cast her eyes accusingly at Sigrid. ''Ally told you and not me?'' She shut her eyes in pain. ''Why?''

''You have to understand, Maggie, she didn't exactly let it slip between classes. I suppose I should explain.''

''Please do,'' said Jane.

''Well, remember when we all drove up to Taylor's Falls for that retreat last January?''

''Yes,'' said Maggie warily, keeping her eyes away from Sigrid.

''If you remember, we had that hideous pep fest, or whatever you call those rah rah meetings where we all have to sing the Kappa Alpha Sigma songs over and over again. Allison and I were both exhausted by the sisterly unity so we decided to go up to her room after it was all over, instead of going out drinking with the rest of you. She had a bottle of Barsac and a bag of chips so we turned out the lights, lit a candle, and proceeded to get drunk. The conversation turned almost immediately to the trip she had just taken with Mitch back to Philadelphia over Christmas break. She told me what a disaster it had been. The conversation moved rather quickly to her childhood. Didn't it ever strike you as funny that she never talked about that part of her life? Anyway, after a while we just stopped talking. We sat there looking into the candle flame. And then," said Sigrid, pausing for maximum effect, "out of the blue, she kissed me."

"My God!" said Maggie. Jane had never seen someone more surprised. "What did you do?"

Sigrid looked at Maggie as if she was an idiot. "What do you mean what did I do? I kissed her back, birdbrain. What did you want me to do, bite her?"

"Sigrid!" Even in the firelight Maggie's face went pale.

"Oh, stick a sock in it, Maggie. Grow up. I've always been curious. I'd never had a woman make a pass at me before. Unlike some other people who *say* they think all of that is just fine and dandy, I really think it is. It's just a question of what's right for you."

Jane was glad Maggie was young. She was sure her blood pressure had shot up at least thirty points.

"And," said Sigrid, deciding to ignore Maggie now and speak only to Jane, "we made love a few times after that." She bit the nail on her index finger. "So I guess you could say I knew."

Maggie reached over and roughly grabbed Sigrid's glass of beer. She took several big gulps before handing it back. "Why did she make a pass at you and not at me?"

Here we go, thought Jane.

"Oh Maggie, leave it alone." Sigrid shook her head wearily.

"Don't patronize me." Maggie's voice was cold.

"I'm not patronizing you. But you don't even recognize it when a guy makes a pass unless he snorts and paws the ground first. How would you ever recognize one from a woman?"

Maggie was not convinced.

"Look Maggs, she never would have tried anything with you. I think she had a pretty good sense of what was possible and what wasn't."

Now Maggie was hurt. Jane figured this conversation could go on forever. She knew Maggie would have to work it all out for herself sooner or later, but they didn't have time tonight. Perhaps she could talk to her about it later. "I've got a couple more questions, if you don't mind."

"Sure," said Sigrid.

Maggie sat silently looking into the fire.

"Okay. Question two. Who knew Allison couldn't swim?"

Sigrid looked up immediately and narrowed her eyes. "Very clever, Jane. I wondered if you'd get around to asking that."

Jane was having a terrible time reading Sigrid. There was an arch quality about her that was bewildering.

Sigrid took a sip of beer. She knocked Maggie on the arm and offered the glass. Maggie shook her head. "Well, I suppose Maggie and Kari both knew. And of course, *I* did." She finished her beer and set the glass down hard on the table. Maggie jumped.

"Anyone else?" asked Jane.

Sigrid's eyes grew shrewd and careful. "Who do you mean? Mitchel Page? It's possible."

"Do you think there's any way Susan Julian could have known?"

Sigrid seemed surprised. "Ah, so she's a suspect now, too. You aren't going to miss a trick, are you?"

"Knock it off, Siggy," said Maggie, forcing herself to comment. "I'm sure Jane wasn't suggesting Susan had anything to do with Allison's death."

Sigrid's smile was like a razor. "Of course not. I'm sorry.

To answer your rather pointless question, then, I doubt Susan knew. But of course," she added helpfully, "one could never be certain of that, could one?"

"I imagine Emily Anderson knew," said Jane matter-of-factly. She wasn't fooling Sigrid but didn't feel particularly comfortable confiding anything either.

"Probably. Have you had the pleasure of meeting her yet?"

Jane shook her head.

"Well then, you're in for a real treat. A grad student in English literature, I seem to recall. She looks as if she'd been hermetically sealed in a library since birth. Wafty and yet nervous. Like she was afraid any minute a book might fall off the shelf and crush her. I will admit that I don't understand what Allison saw in her, but then, I could never figure out the attraction for Mitchel Page either. To each her own."

Jane inspected the comment for veiled jealously. It was possible Sigrid was just being sarcastic. But if she had been jealous, it could certainly have complicated things for Ally.

"Maybe Allison just liked odd people," said Jane.

Sigrid's eyes flashed for a split second and then looked away.

"You mean like her brother," interrupted Maggie. "I always thought he was kind of strange."

Sigrid nodded in agreement. "I've only met him once, but it was quite enough."

Maggie was starting to loosen up a little. "I've seen him twice. The last time was yesterday after the memorial service."

"Yes," said Jane. "I talked with him for quite a while downstairs in the dining hall."

"Oh, was he there?" asked Maggie. "I didn't see him until later."

"When was that?" asked Sigrid. "I never saw him."

"The whole day was so crazy," mused Maggie. "I guess I didn't think much about it. It was after we got back from church. You went straight on to class but I had to run upstairs to see if I could find that paper I'd misplaced. Just as I headed down the second floor hall, out of Ally's door popped her brother. He really startled me. I noticed he had something in his hand, but I really never thought to look at it. Maybe I should have questioned him or something, but everything had been so bizarre all week I never even thought to ask. He smiled, and I smiled, and he walked past me through the hall and down the stairs. That was it. We never actually said anything to each other."

Sigrid stared at Maggie incredulously. Maggie glared right back. She'd had enough of Sigrid for one night. "It's just that it never occurred to me it would be important. Was it?" She looked at Jane.

"I don't know. You both met him once before, is that right?"

"Yes. Once," said Sigrid. "I had gone to Ally's room to tell her something. When I opened the door, he was lying on her bed."

Maggie nodded. "The time I met him he was sitting outside in this fancy sports car. He and Ally had been out somewhere together. He was dropping her off."

The expensive car didn't seem to fit the picture of a reclusive, spiritually searching young man. Edwin was an odd mixture. "How is Kari?" said Jane, changing the topic abruptly.

Sigrid looked up. "I haven't seen her much all week. Why do you ask?"

"Same for me," said Maggie. "Even before Ally died she was spending quite a few nights at her parents' home." Maggie was now shredding Sigrid's napkin. "Did anyone tell you about the problem we've been having with people feeling like they were being watched?"

"What do you mean?" asked Jane.

"Well, it all started the second week of fall term. One of the girls thought she saw something outside her window late one night. She came down to my room and the two of us went in to talk to Mrs. Holms."

"I refuse to call her Mrs. Holms," interrupted Sigrid. "If she can call me by my first name and it doesn't show disrespect, then I can call her by hers."

Maggie listened politely and then continued without comment. "Mrs. Holms thought it was a fraternity prank, and I was inclined to agree. It didn't help Stephanie Wallberg's shattered nerves any, but we decided to let it go. Then, one by one, other girls reported seeing something outside their windows at night. Kari was no exception. And something else. She was sure that at least twice, someone was standing outside her door in the middle of the night. She said she heard the floor creak until the person was standing right outside. Once she got up—mind you, this was like four in the morning—and asked in a normal voice who was there. She said she heard footsteps running quickly back down the hall. By the time she got the door unlocked, whoever it was had disappeared. After that, she felt so creepy she stayed home a lot.''

"I've felt it, too," said Sigrid. "Even down in the green room watching TV. It's this instinctive feeling that someone is watching you. I don't know how else to explain it. And yet, there aren't even any windows in that room.''

Jane shivered. If anything had caused her to think something dangerous was going on, this was it. The house seemed to be the center for something evil. "I don't want to alarm you," she said carefully, "but when you take all of this together, it sounds pretty bad. I think maybe you *should* call the police.''

"No," said Sigrid. "Absolutely not. No police. Look. As a sorority, we've already been damaged. Having a lesbian member commit suicide, and that's how everyone sees it, is bad enough. I may not have anything against gays personally, but something like this can kill a chapter. If we call in the police and they come crawling all over the house, we're going to lose what's left of our membership. I guarantee it. I don't know if you're aware of it, but we've already lost over ten people since last Monday. Once a sorority gets this kind of reputation, it's finished. You know that as well as I do. So, no police. That's final. We have to handle this ourselves.''

"I agree," said Maggie cautiously.

Jane shook her head.

A tall young man with a dark beard came up behind Jane and kissed her on top of her head. She whirled around. "Peter! You startled me!"

"Sorry, sis." He smiled broadly as he pulled up a chair and sat down next to her. "Aren't you going to introduce me?"

Jane was irritated at the intrusion, yet she was glad to see him. They had both been so busy lately that they rarely saw each other. "Maggie, Sigrid, this is my little brother, Peter."

"Glad to meet you, little brother," said Sigrid, studying him.

"My pleasure. Is this a private pow wow?" Peter put his arm around Jane. "You look like you need to smoke a peace pipe, Janey."

"Actually," said Jane, looking at her watch, "I should probably drive these two home. Unless you've got another way. It's almost midnight."

"The witching hour," said Peter, raising his eyebrows at Maggie. "Better be careful. My sister's car turns into a pumpkin after midnight."

"I thought you had an assignment tonight," said Jane.

"I did. Due to my brilliance, we got done early." He winked at Sigrid. "I'm a highly successful cameraman at WTWN-TV."

"And you came over for a bite to eat?" asked Jane.

"Not exactly, though I wouldn't turn that down." He unzipped his suede jacket. "I came to talk to my sister about Thanksgiving. Dad wants to have it over at his place this year. What do you think?"

Jane stood up. "I think I'll take Maggie and Sigrid home, and then I'll come back. We can talk about it over some dinner. In a civilized manner."

"Yes, ma'am," said Peter. "I'm nothing if not civilized."

Jane pulled her car up in front of the sorority. As usual, there were no empty parking spaces.

"Thanks Jane," said Maggie. "This has been a *revealing*

evening." She did not look at Sigrid as she spoke. "If anything new comes up, I'll give you a call."

Sigrid leaned her head wearily against the window. Dry leaves were blowing across the front lawn. She hoped Maggie would simply go to bed when they got inside. The last thing she wanted was another intense confrontation.

"Your brother sure is cute," said Maggie, grabbing her purse from under her feet.

Terrific, thought Jane. Another *cute* man. Just what the world needed. It had been a long day, and she realized what *she* needed was some sleep.

"What was that?" said Sigrid.

"What was what?" said Jane, turning around.

Sigrid sat bolt upright. "Over there. Next to the side of the house. I was sure I saw something move."

Maggie reached up with her hand and wiped a circle in the foggy side window. "I don't see anything."

"You're blind as a bat without your glasses, Maggie. You couldn't see a 747 parked in the front yard from ten feet away."

Once again Maggie was hurt. "That's not true."

"There it is again," said Sigrid, pointing.

Jane turned off the car lights. "Can you tell who it is?"

"No, but I'm sure going to find out," said Sigrid, jumping out of the car and running toward the dark side of the house.

"Wait!" shouted Jane. She reached into the glove compartment and fumbled around until she found an old flashlight. She hoped it would still work. "Come on," she said to Maggie.

By the time Jane got around the car she could see someone dart out of the bushes. The dark figure bolted toward the brick retaining wall that partially enclosed the property. About five feet from the wall Sigrid took a flying leap and caught the runner around the ankles, sending him crashing into the wall. A second later, Maggie and Jane reached them. Sigrid was standing over the crumpled figure, demanding an explanation. Jane clicked on the flashlight. "Elliot! What's going on?"

Elliot squinted up into the bright light and attempted a

cheery smile. "Good evening, ladies," he said, standing up and brushing off his pants. He seemed to be limping slightly. "Chilly night, isn't it?"

Sigrid was furious. "If you ever plan on working another day around here you better have a pretty good reason for all of this."

Elliot blew on his hands. He looked as if he had been out in the cold for quite some time. "An explanation for what?" he asked innocently.

"Cut the crap, Elliot."

"Sigrid! How you do talk sometimes. If you must know, I thought you were the campus police. You scared me. So I started running."

"Really? That's imbecilic! Someone headed for law school ought to be able to do better than that."

"Well, you *did* frighten me, Sigrid." He was slowly recovering his charm.

"Look," said Jane. "I think we deserve some explanation for your behavior. Skulking around in the dark . . ."

"I wasn't skulking." He gave Jane his most wounded expression.

"Elliot," said Sigrid, "I'm going into that house right now and call the police unless you tell me what you were doing out here. You may be a big shot in student government, but that won't mean diddly to the police. And I guarantee you, a police record won't look so good when you're running for governor."

"Governor! That has a nice ring. Don't you think?"

"Elliot!"

"Okay, okay. Calm down." He pushed Jane's flashlight away from his face. "Here's the story. I'm suppose to scout out the best way to get into the house. For my fraternity. We're planning a raid. See, all I have to do is leave a window unlocked, and we can climb through later in the night. I had to figure which was the best window."

"And you had to do that from outside in the middle of the night?" asked Jane.

Elliot gave her his most lavish smile. Christ, thought Jane, does this guy think his smile can solve everything?

"I didn't even know you belonged to a fraternity," said Sigrid curtly.

"He does," said Maggie. "The Tri Betas."

"Of course," snorted Sigrid. "It figures. How come I don't know about all this? I'm the president, and Greek rules say you're supposed to notify me."

"Well," grinned Elliot, "it's just in the formative stages."

Jane was pretty sure he was lying. She had no doubt that he relied on his charm and deep voice to get him out of tight spots.

Sigrid was unconvinced. "Who's the president of that fraternity?"

"Tom Albight. Tall guy. Nice looking. Usually wears a tam. Drives a little red BMW. But," he added, "he doesn't know anything about it either. A few of us guys were going to figure out all the logistics and then present it to him later."

"Am I supposed to believe this?" said Sigrid, raising her voice to a shout. "This is pure crap, and you know it. That's not even the way things are done."

"I don't lie," said Elliot coldly. "That would be wrong."

Maggie cleared her throat. "He's a Tri Beta, remember."

Sigrid looked at Maggie as if she were an annoying fly. "I don't care if he's a Tri *Pod*." She looked back at Elliot. "If I find out you're trying to snow me, you can believe you'll regret it. Maybe I'll just have to call the police and file a report anyway. That would probably be the smart thing to do."

"No, don't do that!" He reached for her arm.

"Let go of me, you creep."

"Sorry." He pulled his hand back quickly. "Just don't call the police. I told you the truth. I swear it." Even in the dark Jane could see Elliot's pleading eyes. The charm had evaporated. "I haven't done anything wrong. I'm only trying to help all of you!"

"What do you mean by that?" asked Sigrid irritably.

"Oh let him go," said Maggie. She felt sorry for the shivering figure standing in front of her. "We've done a lot worse things. Remember what we did to Kappa Sig last spring?"

"But what was it you were saying about helping us?" asked Sigrid again.

"Sure," said Elliot, once again regaining his composure. "You should be glad they sent me. Another guy might have done some damage to the house. Inadvertently, of course. I know the layout of this place like the back of my hand."

Sigrid was sick of listening to him. "Oh go home. I've had it."

"Thanks ladies. See you around." In less than a second he had run across the street and into a dark alley.

"I know it's a chilling thought," said Sigrid, "but if he ever does run for governor, I'm moving to Canada."

12

As soon as Maggie awoke on the following Thursday morning, she knew something had changed. The light streaming into her bedroom through half drawn shades had a different quality of brightness, not like sunlight. She threw back the covers and jumped out of bed. Even before she reached the window, she was certain what she would see. The shade snapped all the way to the top revealing the full wonder of the first snow of the year. Already it looked like almost six inches had fallen. And what was even better, she had no classes until the afternoon. The snow looked heavy and wet, perfect for making a snowman in the front yard.

She searched briefly for her robe and found it crumpled under the typewriter. Pulling it out, she looked into the pocket for her toothbrush. No luck. It must have fallen out somewhere. She reached into her side desk drawer and felt around until she found another. Perhaps today would mark some kind of change. Not only in the weather, but in her life.

Since her meeting with Jane and Sigrid last Friday night, nothing new had turned up. She had racked her brain, trying to make sense out of the strange goings on surrounding Allison's death. But nothing was any clearer. She knew she needed to relax and give her mind a rest. This would be a good day for it. She would spend the morning playing in the snow. It was early enough that nobody would be hogging the bathroom. And by the time she was done getting cleaned up, Adolph would have the juice and cereals set out. She'd go down to the dining room and make a fresh pot of coffee. She might even read the morning paper before it got scattered all over the house.

As she rounded the corner, she became aware of a strange noise. It was an odd sound, almost like a wounded bird. She stopped for a moment and listened. It seemed to be coming from the attic stairway. No one used the attic except for storage. It would be strange indeed if someone were up there so early in the morning. She moved back a few paces and listened again. Squinting up into the dimness, she thought she could make out a small figure slumped against the wall very near the top.

"Who's up there," she called softly. "Is there something wrong?"

No reply.

She took a few steps up the stairs. The small birdlike sounds ceased. "I know someone's up there. It's Maggie." She took another step.

"Don't come up," said a small but firm voice. "I don't want any company."

Maggie knew she could not simply leave. "Who is it? Brook, is that you?"

No answer. She took another step.

"Please, Maggie," the young woman's voice pleaded. "I don't want to talk to anyone right now. Things are just too awful."

Maggie sat down on the steps. "I know I could help if you'd let me," she said softly. "Most things aren't as bad as they first seem."

"This is," sniffed Brook.

Maggie thought for a moment and decided to press a little further. Maybe Brook would finally open up to her. It was worth a try. "Does it have anything to do with Elliot? I know you two have been seeing a lot of each other lately. He seems like a pretty nice guy."

The quiet sobbing lessened. "He's been wonderful."

Maggie waited. That was apparently all she was going to say on the subject. "Have you told him what's been bothering you?"

Again, no reply.

"Brook? Are you okay?"

"No."

"No you're not okay, or no, you haven't told him?"

"Both." Another indelicate sniff.

"Look, I'm not trying to pry, but I know something's been wrong for weeks."

"What do you mean?" asked Brook a little too quickly.

"I mean," said Maggie, "that the first few days of fall term you were a different person. You seemed happy and excited about everything. But something happened. Lately you've been moody and distracted. You don't talk to people anymore." She waited for a response but there was none. "I know you and Kari are pretty close friends. Have you told her what's wrong?"

Again no answer.

"Does Allison's death have anything to do with it? She sponsored you, isn't that right?"

Once again Brook broke down into loud sobs. As soon as Maggie had said the words, she knew it was a mistake. This game of twenty questions was going nowhere. It was probably better just to sit quietly and wait. Maybe Brook would eventually break down and tell her something if she waited long enough. It was worth a try.

For the next few minutes, Brook continued to sob in small fits. By now Maggie's eyes had adjusted to the dimness. She could see a thin body pulled up tightly into itself, face toward the wall. Maggie leaned back and tried to make herself comfortable. After what seemed like an eternity, the crying stopped and Brook eased herself back against the opposite wall.

"You were a good friend of Ally's, weren't you?" sniffed Brook.

"Yes," said Maggie gently. "She was one of the best friends I've ever had."

"She was a good person. Kind. She always knew the right thing to do."

Maggie doubted too many people would share that opinion. She was touched that Brook saw the same qualities in

Allison that she had. "You know," said Maggie tentatively, "you probably feel like you could have talked to Allison about what's bothering you. But we both know that's impossible now. I just want you to know that I'm here if you ever need anything. I want to be your friend. Anytime you want to talk, just come knock on my door."

"Thanks," said Brook with a bit more strength in her voice. "But I don't think anyone can help. Not you, not Ally, not anybody. Please leave me alone now." She said it simply, and yet the desolation in her voice made Maggie shiver.

"All right. I'm going. But just remember what I said. I'm here for you if you need me."

Brook made no reply.

Maggie stood and walked slowly back down the steps. She could feel something was desperately wrong. Not merely with Brook, but something was terribly wrong with the whole house. Something foul and hateful hung in the air. Maybe Jane was right. This was too big to handle by themselves. But on the other hand, the police might not be equipped to handle it either. Maybe what they needed was an old-fashioned exorcist.

After a hot shower and two glasses of orange juice, Maggie had still not been able to shake her mood. The house and everything in it felt diseased. She no longer had any desire to build a snowman, but thought perhaps a walk might do her some good. She stared blankly out the frosted front window, trying to remember where she had last seen her winter boots.

"Just the person I wanted to see," boomed a cheerful voice behind her. Maggie turned around in time to see Gladys Bailey, Kappa Alpha Sigma's longtime housekeeper, bustle out of the kitchen doorway carrying two overstuffed bags of garbage. She set them down next to the buffet table and leaned her stout frame against it heavily.

"How was your *Doctor Who* convention?" asked Maggie, attempting a smile.

"Marvelous! Cosmic!" She clapped her hands together

for emphasis. "My favorite Doctor, Jon Pertwee—he was number three—stayed at the same hotel as me. An elegant man, if I do say so myself." She beamed as if they were related. "I even bought a new sweatshirt with the Tardis on it. It's very warm. I could probably wear it today, but I want to keep it for special occasions." She winked at Maggie and walked over to pour herself a cup of coffee. "I suppose the Iron Maiden had a fit because I was gone so long." She flicked her eyes up to the ceiling. Directly above were Edith Holm's rooms. "I gave her plenty of notice. Even cleared it with the corporation board. She had the okay to hire some- one to come for the time I was gone. Even gave her a couple of names she could call. I've been up since five A.M. cleaning this pit." She pulled out a pack of cigarettes and lit one. "Did she hire anyone while I was gone?" The question was rhetorical. "Of course not. She tries to do everything on the cheap. It's her old martyr trip. I've witnessed it before many times. She tries to do everything herself. Once she realized how much work it is, she simply quits. And then when I come back, I'm welcomed home by *this*." She swept her hand grandly over the room.

"I didn't realize the board had told her to hire someone while you were gone. She should have told me that. I did see her sweep the entryway once."

"Humph," said Gladys, taking a sip of coffee, "that sounds like her usual effort. She huffs around here like she's been personally shoveling coal into the furnace all day. I don't know what that woman would do without an audience." She held the cigarette to her mouth and inhaled deeply. "I wanted to tell you how sorry I was about Allison. The Iron Maiden gave me the news as soon as I got in the front door last night. She couldn't wait." Gladys carried her coffee and cigarette over to the table and sat down. Her watery blue eyes and gargoylelike face looked unusually tired this morning. Mag- gie could easily believe she'd been up since five. "You know, I can hardly believe it. I mean, as I think about it, I must have been one of the last people to see her alive."

"What?" said Maggie, feeling a kind of electric shock. "When was that?"

"Well, it was the night I left for Des Moines. You were all at that big homecoming party. That was the night they say Allison took her life, right?"

Maggie nodded. Of course! Mrs. Holms had said something about going down to say goodbye to Gladys that evening. "What time did you leave?"

"Let's see," she said, blowing smoke out of the side of her mouth directly at Maggie. "My train left at nine. I guess Sally picked me up about eight-thirty. It's not very far to the depot."

"And where did you see Allison?"

"Well now," she said, studying the burning tip of her cigarette, "that's kind of strange. I'd packed my bags for the trip and thought it best to carry them upstairs to the foyer. I don't like to make my daughter help me with things like that. She's got a bad back. I tell her it's from too much sitting. She's a typist you know. Works for a big firm downtown. Anyway, I opened my door—I suppose it was about quarter of eight—and there was Allison sitting across the hall in that small room of yours."

"You mean the rituals room."

"Yes, that's it. I can never remember what you call it. Anyway, there she was, big as life, sitting on an old trunk. I must say, you girls don't keep that room very neat. There was stuff thrown everywhere."

"Did Allison see you?"

"That's what's so funny. Normally she was a very friendly person. It's hard to believe she wouldn't have noticed someone pushing some heavy luggage out of a doorway only a few feet from her. But she never moved. She must have been pretty deep in thought to be so out of it."

"And that was the last time you saw her?"

"No. Actually I saw her again a few minutes later." She leaned across the table, closer to Maggie. "I hauled all my luggage upstairs and decided to make a quick phone call. While I was talking, I realized I'd left my purse sitting on my bed, so when I was done, I raced back down to fetch it. The rituals-room door was still open and the light was on, but Allison was gone. I went in and grabbed my purse. When I got back upstairs, that new girl, what's her name? You know the one I mean. Short, curly blonde hair. Sparkly eyes. The one who wears yellow and black all the time. Kind of an odd combination, don't you think? Reminds me of a bee. I probably shouldn't say anything, but I don't think she looks too well.''

"You mean Brook Solomon?"

"That's the one. She was coming out of the dining room. Her face looked all mottled, like she'd been crying. As soon as she saw me she ran upstairs without so much as a good evening. It kind of upsets me when people aren't friendly. I mean, I'm not some servant. I deserve to be treated with respect. If people snub me, I don't forget it. Anyway, Allison was on the phone talking to someone. Mind you, I wasn't trying to listen, but I was only a few feet away standing by my luggage. And it *was* quiet in the house. I couldn't help but overhear some of what she said.''

Maggie never doubted for a moment that Gladys hadn't heard *all* of what Allison had said. She knew Gladys made it a point to eavesdrop on every conversation she possibly could. Very little of what happened at Kappa Alpha Sigma got past Gladys Bailey.

"Well," she said, thinking for a moment. "It's lucky I have such a good memory. I believe Allison said something like, 'You're not making any sense.' Then she listened for a while. The last thing she said was, 'Okay. I'll meet you in fifteen minutes, but I'm not changing my mind.' Anybody who knew Ally knew that when her mind was made up, that was it. No more talk.''

"And then what happened?" Out of the corner of her eye, Maggie noticed Adolph come out of the kitchen carrying a load of plates for the buffet table. He seemed awfully concerned about arranging them correctly. It was only too apparent that he was trying to listen to their conversation.

"She just came out of the phone closet," said Gladys, "and said hi. She wished me a good trip. You know, she was a fan of *Doctor Who* just like me. That always made her kind of special.'' She ground out her cigarette and immediately lit another. ''You know,'' she whispered conspiratorially, ''all that stuff about suicide. She sure didn't seem suicidal to me. I mean, my impression was that she was pretty mad, not depressed.''

Adolph walked back into the kitchen. He was another person Maggie figured never missed a thing that happened around the house. Between Gladys, Adolph, and Edith Holms, she felt like she was living with the KGB.

''That's about all I can tell you, kiddo. If I think of anything else I'll let you know.''

Maggie couldn't believe how lucky she was to have run into Gladys. She had to get to a phone and call Jane right away. Adolph came out of the kitchen again, this time carrying a stack of soup bowls. Gladys turned around. ''Adolph! I missed your cooking while I was gone!'' She winked at Maggie. ''What's for lunch?''

On his way back into the kitchen he murmured, ''Tomato soup and assorted sandwiches.''

''How unusual,'' smiled Gladys.

After a great deal of thought, Maggie determined her boots were probably somewhere in the front coatroom. As soon as she found them she was going to call Jane and ask if she could come over. Lunch at The Lyme House sounded more appealing than what Adolph was preparing. Just as she succeeded in squeezing herself behind several stacks of chairs and a long folding table, the doorbell rang. She stood up straight, knocking down a heavy box of file folders that had been sitting precariously on the edge of the shelf above her. Crouching down, she crawled out of the closet on all fours. Nobody was around. The grandfather clock in the living room was just striking ten. She stood, rubbing the top of her head, and walked over to answer the door. A gust of snow blew into the foyer along with Jane.

''I was just going to call you,'' said Maggie, helping to

brush the snow off her coat. "You look different in jeans and a hunting jacket." Maggie stood back to get the full view.

"Thanks," said Jane, shaking snow out of her hair. "I'll take that as a compliment. It's really bitter out there. And the roads are getting pretty nasty."

Maggie smiled. "You look like you could use a hot cup of coffee."

"What time is it?" asked Jane. "I'm supposed to meet with Edith Holms this morning about the winter retreat we're planning to have up at my family's lodge."

"I didn't know we were meeting there," said Maggie. "Where is it?"

"It's up near Repentance River. That's the closest town. It's actually on Blackberry Lake. A really beautiful place, even in the winter." She kicked the snow off her boots. "So what time is it? I'd like to have that cup of coffee with you if I have time. You know how upset Edith gets if you're late for a meeting. It's almost worth arriving an hour early. I don't recall ever seeing anyone pout quite like her before."

"It's hard to win with a passive-aggressive," said Maggie seriously. "It's exactly five after ten." She checked her watch, which she had finally found yesterday in a half-filled box of cereal.

"Great. Let's go find that coffee." Jane took off her damp jacket and tossed it over her shoulder. They walked slowly past the bulletin board where Adolph was busily tacking up next week's menu. She stopped momentarily to look at it. Her eyes came to rest on a one-page announcement that he had tacked up directly below it. It advertised a Bible study in south Minneapolis.

"What's all this about?" asked Jane, tapping the sheet.

Adolph turned around. "Good morning, Miss Lawless." His voice was formal.

"Please, call me Jane."

"Jane," he smiled. "It's a Bible study I attend every Wednesday night." He handed her a copy. "I post one of these and leave the rest over by the phone." He pointed to a thick stack resting on the table and cast a furtive glance at

Maggie. "I hope you young ladies will give them out to your
friends when they come over."

Jane took out her glasses and put them on. She read the
heading: *"Wednesday Night Bible Study Series."* Underneath it said, "Holy Law Christian Church of Minneapolis."
It continued: "What is Godly sexuality? Why did God ordain
marriage? What did God personally teach Adam and Eve
about sex? Come learn the sacred meaning and divine purpose for which God created man and woman. This Bible
study is free and open to the public. Seven-thirty in the lecture hall above The Salt Lick Café, 1022 East Lake Street.
Everyone welcome."

Jane handed it back to him, noticing that he seemed unusually distracted this morning.

"You're not interested, I take it," said Adolph, folding it
quickly and stuffing it into his pocket. "In a couple of weeks
we'll be starting a series on prophecy. Maybe that would
interest you more."

"I don't think so," said Jane, trying to sound cordial,
"but thanks." She took hold of Maggie's arm and pulled her
into the dining room. "I didn't know he was religious,"
whispered Jane as they approached the coffee maker. "This
place has more religionists than a revival meeting."

Maggie gave a weak smile. "But you know, it's kind of
strange. Adolph and Susan Julian don't really get along.
Wouldn't you think they would? I mean, they had this extremely heated discussion last week about where the *true*
church really was."

Jane held up her hand. "Please. Spare me the exegeses.
What I *would* like to know is who gave him permission to
post that stuff?"

"Mary Sue Engstrom. She was president last year when
he started as cook. I think Sigrid figured she had to go along
with it, especially after Susan started her Bible study downstairs in the green room. Adolph posts that sheet every
Thursday morning, just like clockwork. I guess he picks them
up at the meeting the night before. It's a toss-up sometimes

which is more interesting, the Bible study topics or the menu for next week. Sometimes the menu loses.''

Jane laughed as she leaned back against the counter. ''He's a funny little man, isn't he?''

''Yeah. But Sigrid doesn't like him *at all*. She'd get rid of him in a minute if he didn't have a contract. Except, he *has* been helpful to some of the girls. He helped Carol Hjermstad with her bulimia last year.'' Maggie poured herself a cup of coffee. ''Maybe I shouldn't say this, but he's also a bit of a gossip. I get the impression Susan Julian knows about it and doesn't like it one bit. She made some comment once about him being too nosy for his own good. And of course,'' she took a sip of coffee, ''he's probably not politically conservative enough for her. Actually, come to think of it, she and Elliot would make a great team. They're both always thumping about morality and politics. And only their kind of politics have any moral base, you know. They're both terribly conservative.''

''I think I've heard that,'' said Jane, pouring her coffee.

Maggie silently regarded the new milk machine. ''Oh! I almost forgot! I've got some incredible news. You need to be sitting down to hear this.''

They moved their cups over to the front table. With growing excitement, Maggie filled Jane in on what Gladys Bailey had told her earlier. As they spoke, Adolph came in and out of the dining room, occasionally stealing a glance in their direction.

''Did she remember if Allison mentioned a name?'' asked Jane. Before Maggie could answer, Mitchel Page marched aggressively past them without so much as a nod. He entered the kitchen and dumped his books on the counter. Jane watched him for a moment before continuing. ''And also, did she say if Allison made the call, or was it a call she answered? That could be important.''

''No,'' said Maggie. ''She didn't mention anything about either.''

''I'd like you to introduce me to her sometime soon.''

Suddenly, the sounds of shouting and a loud metallic crash

exploded from the kitchen. In less than a second, both Maggie and Jane had jumped up and run through the kitchen door. Adolph was nowhere around, but next to his desk in the back of the room, crouched Mitchel Page. He looked ready to dive behind it any minute if necessary. Jamie McGraw was about ten feet away holding a large stock pot above her head.

"I won't talk to you when you're like this," shouted Mitch as he ducked out of the way of another pot. It bounced off the stainless-steel refrigerator door, leaving a fair-sized dent.

"You disgust me," said Jamie, picking up a butcher knife. She moved several feet closer to him before tripping over a stool and landing halfway across the counter. The knife fell to the floor as she tried to catch herself. Maggie quickly moved through the room and helped her off the counter. The sour smell of alcohol and sweat permeated the air around her, making Maggie momentarily nauseous.

"Leave me alone," said Jamie, pulling her jacket down with a tug. She whirled around. "Oh, it's you, Maggie." She steadied herself against the counter and ran a hand through her thick black hair. "I thought I'd come over for lunch."

"Christ, Jamie," said Mitch, getting up from behind the desk, "it's not even eleven, and you're drunk."

"Shut up," she shouted angrily. "I'm not drunk. Tell him to shut up, Maggie."

Maggie put her hand on Jamie's arm to steady her. "Why don't you come out into the dining room and have a cup of coffee? Or, better yet, you can go up to my room and sleep for a while. You'll feel better."

"Sleep," shouted Jamie, as if Maggie were a bigger moron than she had ever suspected. "I haven't been able to sleep since the night it happened!"

Mitch jumped over Adolph's desk and grabbed her roughly around the waist. "I'll take her home," he said, pulling her out the back door. "Don't worry. She'll be fine. Tell the old man I'll be late for lunch dishes."

"Let go of me, you neanderthal!" Jamie protested loudly as he dragged her out the door.

Maggie turned around and looked at Jane. "Should I have let him take her? I don't feel very good about that."

Jane shook her head.

At the other end of the room a door opened and in floated Edith Holms. Today her hair looked almost blonde. "You have a phone call, Jane," she said in her most cultured voice.

Jane was momentarily surprised that anyone would know where to find her. "Oh, I guess I did tell the restaurant I'd be over here this morning. I'll try to make it brief and then maybe the three of us can sit down and talk about the winter retreat."

"That's fine, dear," said Edith, critically examining Jane's attire. She turned her attention to the pots littering the floor. "What have you been doing in here, Maggie?" She sniffed the air. "This kitchen smells like a distillery!"

It was probably that new steam-jacketed kettle, thought Jane as she picked up the phone. It had been giving them trouble all week.

"Hi. This is Jane." She expected the usual litany. It won't heat. It's curdling all the sauces.

"Hello," said a low voice. "My name is Emily Anderson. We've never met, but I understand you came to my parents' house looking for me."

"Yes," said Jane trying not to sound too excited. "I'm delighted you called. I was wondering, could we possibly meet sometime soon?"

There was silence on the other end.

Jane stumbled around in her mind for something inoffensive to say. "I'm glad your mother was able to get my message to you."

"What was it you wanted to talk to me about?" asked Emily warily.

"Actually," said Jane, not really knowing quite how to ask without scaring her off, "it's about Allison Lord. I was kind of hoping you could help me out by answering a couple of questions."

"Questions?" said Emily, her voice an octave higher. "Are

you trying to get my address for Mitchel Page by any chance? Because if you are, I've got a little message for him!''

"I don't know anything about that," said Jane quickly. "Is he trying to locate you?"

"Yes. He's called my parents' house three times. I don't know what he wants from me but I have no intention of talking to him. I hope I make myself clear."

"Please believe me," said Jane firmly, "I don't know anything about that."

"Well, because if you did . . .''

"Please," said Jane. "I'm not a spy. I promise if you'll just see me, I'll leave as soon as you ask. And I won't tell anyone where you live."

"What do you know about Ally and me?" Her tone was guarded. "Who are you anyway?"

"I was a friend of Ally's before she died." Jane didn't want to say too much. The fact that she knew Allison so briefly would only add to Emily's suspicions. "I do know that you and Ally were lovers."

"I see," said Emily. She was silent for a moment. "And do you have any particular problem with that?"

Jane felt the belligerence in her voice. And she understood it. "No," she said simply.

Another silence. "Okay. I guess I could talk to you for a few minutes. You'll have to come to where I live. I don't have a car, and I'm kind of short on money right now."

"That's fine," said Jane, trying to hide her eagerness.

"Right now I'm living in Hudson, Wisconsin. It's just across the river from Stillwater. I have a room above an old drugstore. 115 Elmwood. Come at four tomorrow afternoon. I may be leaving the area soon, so if you want to see me it will have to be tomorrow."

"That's fine," said Jane. "I'll see you at . . ." The line clicked. Emily had hung up. Jane got out a pen and quickly wrote down the address on the back of one of Adolph's Bible study announcements. She wondered if he had any idea how often they were probably used for scratch paper.

13

Nordeen Drug in Hudson, Wisconsin, was located quite a distance from the main part of town. It was an old two-story building that had been badly neglected over the years. Jane parked her car near the front entrance and sat for a few moments looking around the neighborhood. The fading winter sunlight cast deep purple shadows in the newly fallen snow. Without the clean covering the snow provided, she was sure the houses would look ramshackle. She could easily believe Emily had little money. No one would willingly live above such a dreary, and no doubt dirty, drugstore.

The front door creaked unpleasantly as Jane walked into the small, overheated room. The cracked linoleum needed a good sweeping, and the windows could have used a scrub. A heavyset, middle-aged woman sat casually behind the cash register, absorbed in a magazine. She looked up as Jane entered.

"Can I help you?" she said, examining Jane curiously. "You're not from around here, are you." It was less a question than a statement. Still gazing intently at Jane, she reached over the counter and grabbed a pack of chewing gum.

Jane smiled, wondering if perhaps she had just witnessed a petty theft. She supposed a drugstore this far from the main part of Hudson rarely got visited except by those in the neighborhood. "That's right," she said, looking around the store. "I was wondering if you could tell me how I get to the apartment upstairs. I didn't see a door outside."

The clerk nodded toward a narrow stairway in the back by the pharmacy. "There's also an entrance out back, but this one'll be easier for you." She unwrapped the gum and folded a stick into her mouth. "Old man Nordeen used to live up there before he died."

"Thanks."

"You know her?" asked the clerk chewing audibly. "The woman up there, I mean." She nodded toward the stairs.

"No. We've never met."

"She seems pretty upset about something." She unwrapped another stick and crammed it into her mouth.

"What do you mean?" asked Jane.

"She never goes anywhere. And when she does pop her head out, she always looks like she's been crying or something. She keeps that door locked day and night." The clerk chewed loudly. "Except, I've heard her talking to someone. Well, not exactly talking. Yelling is more like it. Some guy has come to visit her a couple of times, and they've had some pretty heated discussions, if you ask me."

"I see," said Jane. She moved a little closer to the counter. "You don't remember anything they said by any chance?"

The clerk stopped chewing. "I'm not that kind, lady. I don't go listening to other people's conversations. I mean, I may have some natural curiosity about what's going on up there. Who wouldn't?"

"So do I," said Jane. "I guess that's why I'm here."

The woman began to unwrap another stick of gum, which sent Jane flying toward the stairs. She couldn't bear to watch the woman's teeth rot and fall out right in front of her.

Everything about Emily Anderson's room was lean and tucked in. Hospital corners on the bed. No frills. Nothing that would give any hint about its occupant. It was almost as if the life in the room had escaped while it still had the chance. A place for everything and everything in its place, thought Jane grimly as she took the seat Emily offered her. They sat together silently for a few moments. Jane could see that Emily's eyes were swollen. And yet, it wasn't just grief. There was something withered about Emily's appearance. She had the transparent look of the very ill. Feverish energy and no substance.

"What was it you wanted to ask me?" Emily's voice sounded brittle. She barely moved her mouth, afraid perhaps that any movement would crack her face in pieces.

"Thank you for seeing me today," said Jane. "I know I've come at a bad time." She wondered what internal price Emily was having to pay for such tight control.

"You didn't tell anyone you were coming here today, did you?"

Jane could feel herself being scrutinized even though Emily had hardly looked at her. "No. I promised I wouldn't tell anyone." She paused. "I know this might sound patronizing, but I do understand a little of what you're going through right now."

Emily turned her head stiffly, regarding Jane with contempt. "You're right. That sounds patronizing."

This is not going to be easy, thought Jane. She didn't know what she had expected from Emily, but this wasn't it. "Okay. I'll get right to the point. I guess the first thing I should say is that I don't believe Allison committed suicide. I want to find out the truth." She waited for a response. There was none. "Is that an opinion you share?"

Emily's swollen eyes looked away. "Yes," she said coldly. "Ally would never have killed herself."

"Do you have any reason to suspect someone might have wanted her . . ."

Emily turned on Jane with the force of an explosion. "Let's stop playing this game, shall we! What is it you want? You want me to say I killed her? Well, I'll tell you who is responsible. If you want to hear the truth, I'll give it to you! It was Mitchel Page! He was like a cancer in our relationship. Always pushing her. Always working the angles. The whole plan was his idea, not Ally's. She didn't need him, *he* needed *her*! It was all crazy. I told her it was crazy." Emily's body shook violently.

"What do you mean when you say a plan? Who was planning what?"

The strange light in Emily's eyes smouldered. "Ally and Mitch were planning to be married. I thought everyone knew that by now. Her dad told her she'd be disinherited if she continued her relationship with me. Somehow Mitch found out. He worked out this little scheme all by himself. I mean, it was just ludicrous. He and Ally would marry. He'd be in hog heaven as Adam Lord's son-in-law and he promised he'd leave Ally and me alone. We could continue our lives with a minimal amount of interruptions. Just an occasional state dinner at Daddy's house. That was all. He said they would never have to see each other except for that. I may be kind of slow, but I didn't get it. We argued about it for weeks. She was sure it would work. For some reason she thought she needed that old man's money. We could have made it! I know we could have! She just wouldn't listen. She seemed frightened. Mitch kept calling all the time. Kept hounding her. Allison was strong, but she wasn't ruthless. I don't think she recognized that quality in other people. She knew Mitch was brutal and that what she was doing was dangerous, but she thought she could handle it. She thought she could handle *him*. Until it was too late. She trusted people. He used that trust and her own fear to manipulate her.'' She broke into loud sobs. ''I hate him. He should be dead, not her!''

Jane let her cry. The intensity of her emotions had exhausted her. She wondered when Emily had last had a decent meal. After a few moments it was apparent that she had no energy left, not even to cry. The light outside was nearly gone now. The only source of light in the room came from the neon Nordeen Drug sign outside the window.

''Why did Ally meet with Mitch on the night she died?'' asked Jane.

Emily sat back and closed her eyes. The flatness in her voice gave her words even more electricity. ''I had finally convinced her that he would never leave us alone once they were married. He would have used our relationship to manipulate her for the rest of her life. At first she didn't believe he would do that. She thought he would keep his word. But she changed her mind, I don't know why. She called him that Sunday afternoon and asked to meet him over at Ernie's Bar. Right before she left, we got into another argument. I wanted to quit grad school and get a job. She wouldn't hear of it. I think she was more scared than I ever realized. But I knew she'd go through with it. It was all so horrible. She slammed out of the apartment and I could hear her car screech away. I sat in that empty room and for a moment I almost hated her.'' Her voice had dropped to a whisper.

''Your father came to visit you that night, isn't that right?'' Jane could see her visibly stiffen. The question seemed to bring her back to the moment.

''Yes,'' she said, tucking her emotions, tightening her control. ''How did you know about that?''

''I talked to him the day I drove to Stillwater to find you. He mentioned that you'd thrown him out.''

Jane knew this might present Emily with a dilemma. She needed to be careful, since this was one thing Jane apparently knew something about apart from what Emily might wish to tell her. If she had lied about anything else, Jane might never know. This was different.

''Yes. We had our usual argument. He couldn't believe I was a lesbian, and I couldn't believe he was a bigot.''

''Had he ever met Allison?''

''No. He knew she was rich and was a member of Kappa Alpha Sigma. That's it.''

''Do you think your father could have had anything to do with her death?''

Again Emily sat back and closed her eyes. ''No. It's impossible.''

''How do you know that? From what he told me he certainly hated her.''

Emily opened her eyes and looked out the frosted window. The room was filled with a virulent quiet. ''Don't bring my father up again or you can consider this little interview over.''

Jane wondered why she hadn't already thrown her out. Perhaps it was some need to finally talk. To get all the feelings out in the open. If she could convince Jane that Mitch was responsible, she might finally convince herself. ''Did anyone call looking for Allison after she left?''

Emily relaxed her grip on the chair. "Yes, I think she did get a call. It wasn't important."

"Do you remember who it was from? Did they leave a name?"

"It was a woman. Let me think. Oh yeah, Ally mentioned her a couple of times. I think her name was Susan."

"I see," said Jane. "Had she ever called before?"

Emily shook her head. "I don't think so. At least, not while I was home."

"Do you remember what time she called?"

"It must have been around seven-thirty. I remember looking at the clock and thinking Ally would be done talking to Mitch by then. I figured she would be calling me or coming back to the apartment, so I told this Susan to call back later."

"Did she call back?"

"Not while I was there."

"Did you go out that evening?"

"Actually, no. I stayed home all night, waiting for Ally to come back. I did take out the garbage. That was all." Emily's voice was steady and calm, yet Jane suspected her last statement was a lie.

"Have you ever met Edwin Lord, Allison's brother?"

"Sure," said Emily. "Ally took me up north to meet him one weekend after we got back from England."

"What did you think of him?"

"He reminded me a lot of Ally. They look so much alike. When we were in London, we searched all over for a set of twelve lead-crystal wine goblets he had asked Ally to find for him. We finally found the right ones in this little shop in Oxford Street. She loved to spend the day shopping in London. I'd never seen such beautiful things before in my entire life. Ally surprised him with a matching crystal pitcher."

Edwin Lord apparently did not eschew the world in quite the way Jane had imagined. He was an odd assortment of paradoxes.

A knock on the door jolted Emily out of her reverie. She jumped to her feet and held a finger to her mouth. "Quiet," she whispered as she moved over to the door. "Who's there?" she asked softly with her ear next to the keyhole.

"It's your dad. Please open the door, Emily. I've got to talk to you."

"Go away," she said angrily. "I've said everything I know how to say."

"Please," said her father. "There's something I haven't told you. Something we've got to talk about."

Emily stood up straight and pushed her hands deeply into the pockets of her frayed jeans. "Are you alone?"

"Yes. I'm alone. *Please* let me in!" His tone was just short of pleading.

She switched on the overhead light and opened up the door. Clarence Anderson walked into the room carrying his heavy winter jacket. Jane stood up and turned around to face him.

"What's she doing here?" he asked, looking startled.

"She was just leaving," said Emily, handing Jane her coat.

Jane nodded and walked to the door. "Thank you, Emily."

"Don't mention it. And remember, if you want to know who's responsible for Allison's death, you don't need to look any further than Mitchel Page."

"Right," said Jane as the door slammed in her face.

It was nearly eleven before Jane pulled into her own driveway. After leaving Emily's apartment she had driven to the restaurant for a short meeting and then stayed to complete the monthly inventory. The steam kettle was still creating havoc in the kitchen, and she had solemnly promised the head chef to get the sales representative out first thing in the morning.

The night was clear as Jane leaned against the hood of her car and looked up into the night sky. It only took a moment before she located her star. Ever since childhood she had always thought of the North Star as her personal star. She vividly remembered the first time someone had pointed it out to her. It was up at Blackberry Lodge. She and her father were sitting on the end of the dock dangling their feet in the water. He had pointed up into the sky and said, "If you can find that star Janey, you'll always know where you are." Many times since Christine's death, Jane had gazed up into the night sky searching for that guiding star. She always found it twinkling back at her. And yet, somehow, she still felt lost.

The snow crunched under her feet as she approached the front door. Glancing up at the second floor, she was surprised to see a light on in her bedroom. That was funny. She was sure she'd turned it off before leaving the house. She stepped quickly inside and closed the door behind her. The kitchen light was also on. She laid down her briefcase and whistled loudly. Upstairs she heard two thumps and a second later both dogs came charging down the steps wagging their tails and being their generally excessive selves.

"What's going on around here?" she asked Gulliver, scratching down the length of his back. Bean was attempting to open her briefcase with his tongue. The meat scraps inside were of more immediate interest than Jane.

"It's about time you got home," said a voice from the second floor landing.

Jane looked up. "Cordelia! What are you doing here?"

"It's all too awful, Janey. Too awful." She vamped her way down the long stairs holding the back of her hand to her forehead. She was wearing pink satin pajamas under a fake zebra skin robe.

"What's too awful?" said Jane, removing her coat and throwing it over one of the dining room chairs. "Please don't stand on ceremony. Make yourself at home."

"What I need is a drink, dearheart." She leaned against the door frame with her hand over her heart.

"I see you've already been in the kitchen foraging." She nodded toward the doorway.

"Yes, well," said Cordelia waving her hand. "Being terrorized made me hungry. Isn't that the strangest thing? I hope you don't mind. I helped myself to some of that cold tortellini salad you had in your refrigerator. It needs more dill."

"Thanks," said Jane, pulling the scraps out of her briefcase. "I'll be sure to make a note of it. What do you want to drink?"

"Oh, whatever." She threw herself down onto the sofa in the living room.

Jane walked into the kitchen with the dogs at her heels and a moment later appeared with a bottle of Armagnac and two brandy glasses. Cordelia had managed to drape herself over the sofa with all the drama of a Victorian painting. This is going to be a long night, thought Jane.

"So," she said, pouring the brandy, "not to put too fine a point on it, but can I assume the pajamas mean you're staying the night?"

Cordelia looked annoyed. "I had the fright of my life tonight, and you're making jokes?"

"Okay," said Jane, easing back into her chair and kicking off her shoes. "I'm listening."

Cordelia sucked in her breath and let it out slowly. "I'm telling the truth! It was nothing less than a personal encounter with the Countess Dracula."

"You mean you finally met Ms. Right and she turned out to be a vampire?" laughed Jane. "You have such extraordinary luck with women."

Cordelia closed her eyes. "I'm serious! Look at this." She pulled out a small metal cross from the pocket of her robe and held it out in front of her.

"Just tell me what happened."

"That's what I'm *trying* to do!" Cordelia flung herself back onto the sofa. "After the performance we gave to-night—it was the third time we've done *The Cherry Orchard*—I decided to go home and hide. To tell the truth, I left after the first act, before someone could call the police. I'm sure there are laws against impersonating a repertory company. Anyway, I took a hot tub and then came down into the kitchen to make myself a cold cheese sandwich, extra mustard, no pickle. I wanted to get in some tube time before bed, so I switched on the TV in the living room. There was a great old Tracy and Hepburn movie on Channel Six. I'd just gotten comfortable when out of a dark corner of the room flew this hideous beast with huge wings." She flapped her arms wildly. "It attacked me!"

"It was a bat," said Jane.

"I know it was a bat," snapped Cordelia.

"So what did you do?"

Cordelia straightened her robe. "What any sane person would have done. I screamed for the cat to kill it and dove under a quilt."

"Well done," said Jane, putting her feet up on the coffee table.

"Thank you. I waited until I couldn't hear any more flapping, and then I ran upstairs, found my crucifix, just in case, grabbed my coat and car keys, and crept back down the stairs. The cat had it cornered in the pantry."

"And so you decided to spend the night over here."

"Yes," said Cordelia triumphantly.

The doorbell rang, sending the dogs flying out of the kitchen. Jane got up wearily and walked into the front hall. She looked out through the peephole. No one was there.

"Who was that?" asked Cordelia, noticing Jane's irritation as she dragged herself back into the living room.

"Want another?" Jane held up the bottle.

"By all means."

"It wasn't anybody. That's the third time in the last week this has happened. The doorbell rings. I go to answer it, and no one is there." She poured Cordelia another Armagnac.

"Don't you think that's kind of scary?" said Cordelia seriously.

"You're just in a scary mood," Jane smiled. "I think maybe its just some kids in the neighborhood playing pranks."

Cordelia looked at the clock on the mantel. "Not too many kids are up this time of night."

Jane felt a twinge of uneasiness but decided it was best not to add to Cordelia's current condition. "At least I didn't see any large-winged beast hovering over the door."

"You're so damn casual about everything, you probably

wouldn't have noticed a vampire at your door selling Girl Scout cookies.'' Cordelia gave Jane a sickly smile.

Again, the doorbell rang. "This has got to stop," said Jane angrily. She flew out of her chair and raced into the front hall, yanking open the front door.

"Hello," said Edwin Lord, smiling shyly. "Have I come at a bad time? I saw the lights on all over the house so I figured you were still up."

"Yes," said Jane. "I am. You didn't by any chance ring the doorbell a few minutes ago, did you?"

"Me?" said Edwin. "No. I just got here."

Jane peeked her head out and looked around. "I guess you better come in. You look cold."

Edwin stepped inside the door and broke into a big grin. "You have dogs! What wonderful little animals," he said, getting down on his knees to tickle them. "What kind are they?"

"Terrier, poodle, schnauzer. They've got a little bit of everything in them I'm told, but mostly terrier."

Edwin rolled Bean onto his back and scratched his tummy. Gulliver pulled at his sleeve wanting to play tug. Both dogs clearly adored him.

"That's kind of unusual," said Jane. "They're usually curious about guests, but then they like to sit back and examine them from a distance."

Edwin flopped onto his back, and both dogs crawled on top of him.

Cordelia wandered in from the living room and cleared her throat.

"Oh, excuse me," said Jane. "I suppose I should introduce you." She looked down at Edwin who had rolled over onto his side with both dogs licking his face lovingly. "Cordelia, this is Allison Lord's brother, Edwin."

"Hi," said Edwin, nuzzling up to Gulliver.

"Delighted," said Cordelia, with infinite condescension.

"Me too." Edwin stood up and held out his hand. Cordelia shook it limply. She eyed Jane with an expression that suggested she was going to be patient, but where did she find these people?

"Why don't we all go into the living room and sit down," said Jane, with her best activity director smile. "Would you like a brandy?"

"No thanks," said Edwin. "I'm driving." Both dogs jumped into his lap without invitation.

"You've started to grow a beard," said Jane, turning on a few more lights.

"Yeah," said Edwin. "I've found it's a lot warmer in the winter if I have one. Especially when I'm outside a lot."

"Edwin lives with a spiritual community of brothers up near Thunder Bay," said Jane. "I believe I mentioned that to you."

"Ah," said Cordelia, smiling at Edwin and then raising her eyebrow at Jane.

"That's right," said Edwin. "But I really love to drive. I try to get down here at least once a month. I guess I like the solitude you have when you're alone out on the highway. I've got a great car that's easy and fun to drive. I'm sure that probably adds to the enjoyment."

"Uhm," said Cordelia pleasantly. "An old Chevy Van, no doubt."

"No, actually it's a Porsche. St. Victor's has a Chevy Van we use for hauling groceries and provisions. I agree, it's fun to drive those, too. Do you have one?"

Cordelia continued to smile while clenching her teeth.

"Yes," said Jane, glaring at Cordelia. "Cars certainly are important items in the scheme of things."

"That's true," said Edwin seriously. "We've got to design cars that are more efficient and don't pollute the environment. Take this Porsche I drive . . ."

"Let's not," said Cordelia, pouring herself another brandy.

Edwin tilted his head, studying her for a moment.

"Was there some reason you dropped by?" said Jane, changing the subject. "I mean, it's kind of late for a social call."

"Of course," said Edwin. "I'm sorry. I just got into town and came right over. I wanted to give you this." He pulled a small leather diary out of his jacket and handed it to Jane. "It's my sister's." He waited while she looked through it briefly. "After the memorial service I drove over to Ally's sorority. The front door was ajar so I went in. I'd been there a few times before, so I knew where her room was. I mean, that house was deserted! I'd think they would try a little harder to keep their doors locked. I could have been anybody! Anyway, I just wanted to look around her room. Maybe take something that belonged to her. While I was looking through her books, I came across this diary. I suppose Emily might like to have it eventually, but I decided to take it to prevent it from being shipped back to my father. Knowing him, he'll probably have everything burned." He petted the dogs who sighed contentedly in his lap. "I've read the whole thing a couple of times. It's funny. I thought I knew her, but I discovered things she never told me. I suppose that really isn't so strange when you think about it." He looked away. "There are some sections missing. They've been pulled right out from the binding. I suppose Ally did that for some reason. You mentioned you wanted to get to know her better, so I thought you might find some value in reading it. I don't think she would have minded."

Jane turned the small volume over in her hands. She had already noticed the beginning date was last January the first. Allison had probably started it while she and Mitch were in Philadelphia over Christmas break. She looked at the date of the last entry. It was dated several days before her death.

"Thanks so much, Edwin. I really mean it. This could help me a great deal." Out of the corner of her eye she could see Cordelia about to erupt.

"You know anything about vampires?" asked Cordelia, flapping her arms. "You look like you might have some first-hand knowledge." Jane could tell the Armagnac was taking its toll.

"Vampires?" said Edwin, turning toward her in confusion.

"I saw Emily this afternoon," said Jane, ignoring Cordelia.

"You did? How did you find her? She's moved out of her apartment."

"She called me yesterday. I think she wanted to make sure I wasn't just getting her address for Mitchel Page. I assured her I wasn't, and I guess she believed me. She agreed to meet with me earlier this afternoon."

"That's great. Can I have it?"

"Her address?"

"Of course." He scratched Bean's head and smiled.

"I'm not sure." Jane felt a little uncomfortable about the request. "I really don't know if she would want me to give it out."

"Oh, we're old friends. Ally brought her to see me up at St. Victor's, and we had a really good talk. Actually, the night Allison died the three of us were supposed to have dinner together."

"Really ?" said Jane. "I didn't know you were in town that night."

"Yup. I was at a restaurant in Dinkytown waiting for them. It's just a few blocks from the sorority. They serve pasties. Have you ever tried one?" He looked at Jane and then at Cordelia.

"I would have figured you more as the blood sausage type myself," said Cordelia.

Jane glowered.

"Blood sausage? No, I don't believe I've ever tried that."

"You were saying?" said Jane.

"About the dinner? Well, it never actually happened. I waited until almost eight-thirty before calling their apartment. We were supposed to meet at eight. There was no answer, so I waited around until nine or so before leaving. I think I made one more call before I left. I especially like to drive at night, so I had planned to leave right after dinner. I had to be back up to St. Victor's by the next morning."

"You said you called Emily and she wasn't there?"

"That's right. I figured she'd gone with Allison to see Mitch. They had some kind of meeting with him."

"Do you know anything about Mitch?"

"Only that Father treated him like the son-in-law he wasn't at the memorial service. I mean, I know he and Ally dated and that she broke it off with him sometime last year. It's all in the diary." He pointed to the book resting on the coffee table. Jane wondered why he didn't know about their forthcoming marriage, if it was true. Perhaps Allison had been too ashamed to mention anything, since the whole scheme was nothing but a swindle. Yet she must have included something as important as that in her diary. Unless, thought Jane, this was part of what was missing. Why would Allison tear sections out of her own diary? It seemed more logical that someone else had.

Cordelia yawned theatrically.

"Are we boring you?" asked Jane curtly.

"No no. Please continue." She waved her hand.

"I never saw Allison again after that day," said Edwin softly. "I mean, I left to get back up to St. Victor's and got word of her death several days later. It was Emily who finally called me with the news. So you see, I do consider her my friend. I would like to talk with her while I'm down for the weekend."

Jane got up and walked slowly over to her briefcase. Cordelia was obviously frightened, but certainly not of Edwin. "Let's see," she said looking through her appointment calendar. "Here it is." She repeated the address.

Edwin got out a notebook and pen from the pocket of his flannel shirt and copied it down. "Thanks, Jane. How are you coming with your investigation? Have you turned up any leads?"

Jane leaned down to pick up Bean, who had jumped off Edwin's lap and was scratching at her leg. "It's slow. I've got nothing I can really put my finger on yet. Just some hunches."

"Well," said Edwin, rising and walking into the front hall, "let me know how you progress." He glanced into the dining room. "What a beautiful breakfront. This really is a lovely old house." He walked over to examine it more closely. Jane turned on the light so he could see the detailing. "And a bay window! Don't you love those?" He moved to the window and peeked out through the curtains. "You've got quite a large lot here. Must be two hundred feet between this and the next house."

"That's one of the things I like best about this house," said Jane. "I've got lots of privacy."

Cordelia padded into the dining room, pulling her zebra robe tightly around her. Edwin turned in time to see her enter. "You know, you remind me of someone I knew in high school."

"Thank you," said Cordelia formally. "And you remind me of a zucchini."

Jane groaned.

"No," said Edwin clapping his hands together and laughing. "I agree! I often think in terms of vegetables when trying to describe people." He turned his full attention on Cordelia. "You, my dear, are an eggplant."

Cordelia's mouth dropped open.

"I think it's time to call it a night, Edwin. I've got an early meeting in the morning."

"Sure, I understand. I know it's late." He took one more look at the bay window and then walked past Cordelia into the front hall.

"Thanks again for the diary," said Jane as she unlatched the front door. "Good luck talking to Emily. She's pretty upset."

"I imagine," said Edwin sadly. "She's a smart young woman. Sometimes only time can help." He nodded to Cordelia and then left.

Jane held up her hand as she shut the door behind him. "I don't want to hear about it. I'm going to bed."

Cordelia was almost speechless. "How could you stand there and let him call me an eggplant!"

14

The next night the Richard III party was in full swing.

"The only reason you didn't like him was because he called you an eggplant." Jane picked a smoked oyster off a plate filled with seafood and freshly cut lemon slices.

"That's not true," said Cordelia, slapping Jane's hand for ruining her perfect arrangement. "Here, take this plate out into the other room." Cordelia picked up another tray of canapes and backed through the swinging kitchen door out into the dining room.

"Wonderful punch." An older woman winked, hoisting up her hump. "And the mustard meatballs!" She kissed the air over Jane's shoulder.

"Who was that?" whispered Jane as soon as she had passed on into the living room.

Cordelia made a space on the dining room table for the seafood. The entire table was filled to overflowing with plates of appetizers, cakes, and even a roast goose. "That's Cynthia Melling. She was Joan in last year's production of Shaw's *Saint Joan*. Isn't she gorgeous?" She poured herself a glass of punch. "Want some?"

"No thanks," said Jane, watching Bean lick out of a glass someone had foolishly set down on the floor.

"That was a stroke of genius bringing those dogs as your date. Where did you find Gulliver's sweater and hat?"

"In an old trunk," said Jane, noticing Gulliver edging ever closer to a plateful of meatballs.

"Blanche will never be the same, I assure you. Last time I saw her she was peeking out from one of the bookcases next to the fireplace. She's the first cat I've ever seen trying to pretend she's a condensed version of *War and Peace*. Now, back to Edwin Lord. I don't feel any need to forgive someone who has compared me to an eggplant. But that would never cloud my inner sense about someone, and I don't trust him.''

"Turn up that music," yelled a woman standing in the center of the living room. A moment later the volume on "Saturday Night's All Right for Fighting" rose to a thunder.

"Isn't that your date for the evening?'' shouted Jane. They both watched as Andromeda jumped around the room waving a feather boa she had whisked away from an older man sitting on the couch.

Cordelia leaned over and yelled in Jane's ear. "How can you tell!'' Blanche jumped off the mantel and scrambled through the room pursued hotly by both dogs. Cordelia pointed toward the kitchen and shouted, "Follow me!''

Once inside, the music was somewhat muffled. "This still isn't any good for talking. Let's go upstairs.'' She led the way back into the dining room. Several people were standing on chairs blowing bubbles over the crowd.

"Come on and dance,'' shouted Andromeda from across the room.

Oh my god, thought Cordelia. She's actually got a lamp shade on her head. How trite. She gave her a little wave and blew a kiss. "Later,'' she mouthed, not wanting to strain her voice for such a silly person. She grabbed Jane's arm and pulled her through the crowd up the steps to the second floor landing. "In here,'' she said, knocking on the bathroom door. There was no answer.

"Cordelia, we can't sit in there. People may want to use it.''

"Naw,'' said Cordelia switching on the light. "Don't worry.'' She shut the door and turned the bolt. "Now, back to Edwin Lord. I'll just say one thing more and then we can consider the topic closed. He has shifty eyes.''

"He has what!''

"You heard me. And he seemed awfully interested in your house.''

''Now really, just because he noticed the breakfront . . .''

''You weren't watching him closely. I was. He was looking all over the house.''

''He *sat* in the living room the entire time.''

''Yeah, but his eyes! As I said, they were shifty.'' She hissed the word.

Jane shook her head and laughed. ''You brought me all the way up here to tell me *that*? The interior of my house is beautiful. Did it ever occur to you he's just interested in things?''

''No,'' said Cordelia flatly. ''Have a seat.'' She nodded toward the toilet. ''I've got some other news you might be interested in.'' She sat down on the edge of the tub.

''Okay, spill it.'' Jane wanted to get this over with. She'd had about all the festivity she could stand for one evening, and she wanted to go home.

''Kindly refrain from using that kind of metaphor in here,'' said Cordelia delicately. ''Your humor usually isn't so crude.''

Someone knocked on the bathroom door. ''This room is occupied,'' shouted Cordelia.

Jane shook her head.

''Okay, here's the news. I didn't want to say something yesterday because I wasn't sure of anything yet. But now I have proof. Susan Julian *did* go out the night Allison died. She lied when she told you she'd stayed home all evening.''

Jane was amazed. ''How did you find that out?''

''Simple. I happen to have an old friend who lives in the same condominium complex she lives in. I knew it was a longshot, but I called him. It seems he knows her. Not very well, but that was at least a start. His unit is just down the hall from hers. I talked to him this afternoon and he said the night in question he had been out to dinner celebrating. His divorce had become final that Friday. He was out of town on business until Sunday, so as soon as he got back he wanted to party. I think I should point out that this was not a date he would have easily forgotten or gotten mixed up, even though it was two weeks ago.''

"Good point," said Jane.

"He said he got home about eight. He had another date that he had to get ready for. The man has tragically bad taste in women, if you ask me. Anyway, he pulled into the parking ramp and nearly got sideswiped by Susan's BMW, which was pulling out at the speed of light. It would appear she drives about as well as she thinks. He got out of his car and screamed at her, but she just kept going. That's it. That's the proof. All I ask is that you let me know so I can be there when the police pick her up."

"Pick her up?" said Jane.

"Right. I want to be there when the police slap on the handcuffs."

Jane looked up at the ceiling. "Cordelia, that isn't proof of anything."

"Of course it is! She lied! Nobody would do that unless they wanted to hide something. It's perfectly obvious."

"It won't be to the police."

Another knock on the door.

"We'll be out in a minute."

"*We'll* be out!" repeated the voice.

"Get your mind out of the gutter," snarled Cordelia. "Well, I did my best. The ball is now in your court. Just don't take your eyes off that woman in any dark alleys. Mark my words, she's hiding something."

"It's not that I'm saying your information isn't important," said Jane, standing up, "it's just that I'm not sure where it fits."

Cordelia opened the door to a chorus of cheers. She grabbed Jane's hand and pulled her through the crowd. "You've got to see something before you leave." Two people stood outside Cordelia's bedroom talking intimately. Cordelia tapped the man on the shoulder. "Excuse me."

"Wonderful party," said a young woman Cordelia had never seen before. They moved on down the hall.

"Remember I said Andromeda wanted to get together with me for old times' sake?"

"Right," said Jane. "I remember."

"Well, you want to see what she had with her tonight when she appeared at my door? I mean, this really tells me she has a grip on who I am and what's important to me."

"I'm ready," said Jane.

Cordelia pushed open her bedroom door. There, as big as life, stood an exercise bicycle with full electronic functions.

"What a wonderful gift," hooted Jane. "I mean, it's really *you*."

"Gift," snorted Cordelia. "Not only is it *not* a gift, she wants me to pay retail!"

Mozart's *Mass in C* was playing on the university radio station as Jane pulled out of Cordelia's driveway. She had apologized for leaving so early, pleading a headache, and Cordelia had understood.

The cold night air was a tonic after the overheated and smoky interior of Cordelia's house. The dogs flopped down on the backseat, exhausted by several hours of nonstop cat stalking, with only an occasional foray into the living room for food. Jane smiled as she turned around to look at them. At least *they* had had a good time.

The wind had died down, and the night was still and cloudless, revealing a three-quarter moon sitting just above the bare treetops. As she drove along Minnehaha Parkway, she began to reflect on the last two weeks. Next week was Thanksgiving, and nothing was any clearer about Allison's death now than it had been two weeks ago. To be honest, she did have more information as well as a better sense of who might have had a motive, and yet beyond that, nothing. Something was missing. She had a feeling Allison's death was not a premeditated murder, but without proof, she couldn't even be sure of that.

And what about all the strange goings-on over at the sorority house? The stealing had stopped, but some still complained of feeling like they were being watched. Kari and several other girls had even given up their membership and moved home because they no longer felt safe at the house. Did it really all tie together, or was it just random circumstance? No doubt, Cordelia was right about Susan Julian. The fact that she'd lied about where she was the night of Allison's death did suggest she had something to hide. But what? There were too many questions and not enough good answers. Perhaps tonight she would have a chance to get a bit further into Allison's diary. So far, most of what she'd read wasn't new.

Jane's mind felt thick and slow. She struggled to make sense out of each new thought. As she pulled into her driveway, she barely noticed the light on again in her bedroom window.

Both dogs jumped into the front seat as soon as Jane opened the car door. They scrambled across her to get out. A little rest and their energy was once again boundless. She unlatched the gate and let them run into the backyard to perform their evening duties. They might as well get it over with right now so that she wouldn't have to make a trip back downstairs before bed. She entered the kitchen through the back door and switched on the overhead light. It was chilly in the house. She hoped nothing had happened to the monstrous old furnace in the basement. The temperature was already down in the single digits and might even fall below zero before morning.

She glanced out the kitchen window to make sure the dogs were getting down to business. Bean was over by the garage looking for the perfect spot. She couldn't see Gulliver. He must have gone around the side of the house. She entered the dining room and immediately felt an even greater change in temperature. Something was wrong. She stepped closer to the bay window and felt her foot crunch on something hard. Glass! The bay window had been shattered! A cold shiver rumbled through her body. She turned to look up the stairway and saw the light on in her room. This time its meaning did not go unnoticed. She heard the unmistakable sound of a creaking floor. Whoever had broken into the house was still upstairs. She crept back into the kitchen and picked up the phone, dialing 911.

"Hello," she whispered, hoping the dogs would not bark

and give her presence away. "I live at 4532 Bridwell Lane. Someone has broken into the house. I just got home and found broken glass all over the dining room floor. I can hear someone walking around upstairs."

"Okay," said a strong female voice. "Get out of the house *now*. I'll send a squad car right away. Leave now!"

Jane left the phone dangling from the wall and backed out of the kitchen door. The frigid night air instantly surrounded her, prickly with her own fear. She motioned for the dogs to come. Bean obeyed, but Gulliver seemed intent on examining the bushes under the bay window.

"Come here, Gulliver," she called. "Get over here." Gulliver stopped his sniffing and raised his small head. He was listening to something. She picked Bean up and started toward him. A second later he began to bark. Before she could stop him, Bean squirmed out of her arms, and the two dogs disappeared around the north side of the house. The snow from a wide cement walkway was piled high under her bedroom window. Jane waded into the snow in the middle of the yard and caught sight of them standing by the fence barking hysterically. She looked up and saw a dark figure hanging from her window. The figure dropped onto the pile of snow as the dogs tore at the fence with their paws. The intruder ran around the next house and disappeared. A moment later flashing lights drew her attention back to her own driveway.

"He just came out my bedroom window," she yelled pointing to the north side. "He took off that way." She gestured toward the next house over. One of the policemen leapt the fence and ran around her garage. The other shone his flashlight in Jane's face and introduced himself as Sergeant Kirkanen.

"Sorry, miss." He lowered the flashlight. "Are you the lady that called 911?"

"Yes," said Jane, trying to control her shivering.

"Why don't you wait here for just a moment while I go in and check out the house."

Jane nodded. Both dogs bolted from around the north side. Jane bent down to intercept them.

The sergeant entered the house through the kitchen, and soon she could see lights go on all over the house, beginning with the basement. She waited silently, hugging the dogs to her. She knew she was shivering more from fear than from the cold.

"You can come in now," called the sergeant a few minutes later. He waved at her from the doorway.

Jane got up and moved stiffly into the harsh kitchen light.

"They've gone. I checked everything out. We'll want to get an idea of what's been taken," he said matter-of-factly.

"I suppose this happens all the time," said Jane, fixating on the gun at his side.

"Often enough. Nothing seems to be out of place downstairs. Of course, that doesn't mean something hasn't been taken. But I think we should start with your bedroom. I'm afraid it's been pretty messed up."

Jane climbed the stairs, feeling out of place in her own home. Everything was strange. Nothing seemed familiar. Entering her bedroom she was unpleasantly aware of the smell of the intruder's sour sweat. The contents of her dresser and desk were scattered on the floor. It looked like someone had gone through the closet, but she didn't immediately see anything missing.

"Try your jewelry, miss. That's often what they're looking for."

Her jewelry case was in the night stand. She sat down on the bed and pulled out the second drawer. "No, everything seems to be here." She touched Christine's ruby ring. She opened the top drawer and for an instant, stopped breathing.

"Is there anything wrong?" asked the sergeant moving a little closer.

"It's my diary." She looked up. "And the diary that belonged to a friend. They're both gone." Her face drained of color.

Sergeant Kirkanen wrote something down in his note pad. "Anything else?"

Jane looked around the room at the mess. "Not that I can see." Both dogs hopped up on the bed and sat down next to her.

"Do you know why someone might want to steal the diaries?"

Jane shook her head.

"You might want to look around the rest of the house, but sometimes in cases like these, they're just looking for one thing."

Jane nodded. She wondered what he meant by "in cases like these."

"Do you live alone?"

Jane looked away. "Alone? Yes."

The policeman's partner entered the room looking out of breath. He introduced himself as patrolman Maki. Both dogs growled softly. "He got away. I never saw him. But I did pick this up in the alley." He held up a University of Minnesota ski mask. The maroon and gold colors were unmistakable. "Do you recognize it?" He looked at Jane.

"No," she said wearily. "I've never seen it before."

"Were you out earlier this evening?" asked the sergeant.

"Yes. I was at a party."

"It's possible that whoever broke in here tonight has been watching your house. Were the dogs with you?"

"Yes."

"It was probably a good thing they were. They might have been hurt. Someone must have wanted those diaries pretty badly."

Jane reached over and drew both dogs closer. She looked back and forth between the guns resting on the two policemen's hips. It seemed obscene that these guns should be in her bedroom.

"We'll have to file a report," said Sergeant Kirkanen. "We can send someone out tomorrow to take fingerprints if there are any. It's my guess there aren't. I suggest you tack something up over that hole in your window downstairs and spend the night with a friend. You can come back tomorrow and clean up. In the daylight things won't seem quite as frightening.''

"Yes," said Jane numbly. "I'll call my brother. Thank you." She couldn't bear the thought of returning to Cordelia's yearly attempt at being arrested.

"Are you okay, miss?" asked patrolman Maki.

Jane got up from the bed. "I'm just a little shaken."

"Have someone come with you tomorrow when you come back to the house. It will make things easier."

"Thanks," said Jane.

She followed as the sergeant led the way back down into the dining room. "That's a particularly beautiful bay window you've got there. Reminds me of my grandparents' home in Duluth."

"It's the best way to break into your house unnoticed," said patrolman Maki. "I walked around the house a few minutes ago when I was outside. It would have been the window I would have picked."

"You might want to put some bars on that one," said the sergeant.

Bars? thought Jane. She shuddered at the idea.

The policemen walked through the kitchen and out the back door. "Do yourself a favor," said Sergeant Kirkanen, turning around for one last look. "Don't stay here alone tonight."

"No," said Jane softly. "I won't."

The two men walked down the back steps and out to their squad car.

Jane closed the door behind them and sat down at the kitchen table still shivering. Christine, she thought silently, I need you.

15

On Wednesday, the day before Thanksgiving, Maggie was sitting in Walter Library doodling on some notes for an early ancient civilization final. *If I can just concentrate for another half hour,* she thought hungrily, *then dinner will be on the table when I get home. That will be my reward for thirty more minutes of agony.* Her stomach growled pitifully, causing a young woman several chairs away to look up and smile. Maggie wondered if her boredom was as apparent as her hunger. Ancient civilization was not her best subject. All quarter it had been a struggle to concentrate on such things as the rise of Mesopotamian civilization or the reign of Suppiluliumas. This afternoon she was trudging her way from the reign of Shalmanezer III through Sargon II. She was finding it slightly less interesting than reading the ingredients on the back of a bottle of shampoo. During the last hour, her doodle had begun to take on epic proportions. It was a terrific doodle. One of her best efforts. She could imagine it framed and hanging above her bed. It would always symbolize her fitful attempts to concentrate on something consummately dead and boring while life was flying past her, demanding full attention. And besides, what kind of parents would name a little baby Shalmanezer?

"Excuse me, miss," said a thin voice behind her. Maggie turned and found a tall, gangly young man holding out a piece of paper to her. "A girl out in the lobby asked me to give this to you." He nodded toward the entrance. Maggie took the paper, examining it briefly. Her name was written on the outside along with the word "private."

"Thanks," she said, looking up, but he had already left. She unfolded the paper and read silently:

Maggie, I'm desperate. Will you meet me in the stacks on level C? Walk back to the east corner. I'll meet you there. Be sure no one follows you. Please come.

Brook Solomon

Maggie crooked her neck trying to see out into the lobby. This was all very unusual. Perhaps Brook had finally decided to explain the mystery of what had been bothering her all term, but why such an odd time and place? And why all the secrecy? Well, thought Maggie, sensing that her liberation from Sargon II was at hand, anything is better than ancient Mesopotamia. She gathered her notebooks and headed off toward the elevator, noticing that the young man who had delivered the note was sitting at a back table, his nose deep in a book. She doubted he doodled very much. He looked like the type who was trying to escape *into* a library instead of out.

A few minutes later she emerged on level C and found herself staring at row after musty row of stacks. The air was pungent with the itchy smell of dust. The room, which was actually more of a vault, was frighteningly quiet. She had dated a boy last year who boasted about the many times he had slept in the stacks. She tried to envision him lying on the wooden floor, snoring.

She walked to the end of the room and turned east. The floor squeaked somewhere behind her, making her aware that she was not alone. She turned around slowly, expecting to see Brook. No one was there. She took a few more steps down a narrow passage and heard the floor squeak again. "Brook, is that you?" Her voice cut through the thin air like a razor.

"Over here," whispered someone. Maggie turned toward the sound. There, about ten feet away, stood Brook, peeking out from behind an immense ladder.

"Was that you making the floor squeak?" whispered Maggie somewhat angrily. "You scared me."

"I wanted to make sure no one was following you."

"Who would follow me?" Maggie tried not to sound annoyed, but all this cloak and dagger stuff was simply too much on an empty stomach.

Brook held her finger to her lips and motioned for Maggie to follow. They walked silently back to the elevator and Brook positioned herself so that she could see both it and the stairway. "I needed to find someplace where we could be alone." The fluorescent lights made her look unusually tired.

"What's all this about? Why all the secrecy?"

Brook fidgeted with the zipper on her jacket. "Now that I've got you here, I'm losing my nerve. I've gone over this a thousand times in my mind."

"Just begin at the beginning," said Maggie.

"The beginning?" Her voice was flat and emotionless. She looked down at the floor. "Okay. The beginning." She took a deep breath. "Last year, my senior year of high school, I did something really stupid. Something I'll regret for the rest of my life." She paused, pulling off her fur cap and shaking out her hair. "There was this teacher. His name was Mr. Van Horne. He taught senior English, and I took his class second trimester. Looking back on it now, I can't believe I was so incredibly gullible. I developed this terrible crush on him. It was quite obvious to all my friends, so I guess it must have been obvious to him, too. Anyway, he was about fifty, divorced, and terribly sexy. At least I thought so. One afternoon last winter, after school was out for the day, I went up to his room to discuss an assignment he'd given us. I was having some trouble, and I thought maybe he could help." She shook her head angrily. "See! Do you see what I'm doing? I'm still lying to myself. I went to his room just to see him. He was erasing the blackboard when I walked in, so I picked up another eraser and began helping. We got to talking about a party he was giving that evening. It was Friday. He said it was an end-of-the-week celebration. I remember holding my breath. If he brought it up, maybe that meant he was going to invite me. I mean, I never really expected it, but then he got real close—he didn't touch me or anything—but he invited me! I couldn't believe it.

"I went to that party. I went to a lot of his parties after that. He never touched me, though I always felt he eventually would. He'd just get real close. I suppose, looking back now, he was simply enjoying the power. He was playing with me. There was another man at all the parties. His name was Tim Newman. He was younger, probably in his early thirties, and he lived in this beautiful house out on Lake Minnetonka. You know, I can't believe I was so dumb, but I thought I could handle anything. I talked easily and convincingly, and I really thought I was street smart. And, though I've changed my mind since, at the time I thought people were basically good. God, I was so naive." She walked over and sat down on the stairway. Maggie followed.

"This Tim was really smooth. I didn't see it as smoothness then; I just thought he was nice. There were always drugs at the parties, but I never did any. I took pride in thinking drugs were dumb. I was too smart for that. Actually, I drank quite a lot, but I thought that was different. Anyway, Tim said he admired me for not getting into the drug scene the way others were. I liked him for that. Not, of course, the way I liked Mr. Van Horne. But I thought Tim was my friend. He invited me out to his house a few times for a couple of his parties. They were a little wilder than Mr. Van Horne's, but no one ever tried to push me into anything. I felt completely safe. There were always a lot of older men, nobody my own age.

"One Friday night, it must have been late March, Tim called me at home, which was unusual. He had never done that before. He asked if I'd like to come out and watch some movies. We'd done that a few times. He had this huge TV screen. Anyway, I was really bored that evening. Nothing was going on, so when he called, I said sure. I'd be out in about an hour. I lied to my parents, which I did all the time. I was really good at it. I felt kind of lousy because they trusted me, but if I'd told them the truth they would never have let me go. When I got to his house I guess I expected to see other people. But it was only Tim and this other guy I'd never seen before. He was more my own age. The more I talked to him, the more he gave me the creeps. I think it was probably the way he was looking at me. Tim offered me a glass of wine, and I took it gladly. After a few sips I remember feeling kind of funny, and the next thing I remember I woke up in this huge bed. My whole body ached, and I had scratches everywhere except my face. I felt like I'd been beaten up. I *had* been beaten up! And I had this horrible headache. Tim was standing next to the bed behind a video camera. He had it sitting on a tripod. I'd seen him use it before at parties just for fun. The other guy was gone.

"I started to cry, and Tim sat down on the bed next to me. He just watched. His expression was totally blank, I remember that vividly. He didn't even try to cover me—I was naked—or try to console me or anything. Finally, he said, 'You better shut up, bitch, before I shut you up.' He said it with no emotion. For some reason that made it even more threatening. If you can believe it, this was the first time it ever occurred to me that I should be afraid of him.'' She closed her eyes with the pain of her own stupidity. A second later she started to cry.

"We all make mistakes," said Maggie. "It's all right."

"No! It's not all right!" shouted Brook. She jumped up and flung herself hard against the metal elevator door. "It will never be all right. Don't you understand?" she said, whirling around. "This guy Tim did that for a living! He sold these little taped documentaries to video stores all over the country. Not only had I been raped and beaten, but it was all on tape for the enjoyment of any guy who felt like indulging in a little vicarious sexual brutality. He said if I told anyone, he'd send a copy to my parents and also to my brother, who he knew was a priest in Boston. And of course, he said Mr. Van Horne would be the first to receive a tape if I didn't keep quiet. I couldn't believe anybody was so horrible! He threw my clothes at me and told me to get dressed. He made me take this pill so I wouldn't get pregnant. And then he threatened me again. Before I left he said he'd kill me if I told the police. By that time, I believed he meant it.

"The rest of last year was a nightmare. I couldn't let my grades drop or people would know something was wrong. I practiced smiling and looking happy in the mirror at night. I don't think anybody ever guessed something was wrong except my mother. I started drinking a lot more, which led to some pretty awful situations. I didn't have any respect for myself anymore, so I pretty much slept with any guy who asked. I already felt like a slut, so I decided to act like one. At least I think that's what I thought. I was pretty messed up. In just a few short months I had earned quite a reputation. And somehow, I found this out later, someone had bought a copy of that video and was showing it around. People actually *knew* about it! I spent most of last summer going to video stores and buying or stealing any I could find. God, that was degrading. They were always kept under the counter, and you had to know how to ask. I got real good at it. I was number six in a series of bedroom rapes called North Country Vixens.

"I really thought I'd gotten all of them," said Brook, letting her head lean back heavily against the elevator door. "I vowed to make a fresh start at the university this year. The sorority would be a new place to live. I'd make new friends. I wouldn't associate with anybody from my old school. And then, I ran into Elliot Kratager. You'd just hired him as a busboy. Mr. Perfect. He'd been student body president at my high school last year. When I saw him I nearly quit then and there. I figured he must know about the video and before long it would be all over the house. All over campus for that matter. He acted pretty smug around me during rush. Everytime I saw him talking to someone, I was sure he was telling them about me. But then, when I was chosen to be a pledge, I figured maybe I'd stick it out for a while. Maybe he hadn't said anything after all. Or better yet, maybe he didn't *know* anything. Ally had been such a good friend and had tried so hard to get me into the house. I couldn't disappoint her. So, I formally pledged Kappa Alpha Sigma. Then, about a week after I was all moved in, the newest nightmare started. I got this little note in my box. I don't remember exactly what it said, but the point was if I left some money—about three hundred dollars—under a brick outside next to the back deck, nobody would need to know about *my past*. No matter how hard I tried, I couldn't make it go away!'' She closed her eyes.

Maggie wished she could somehow make this easier for her.

"There was some weird stuff in the note. I can't remember exactly. It was all crazy, but I couldn't ignore it. I just could never seem to get away from that awful night.''

Maggie stood up. "No,'' said Brook quickly. "I have to finish this.'' She walked back over to the stairs and sat down wearily. "I didn't have much money, unlike some of the other girls. My parents aren't as well off as it looked to the pledge class advisors during rush. Mom has been ill off and on for the last three years, and that's eaten up a lot of their savings. I was on a strict budget. I used up all my book money to pay the three hundred dollars. I figured Elliot had to be behind it since he was the only one in the house who could possibly have known. I put the money under the rock just like I was instructed, and the next day I asked Elliot if I could speak to him. I demanded to know if he was going to blackmail me for the rest of my life because of that video. At first he was kind of snotty. He said he knew about it of course, as well as my reputation. He told me he thought I was pretty sleazy—not in those exact words, but I got the point. But he said he never had any intention of trying to blackmail me. He seemed irritated that I would even suggest it. I guess I believed him. I didn't say anything about the note. After we got that out of the way, we actually sat and talked for quite a while. And something I said must have impressed him favorably because after that, he was almost nice to me. We would sit and talk fairly often after he had finished the dinner dishes. And he insisted on taking me to the memorial service after Ally's death. I was surprised when he asked me for a date. I think everyone already thought we were a hot item, but that wasn't true. He's been wonderful.''

Maggie shook her head. "That's all pretty gruesome. I can see why you've been so preoccupied."

"That's not all of it," said Brook, nervously looking up the stairs. "There's more. About a week after the first note, I got a second. It had all the same crazy stuff in it, but this time I was asked for four hundred dollars. I was given another location in which to hide it. But the problem was, I didn't *have* four hundred dollars. I had no idea where to get it." She looked away and began to wring her hands. "I'm the one who stole that camera and gadget bag from the front coatroom. I took it to a pawnbroker over on Cedar Avenue and got just over four hundred for it. I know it's worth more than twice that. I kept the ticket, thinking I'd buy it back as soon as I could. I paid off the blackmailer and hoped it would be the end of it. Somehow, I knew it wouldn't.

"Several weeks later, I got another note. This one said something about my repentance not being real. What the hell did that mean? I was given a week to get the money. I can't tell you how desperate I felt. I don't ever remember stealing anything before in my entire life. Several nights later, I noticed Lilly Sandvic wearing that emerald pendant her parents had given to her for her birthday. I could tell it was expensive. I felt awful, but the next night, while everyone was at dinner, I snuck into her room. I knew where she kept her jewelry. I got almost six hundred for it and paid the blackmail. I kept the extra two hundred under my mattress. Just in case. But there were no more notes until right around homecoming. Someone slipped one under my door while I was out. This time they wanted five hundred. I nearly went crazy. I didn't know what to do! I couldn't go on stealing, but where else could I get the money? If I told anyone, everything would come out. I was terrified it would kill my mother. She was back in the hospital at the time. I trusted Elliot, but not enough to tell him. I know Allison knew something was wrong. She tried to talk to me about it, but what could I tell her? The night of the big homecoming party at Sigma Nu, I put in an appearance, but left after only a few minutes. I ran back to the house and went immediately down to the basement to the rituals room. I'm ashamed to say that I had stolen your keys, Maggie, several nights earlier. You had left them on your books on top of the buffet when you went to make a phone call. I could never figure out why you didn't miss them.''

Maggie smiled weakly.

''I knew there was a money box in the rituals room so I unlocked the door with your keys. It was pretty well hidden, and I was in a panic, so I made kind of a mess. But I finally found it. I broke off the lock with a screwdriver. Just as I was about to count it, I heard this voice behind me say. 'What's going on here!' I turned, and there was Allison. She didn't look angry, just surprised. I started to cry, and the strange thing was, I couldn't stop myself. I couldn't even talk. Ally came in and shut the door. She just held me. Everything that had happened since last year seemed to come together in that moment. My body ached just like the night I woke up in that awful man's bed. It was such inarticulate pain. All I could do was cry like a baby. We finally sat down on the trunk and I told her everything. It just poured out. Afterward I felt like a zombie. I had no emotion left. I remember Ally sat thinking for a few minutes, and then she told me to go on up to my room and try to get some rest. She said she'd take care of everything. She made me promise that I'd see a counselor. I knew she was right. I don't know quite how to say this, but it was the first time in a long time that I had trusted anyone. It almost felt like she had given me back my life. I believed in her goodness and in her ability to make everything right again.

''I slept till late the next morning. I woke up feeling rested for the first time in months. That nagging inner nervousness I'd lived with for so long was completely gone. I got dressed, went downstairs, and the first thing someone said to me was that Allison was dead. A suicide. I must have come back upstairs to my room, though I don't remember doing it. All I remember was sitting on my bed staring at a bottle of prescription sleeping pills my mother had given me last summer. Nothing seemed real. Nothing made any sense. It was all like a dream. I lay there for a long time knowing I had the power to end it all if I wanted. While I was contemplating my own death, someone knocked on the door. It was Carolyn Harris coming to tell me the *big* news. Had I heard? Allison was a queer! A dyke. She'd been going to move in with some girlfriend of hers and be man and wife, or wife and wife as Carolyn put it. Wasn't it all too funny. Allison was a pervert. What a joke. I started to laugh, and I couldn't stop. I think I must have gotten hysterical because Mrs. Holms appeared. I remember seeing her bending over me. She asked if I wanted someone to call my parents. *That* brought me back to reality pretty fast. I said absolutely not and asked everyone to leave. After they were gone, I picked up the sleeping pills and put them away. It was funny. I knew *I* was a pervert, and now everyone was saying Allison was one, too. The world was simply filled to the brim with perverts. It was a sickening feeling.'' Brook's laugh was mirthless even now. ''I stole the silver candelabra out of the buffet case. No one has even noticed that it's gone. I hocked it for around three hundred dollars and combined it with the two hundred under my mattress and paid off the blackmailer. Since Ally's death, I haven't received another note. Not until last night when I got home.

''I found writing on my mirror just inside the door. It was written with some of my lipstick. This time they want two hundred dollars, and once again I don't have it. I can't stand the thought of stealing again. I took out the pills this morning, but it's strange, I knew I wouldn't use them.'' She looked hard at Maggie. ''Can you help? I've got to find out who's responsible for writing the notes and stop them somehow. I don't think they'll ever stop if I don't *do* something. At first, I believed what everyone said about Ally's death. But now, I'm not so sure. I think she *knew* who was sending me the notes. I think she tried to help and got killed for it. I have this terrible fear that now that I've told you all this, *you* will be killed!'' She reached over and took hold of Maggie's hand.

"I don't know what I'd do if something should happen to you."

"Nothing's going to happen to me," said Maggie softly. "Don't worry."

"But I *am* worried. I've been worried something would happen to Elliot, too, since he knows so much about my past." She pulled her hand away and began to rub the back of her neck.

"But he doesn't know about the blackmail?"

"No. I've never told him anything about that. I've been given several weeks to come up with the money this time. I'm almost positive Ally met with the blackmailer that night. I think she told them I didn't have much money. That I'd been stealing to get it. Because, the note on my mirror actually instructed me *not to steal*. How could they know I'd stolen the money unless Ally had told them? And the only time she could have done that was the night she died! I'm almost at a point where I don't care if people find out about the video, except for my mom. Will you help me? You've got to promise not to tell anyone." Her eyes implored.

"Of course I'll help," said Maggie gently. "But with one condition. There is someone we have to tell, and I won't help you unless you agree to it."

"Who?" said Brook cautiously.

"Jane Lawless."

"You mean the alum?"

"Yes. You're not the only one who suspected Ally's death wasn't a suicide. She's been doing a little private investigation into Allison's death. She never believed it was a suicide."

Brook looked genuinely surprised. "That's amazing. Okay," she said tentatively. "But no one else. Especially not Sigrid. I know you're a good friend of hers, but I don't like her. She's too sarcastic or something. I never know how to take what she says."

"I'm really sorry you feel like that," said Maggie. "Sigrid is a remarkable person in her own way. But I promise. I won't tell her anything."

They both stood and walked to the elevator. "So, what should we do first?" asked Brook, pushing the DOWN button. Her hand shook slightly.

"I'll call Jane. She may want to talk to you personally. But I don't think she'll have much time until after Thanksgiving. Maybe on Friday." The elevator doors creaked open, and they both got on. Maggie pushed the button for the lobby.

"I'll be at home tomorrow. My brother is flying in tonight from Boston. If you need me you can reach me there."

Maggie felt the elevator drop a little too fast. She had never liked the elevators in Walter library. "Sigrid and I have been invited to Jane's father's house in St. Paul. Actually, her brother Peter called with the invitation. I think he kind of likes Sigrid. He asked her to be his date, and I'm to bring along someone if I want."

The doors opened onto a crowded lobby. Maggie was glad to step out onto solid ground. "Let me know when Jane wants to talk to me," said Brook, looking furtively around the room. "And remember, you promised not to tell anyone else."

Maggie nodded silently as she watched Brook weave off into the crowd. She looked at her watch. It was nearly six. Damn. She had missed dinner again. It would be cold cereal and popcorn again tonight. Oh well, it might be just as good as Adolph's hot dinner. Maybe even more nourishing.

The walk home allowed Maggie to clear her head and think. She unlocked the front door of the sorority and entered the brightly lit foyer, shaking the snow out of her damp hair. Mitch and Elliot were busily clearing tables in the dining room, and she could see some people still talking in small groups around the dinner tables. She walked into the phone closet and closed the door halfway. Jane was no doubt at the restaurant, so she dialed the number of her private office. With any luck, she would answer.

"Hello," said a distracted voice.

"Jane, this is Maggie."

"Hi! What a nice surprise. I didn't think I'd hear from you

before tomorrow. You're still planning to come for Thanksgiving dinner, aren't you?''

"Absolutely! I'm looking forward to it."

"Good. Peter is planning to pick you and Sigrid up about two."

"I'll be ready. The reason I called is that I've got some incredible news! It's about Allison. I spoke with Brook Solomon a few minutes ago. I know this may sound crazy, but apparently she is being blackmailed. She was the one who made all the mess in the rituals room. Ally discovered her there and prevented her from taking the chapter dues. It's kind of a long story, but Brook told Ally everything, and she was under the impression that Ally must have known who the blackmailer was. She thinks there's some connection between that and her death. I won't go into it all now, but I think we need to talk.''

"What was she being blackmailed for?" asked Jane.

Maggie could hear shouts of laughter from the dining room. She reached over to pull the door completely shut and jumped back at the sight of Mitchel Page staring back at her through the half open door. Her hand froze.

"Maggie, are you there?"

She jerked the door shut and sat motionless. Why hadn't she been more careful?

"Maggie, is something wrong. Are you there?"

"Yes," she whispered. "But it's Mitchel Page. I think he heard me tell you about Brook. It's all supposed to be a secret. Oh Jane, did I just do something terrible?"

"You may have. Listen to me. Try to find him. Ask him if he heard what you said. It can't hurt. There should still be plenty of people around after dinner, so I don't think you'll be in any danger. See what he has to say for himself."

"Okay," said Maggie, summoning her courage. "I'll do it."

"And call me back. If I don't hear from you in half an hour, I'm going to call the police. I mean it. This is not a game. Someone broke into my house over the weekend and stole my diary as well as Ally's."

"Jane, how awful!"

"Whoever is behind this means business. I want you to be careful, Maggie. And call me as soon as you're done talking to him."

"I'll be fine," said Maggie confidently. "I'll call you right back." She hung up the phone and opened the door gingerly. Mitch had gone. She walked into the dining room and surveyed it carefully. He seemed to be nowhere around. Sigrid waved at her from one of the back tables. Maggie waved back but didn't stop to talk. She wanted to check out the kitchen. Wednesday was Adolph's early night. He usually left right after dinner so that he could make it to his Bible study on time. Elliot and Mitch were left to clean up. Maggie entered the kitchen and was amazed at how little had been done on the evening dishes. No one seemed to be around. As she turned to go she heard a groan somewhere behind her. She walked around the center island and was surprised to find Elliot on the floor propped up against Adolph's desk. He was rubbing his jaw.

"What happened?" asked Maggie, helping him to his feet.

"It was that asshole you employ here as head busboy," said Elliot, feeling the back of his head and finding a lump. "I guarantee he'll pay for this." He leaned against the desk and felt his jaw again.

"Why did he hit you?" asked Maggie incredulously.

"He came in here accusing me . . ." Elliot stopped talking long enough to allow his tongue to examine one of his lower teeth. Maggie wondered if he wasn't also reconsidering what he was about to say. "Accusing me of something stupid. He has a hard time with reality. I think he must prefer cartoons."

She was just about to ask him what he meant when Sigrid sauntered into the room. "My, but your management style is brutal, Maggie. I don't think hitting the hired help is any way to motivate them."

"What?" said Maggie turning around. "I didn't hit him. Mitch did."

"Ah," said Sigrid watching a trickle of blood ooze from Elliot's left nostril. "Mitch did. Of course, I should have known. I suppose it was entirely unprovoked." She handed Elliot a napkin.

"Entirely," said Elliot, flashing his slightly damaged imperial smile.

"Do you want me to call the police?" asked Maggie. "I think you have the right to press charges."

"No, no." said Elliot quickly. "I'll settle this my own way."

"I'll just bet you will," said Sigrid, moving closer to examine his jaw. "It occurs to me that Mitch may not be through with *you* either."

"The police might not believe me," said Elliot, looking at Maggie. "But of the two of us, who would you believe?" He winked at Sigrid.

Maggie honestly had no idea.

"I think in your case, Elliot, I wouldn't even believe a lie detector." Sigrid's tone was cheerful, but the acid was unmistakable.

Elliot continued to smile.

"If you feel like you're going to be okay, I've got some business I need to take care of," said Maggie, turning to go.

"Anything I should know about?" asked Sigrid, moving to block her exit.

"Not really. Peter Lawless is picking us up at two tomorrow afternoon."

"I know," said Sigrid. "I talked to him just before dinner."

"I see." She looked at Elliot, who was still holding the napkin against his bloody nose. "I'll talk to Mitch about this after Thanksgiving." She nodded to Elliot and headed out into the dining room. Sigrid followed.

"Want to go downstairs with me to see Gladys?" asked Sigrid, pouring herself a cup of coffee. "Did you know she hurt her back last weekend? She said she had a bad dream and fell out of bed. I thought maybe we should pay her a little visit."

"I'm sorry to hear that," said Maggie, looking at her

watch. She needed to call Jane right away. "Let me make one short phone call and I'll be right down."

Sigrid's look was more than skeptical. "Okay. But help me out this time, will you? Don't let her go on and on about *Doctor Who*. Try to change the subject. And don't bring up her daughter either. She's good for six hours without a break on that topic, too. Let's keep it real simple. Politics and religion. What do you say?"

Thanksgiving day was unusually cold even for Minnesota. By mid afternoon the thermometer had barely climbed to five below zero. Squirrels and birds huddled in the boughs of pine trees as the growing darkness prevented them from searching out any more food. The smell of wood fires and roast turkey warmed houses against the bitter night wind. Near the University of Minnesota, a car sped quickly down Washington Avenue and turned left at Seven Corners, heading for the Tenth Avenue Bridge. No one noticed as the car turned off before the bridge and drove more slowly down to the river. The car's passenger door opened abruptly and a body was pushed out into the snowy darkness. It rolled down an embankment and came to rest against a large elm. The door closed and the car sped off, leaving the body alone on the bank of the river. Light snow drifted onto the exposed face and hands. Eyelashes fluttered for one brief moment, and then, the whole world was silent.

PART THREE

Sacrifice

This is the thing which the Lord commanded that ye should do: and the glory of the Lord shall appear unto you.

Leviticus 9:6

16

What is that incessant noise? Why the fuck doesn't someone make it stop! God, it must be some sort of punishment. Please someone, make it stop!

Jamie opened her eyes, vainly attempting to focus on a spinning object directly in front of her face. She closed her eyes again and rolled over onto her back. The noise was becoming less a hard thud inside her brain, and more of a metallic drip. My God, she thought, it's the damn faucet. She laughed mirthlessly, laying an arm heavily across her eyes and pressing down hard. She gave herself a moment to muster her courage before once again trying to open them. This time the room seemed less to spin than to bob. Christ! She was lying on the bathroom floor. How long has it been this time, she wondered? The smell of vomit filled the room with an overpowering rankness. She felt her clothes and found them damp. When did I get home last night? she thought, vaguely recalling that yesterday had been Thanksgiving.

It all began to come back to her now as she lay shivering on the cold tile floor. She remembered the Thanksgiving meal her parents had been planning for weeks. Mitch was there. She closed her eyes and propped herself up against the bathtub. She and Mitch had arrived at her parents' house around two yesterday afternoon. Her father had been in an unusually festive mood. He had offered to fix them both a Tom and Jerry. Damn him! *One* Tom and Jerry. He'd probably formed some magical equation in his mind. If we only offer little Jamie one drink then everything will be fine. No

scenes. He must have *needed* to fix that one drink just to
prove things could be normal. Normal? She couldn't remember what that meant anymore. Dragging herself to her feet,
she stumbled into the living room, her head throbbing and
her mouth feeling like it had been stuffed with dry oatmeal.
She wandered around, kicking clothes and dishes out of the
way until she found her clock. It was almost seven A.M. God,
what happened last night? She sat down carefully on the edge
of the couch and lit a cigarette.

She had promised Mitch weeks ago that she'd quit drinking after that awful homecoming weekend. She never wanted
to think about it again. It had been a nightmare. He told her
they would be finished if she didn't get a grip. He was right,
and she knew it. Yet, in her lower moments, she wondered
if her past problems wouldn't provide him with the perfect
excuse to dump her, even if she did stop. He could say her
recovery was only temporary. And maybe he would be right.
After all, drinking wasn't a sin, was it? It may have gotten a
little out of hand lately, but that could happen to anyone
who'd been under the kind of strain she had. The one drink
her father offered yesterday had relaxed her for the first time
in weeks. She felt calm and in control. No one noticed when
she excused herself to go up to the bathroom. She'd remembered a bottle she had cleverly hidden in her old room months
before. After several trips to the bathroom, she could feel
everyone's eyes watching her. At some point, Mitch had
started to look angry. He had followed her up to the bathroom, and there was a scene. She remembered her father
coming up behind them and screaming at Mitch. It was always the same. He was furious and blamed Mitch for everything. Mitch hadn't said a word but simply had left. She
could still feel that cold desperation as she watched his back
disappear down the stairs. She'd shrieked and cried, blaming
her parents for interfering in her life. They *had* interfered!
God, she hated them. Her father tried to block the door, but
she managed somehow to get out to her car and drive away.
She looked for Mitch, driving around for hours. She'd finally
stopped at Ernie's Bar, hoping it would be open. She remem-

bered having a couple of drinks just to keep up her spirits.
But then what? It was all vague. Maybe she'd talked to some
guy at the bar. But how had she gotten home? Mitch must
be furious with her. He'd been so preoccupied yesterday.
What had he said? Something about getting even with someone? Or had she dreamed it? Maybe he'd said he was going
to get even with *her*. Everything was so muddled inside her
brain.

She crushed out the cigarette on top of the coffee table and
ran her hand through her thick, greasy hair. God, I can't go
on like this. She laid down on the couch and drew her legs
and arms up tightly into her body. Slowly, very slowly, she
rocked herself until she fell asleep.

"How would you feel about waxing the front hall this
morning?" asked Edith Holms, sniffing elegantly above her
cup of morning tea. She watched Gladys clean out the fireplace grate as she reclined leisurely in an old armchair. "Actually, Gladys, I haven't wanted to say anything, but I was
under the impression you were to do it every other Tuesday.
I'd hate for anyone on the house corporation board to see it
looking like that." Her tea was beginning to cool, which
invariably annoyed Edith. She longed for a different age,
when servants could be summoned to bring out more hot
tea, and of course that cornerstone of civilization, toast
and jam.

"I'll get to it when I get to it," said Gladys curtly.

Ignoring the insulting tone, Edith continued to sip her tea.
"I think the second floor bathroom also needs a little extra
attention. This will be a good day to get things done without
bothering the girls. Most of them will still be at home after
Thanksgiving. Did you have a nice day yesterday, dear?"
She adjusted her head scarf.

Gladys hated to see that wretched scarf trotted out every
week or two. It was obviously meant to cover her hair against
all the sooty housework she would be doing. And as everyone knew, sipping your morning tea was dirty business. "My
Thanksgiving was just peachy, thank you, Edith." She fluffed

up the couch pillows and in the process found an empty beer bottle hiding between two of them.

"Ah," said Edith, rising to take it from her. "I'll have to speak to Sigrid about this." She sat back down, draping herself elegantly in the wing chair nearest the fireplace.

Gladys pulled out the vacuum cleaner.

"Well, if you're going to turn that thing on," said Edith, not even trying to hide her pout, "we'll just have to finish our conversation later."

Gladys switched on the machine with a small sense of victory. What conversation, she thought to herself as she pushed the roaring vacuum ever closer to Edith's feet. Edith rose with infinite grace and walked slowly out of the room. As she floated into the front hall the doorbell had the audacity to ring. It was all so irritating. Why didn't the girls ever remember to take along their keys when they went out? She opened the heavy door and was surprised to find Kari standing outside in the bitter cold. "What a pleasant surprise, Kari. Do come in." She stepped back. "You look chilled to the bone, dear. We'll just fix you right up with a hot cup of tea."

Kari seemed ill at ease as she stepped into the front hall. "I'm afraid I don't like tea, Mrs. Holms. But thanks anyway."

"Is there some problem, dear?" Even Edith could tell Kari's manner was strained.

"No," she said, looking around carefully. "It's just that this is the first time I've been back here in a while. I gave up my membership, if you recall."

"Yes," said Edith, pursing her lips. Such a frivolous way to treat such an honor.

"I just felt too creepy staying here. Especially after Ally's death. And that face I thought I saw outside my window a couple of times really freaked me." She reached up and smoothed back her hair. "I'm supposed to meet Jo Jo Steadman here this morning. We've made plans to go out to breakfast."

"How nice," said Edith, turning just in time to see Jo Jo

bound down the stairway, tucking her blouse in as she came. "Sorry I'm late, Kari. Hi, Mrs. Holms." She darted into the coatroom and appeared a moment later, one arm thrust into a short camel-hair jacket. Edith sighed the sigh of the old wearily watching the hopeless energy of the young.

"Did you have a nice Thanksgiving, Mrs. Holms?" asked Jo Jo.

"It was very nice, dear, thank you." Edith noticed Kari inch closer to the front door. Very odd behavior indeed.

Again the doorbell chimed, sending Edith's blood pressure up another ten points. Jo Jo leapt in front of Kari and pulled open the door. "Jane! Come on in and join the party." Jo Jo held the door open.

Jane was more than surprised to find Kari standing in the foyer after all these weeks of being absent from the house. "It's really nice to see you again, Kari." She stamped the snow off her boots.

Kari managed a little nod.

"Well, we're off to breakfast," said Jo Jo brightly. "Wish us luck." Her energy was infectious. "Every time someone eats at Rayburns they come back with food poisoning. We're hoping to be the exception that proves the rule!" She sailed out the door, Kari following silently.

Jane turned and once again found Edith critically studying her choice of morning attire. Perhaps people over thirty shouldn't be wearing jeans. Whatever it was, Edith seemed continually stressed by her taste in casual clothing. "Good morning, Edith. I'm supposed to meet Maggie and Brook here at ten." She watched as Edith self-consciously adjusted her head scarf. That silly thing makes her head look like a muffin, thought Jane. Maybe the toaster needed to be de-crumbed.

"That's odd," said Edith. "I haven't seen either one of them since yesterday. But I'm sure if they made the date, they'll be here shortly."

Jane glanced from the beer bottle in Edith's hand over to the clock above the phone. It was already after ten. She noticed that Adolph was taking down last week's menu and putting up the new one. His usual Thursday morning ritual was one day late this week because of Thanksgiving. Jane excused herself and walked over to the bulletin board. Adolph nodded stiffly as she approached. He held up the advertisement for next week's Bible study and centered it before pushing in the thumb tack. Jane read it silently over his shoulder. "REVELATION IS THE KEY! Have you ever wondered what the Bible has to say about *today's* events? Does Bible prophecy have anything to do with *your* life? The book of Revelation is the key that unlocks the door of Bible prophecy! How can you prevent yourself from becoming Laodocean? This and other vitally important questions will be answered in our study." The usual information about time and place followed.

Adolph took a thick stack of flyers out from under his arm and set them down next to the phone. "Would you like to take a copy with you?" he asked, picking one off the top.

Jane smiled. "No thanks. Really." She reached into her bag and felt around for her glasses. "Did you have a nice Thanksgiving?"

"Very nice," said Adolph, smiling a bit smugly. His usual shyness was noticeably absent today. "I have no family here in town, but the woman I rent a room from invited me to have dinner with her. She fixed ham instead of turkey, but that was all right with me. I'm not hard to please."

He glanced into the living room where Gladys had just finished running the sweeper. His smile faded visibly. Jane turned to see what had caused his mood to change so abruptly. She wasn't surprised to see Gladys. Their mutual dislike had been apparent from the first time she had seen them together. It was probably a personality clash of some sort.

Adolph excused himself quickly and walked back into the dining room. As he disappeared around the corner, the doorbell sounded again. Jane walked back into the front hall, nearly bumping into Mrs. Holms, who had also heard the bell. Edith stepped back as Jane swung open the door. A tall, burly man in an expensive wool topcoat stood outside ready to ring the bell again. She recognized him immediately.

"Detective Trevelyan!" Her surprise was genuine. "Please come in." She stepped back, allowing him to enter. He was followed by a huge uniformed policeman. Jane could feel her heart beat heavily.

Trevelyan nodded to Jane. "Miss Lawless. How nice to see you again. I wish it could be under better circumstances." He held his mouth tightly as he motioned for the policeman to stand next to the door.

Edith gave the detective her most Edwardian nod. Gladys, seeing the police from her vantage point in the living room, pulled her sweater more tightly around herself. Jane noticed the gesture and wondered if it was the cold air she meant to protect herself from, or the policeman.

Trevelyan was about to offer an explanation when the door suddenly burst open. Sigrid, Maggie, and Jane's brother Peter came trumpeting into the room carrying a huge tree. They laughed and pushed their way unsteadily into the living room. "Make way for the official Kappa Alpha Sigma Christmas tree," shouted Sigrid. Maggie looked around smiling. "What do you think! It's a beauty, isn't it?" They leaned it against the back wall and stood back to admire their purchase.

"We got it at a Christmas tree lot Sigrid found yesterday on Washington Avenue," said Maggie over her shoulder. "Isn't it perfect?" She inched backward into the foyer, managing to pry her eyes off the tree long enough to turn around. Everyone's grim expression seemed to startle her. "You don't like it?" She looked carefully from face to face. Only then did she notice the policeman. "What's going on?"

"You probably remember Detective Trevelyan of the Minneapolis Police Department," said Jane, making introductions all around. She ended with her brother Peter. Maggie did seem to recognize him now. Why on earth was *he* here?

"Do you still employ Mitchel Page as a busboy at your house?" asked Trevelyan, getting right to the point.

"That is correct," said Edith with great formality. "He is our head busboy." She reached back and took hold of the staircase. Jane looked around and noticed that Gladys was gone.

Detective Trevelyan took out a small notebook and jotted something down. ''Yes,'' he said, looking up. ''I'm sorry to have to tell you this, but his body was found down by the river earlier this morning. It looks like he's been dead since sometime last night. From the preliminary examination, it would appear he died of exposure. He'd been drinking heavily. We found a bottle in his jacket pocket. We're testing it for fingerprints right now. It looks like he may have had too much to drink and fallen down a steep embankment. It may have been an accident, and then again, it may not.''

Jane fixed an empty gaze on the front door, trying to absorb what she had just heard. She could feel her entire body vibrating with the intensity of a lightly tapped bass drum.

Trevelyan looked from face to face. The young woman named Maggie seemed to have entirely wilted. She stood looking nowhere in particular, chewing on her lower lip. Only Sigrid, the house president, met his eyes without so much as a blink. ''We won't know until an autopsy is performed what actually caused the death. It's going to take many hours for the body to thaw before we can do one. But, I'll be straight with you. This is the second death associated with your sorority in the last few months. I don't like the way it looks.''

''What are you suggesting, Mr. Trevelyan?'' Edith's voice was stiff. Her face had gone completely white except for the rouge on her cheeks. The small circles of red made her look silly, rather like a circus clown.

''I'm saying we're going to investigate this thoroughly. Very thoroughly.''

Maggie could feel her knees weaken.

''When was the last time any of you saw him?''

''Wednesday night,'' said Maggie automatically. She glanced at Jane.

''Was there anything unusual about that evening?''

Maggie looked away.

"What happened Wednesday night?" asked Trevelyan, looking hard at Maggie.

"There was a fight." She paused, searching Sigrid's face for support. "He and our other busboy got into a fight. Sort of. I mean, I came into the kitchen after it was all over. Mitch had apparently hit him and then left."

"What is the other young man's name, and where can we find him?" He held his pencil above the note pad.

"His name is Elliot Kratager," said Sigrid, spelling the last name. She gave the name and address of his fraternity. Jane watched her carefully. Was she mistaken, or did Sigrid's eyes have the audacity to twinkle?

"Did they often fight?" asked Trevelyan.

"No," said Maggie. "I'd never even seen them angry with each other before."

"What was the fight about?"

"I don't know. Elliot wouldn't really say."

"He wouldn't say?" said Trevelyan, looking up.

Maggie shook her head.

"I see. And what about Mitch's girlfriend." He checked his notes. "Jamie McGraw. Have you seen them together recently? She's a member of your sorority, I believe."

"That's right," said Maggie, looking again at Sigrid for help.

"As far as I know," said Sigrid icily, "they were the picture of the happy couple. Romeo and Juliet."

Trevelyan looked up, openly studying her.

Maggie was unnerved by Trevelyan's blatant appraisal. "Jamie doesn't live in the house," she added quickly. "She has her own apartment. I can get you the address if you'd like." She hoped she'd broken his train of thought. Why did Sigrid do things like that? It was just plain stupid.

Trevelyan turned his attention to Maggie. "Yes," he said formally. "We already have her address."

Maggie felt certain she shouldn't volunteer anything about Jamie's little drunken episode in the kitchen. And anyway, Jane didn't seem overly anxious to say anything either.

"Do any of you remember if Mitchel had seemed upset or depressed about anything lately? Anything at all?"

"Do you think it might have been a suicide?" asked Jane.

"We can't rule that out. There were no obvious marks on the body. Kind of like your friend Allison Lord." He raised an eyebrow. "I've been doing police work long enough to trust my instincts. Miss Lord's death seemed explainable, but I've got bells and sirens going off about this one. It doesn't smell right. There will be an investigation, I assure you. The problem is, we have little to go on when there are no clues found at the scene. It makes it difficult to prove anything even if we do find a suspect." He flipped his pad closed and put it away inside his coat pocket. "I'll want the names of anyone he works with here. And any of his close friends, if you know them." He looked over at Edith. "Perhaps you wouldn't mind getting that information for me. I'll have someone stop off later in the day to pick it up."

"Of course," said Edith, stepping away from the stairs.

"Does he have any family in town?" asked Jane.

"Yes. I've just spoken with his uncle. He lives over by the Veteran's Hospital. It seems Mitch's parents both died when he was very young. His uncle raised him, and from what he said, I gather they didn't get along very well. Mitch left when he was fifteen. The uncle didn't even seem surprised when I told him his nephew was dead."

Maggie shivered.

"Thank you all for your time." He pulled out a card and handed it across to Edith.

The phone began to ring, sending Maggie backward into the phone closet. "Hello, this is Maggie. Can I help you?" She continued to watch as Edith and Jane showed Trevelyan and the police officer out.

"Hi," said a young female voice. "This is Beth McGraw. I'm Jamie's younger sister. Is this Maggie Christopherson? Do you remember me? Jamie brought me over for dinner once last year. We sat at your table and talked for a long time."

"Sure," said Maggie, trying to reorient herself. She remembered a younger, less aggressive version of Jamie. Dark, small-boned, with a sensitive mouth and deeply set eyes. "I remember you very well. Are you looking for Jamie? I don't think she's here."

"No," said Beth quickly. Her voice sounded tense. "Actually, I was hoping to talk to *you*. I wonder if we could meet somewhere today, away from the sorority. I know this may sound strange, but I need to talk to you alone. It's terribly important."

"Okay," said Maggie, watching Jane approach Peter and Sigrid. "Let's see, I've got some time right after lunch. How about around one?"

"One is great," said Beth. "I don't have school today, and I know I can get the car from Mom. Maybe we could meet at the Madison Grill. It's quiet there. Do you know where it is?"

"Sure," said Maggie, wishing she could hear what Sigrid was saying to Jane. "I'll meet you at one."

"Thanks Maggie. Thanks a lot. This could be a matter of life and death." She hung up.

"What?" said Maggie. "What did you say?"

"I just don't know what to do," said Beth several hours later as they sipped their coffee in one of the dark back booths at the Madison Grill. "My parents have cut off Jamie's tuition money because she won't see a counselor. Jamie doesn't think her drinking is that bad. Certainly not bad enough to warrant a shrink."

"I suppose not," said Maggie, warming her hands over her coffee cup.

"You know, ever since she was fired from that last job, I don't know where she's been getting money to live on. Maybe Mitch has been paying her rent or something, but I don't think he has much money either. I don't think my dad has any idea how bad her grades are right now. And she never cleans that apartment. It's a pit! My parents won't go over there anymore."

Maggie nodded. She and Sigrid had been there a few

months ago. She remembered Sigrid making some comment about it looking like a sanitary landfill.

"I try to cover for her, but it's getting harder and harder. She absolutely destroyed our Thanksgiving meal yesterday. She must have had a bottle hidden somewhere upstairs. Dad refuses to believe the problem is just the alcohol. He prefers to think she drinks because she's so unhappy with Mitch. They both think she could control the drinking if she'd only try harder, if she had the right incentive. That's why they took away her support. I guess I don't see it that way, but I can't go on protecting her. I don't believe for a minute she can control the drinking. And you probably know as well as I do how out of control her temper can get after a few drinks. It really scares me. I know I'm asking a lot, but do you think *you* could talk to her?"

Maggie squirmed in her seat. "I don't know, Beth. I don't see why she'd listen to me."

"The sorority means the world to her! She was so happy when she was picked to be in charge of rush this year. She did a good job, didn't she?"

"Sure," said Maggie, remembering Jamie leading the singing out on the front lawn. "She did a fine job."

"Everything started out so well this year." Beth shook her head. "She promised me she was going to turn over a new leaf. No more booze. And she kept her promise until the night of the big homecoming party at Sigma Nu."

"I don't remember her drinking so much that night," said Maggie, motioning for a refill of coffee. "She and Mitch were there together, I think. He came a bit late because of the meeting he'd had with . . . It's kind of a long story. Did you ever meet Allison Lord?"

"No," said Beth, leaning back to allow the waitress to reach her cup more easily. "I don't think I know her. Anyway, I remember that night vividly." She took a sip of coffee. "She'd been home all afternoon getting ready for the party. Mom and Dad were driving to some friend's house in Long Lake for dinner. I was alone in the house that evening. Around ten, a friend called. She wanted to go out for a burger after she got off work, so about ten minutes later I heard her honk. I came out through the garage and was surprised to find Jamie's car in the driveway. I walked over to look inside. The car was kind of askew. I mean, she'd pulled it in at an angle. I think the front end crushed some of Mom's marigold patch. Anyway, there she was inside the car slumped over the wheel. When I opened the door, the smell of alcohol nearly gagged me. I mean, she smelled like she'd been bathing in it. I suppose she'd probably spilled some in the car seat. I knew Mom and Dad would have a fit if they found out, so my girlfriend and I took her home. She drove her car, and I drove Jamie's. I was just praying we wouldn't get stopped by the police because the car smelled so bad. We got her up to her apartment, and she threw up a couple of times in the bathroom. It was disgusting. And she kept mumbling things the entire time.''

"Mumbling? Do you remember anything specific?'' The significance of Beth's story was just now beginning to dawn on Maggie. If it was true, and she had every reason to believe it was, then Mitch had no alibi for the night of Ally's death. He had told the police that he and Jamie were together all evening. That, apparently, had been a lie. But what did it matter now? He was dead himself. Unless? Maggie tried to put the thought out of her mind. It couldn't be.

"No, I don't remember anything specific. It was too long ago, and even at the time I don't think it made any sense.''

Maggie couldn't shake the thought. Was it possible that Mitch was trying to protect Jamie, instead of the other way around? "Do you know where Jamie was last night?'' asked Maggie. Her discomfort was growing by the minute.

"No, no idea. She left before we even sat down to dinner. Remember I told you she had a bottle stashed somewhere upstairs? Well, I should tell you the whole story so you can get an idea of what she's been like.''

Maggie sat back and folded her arms in front of her.

"Okay. Mom and Dad and Mitch were all sitting in the living room. I had just brought in a tray of appetizers.''

"Mitch was at your house for Thanksgiving?''

"Yes," said Beth, cocking her head slightly. "I thought I told you that. I mean, it's no secret that he and Jamie were serious."

Maggie nodded slowly. "Go on."

"Well, like I said, I came into the room with the appetizers. Just after I'd passed them around, Jamie kind of staggered into the room behind me. She had been upstairs. It looked to me like she was pretty blitzed, but I didn't see how it was possible. Dad said he was only going to fix her one drink. Anyway, we all sat around talking, Jamie occasionally excusing herself and going back upstairs. I think it dawned on Mitch first what was happening, and the next time she excused herself, he followed her. It wasn't long before we heard all this shouting. Dad got real red in the face and ran upstairs. Mom followed. The next thing I knew, Mitch came flying down the stairs and out the door. I could hear Jamie crying. Dad was shouting. I think he tried to prevent her from leaving, but she got by him and stumbled down the stairs. She grabbed her coat and left."

"What time was that?" Maggie didn't want to sound insensitive, but she needed to know.

"Oh, let's see. I guess around three. Jamie left about five minutes after Mitch. Why are you so interested in the exact time?"

Maggie saw no reason to keep Beth in the dark about what had happened to Mitch. "I'm afraid I've got some bad news, Beth." She paused, not quite knowing how to say it. "Mitch died last night."

"Maggie!"

"The police came to the house this morning with the news. Someone found his body down by the river. It looked like he'd been drinking. The police don't know how it happened, but I'm sure they'll want to talk to Jamie."

Beth shook her head back and forth very slowly. "I've got to get to her apartment before the police. It's possible that she's there even if she's not answering the phone. It would be awful to find out from a stranger. I've got to go. I'm really sorry. Please think about talking to her, Maggie. I really think she might listen to you.'' She threw a dollar down on the table and fished in her purse for the car keys. ''Thanks for listening to all my rantings. I'll talk to you soon.'' She turned and ran out of the restaurant.

The waitress came over again to see if Maggie wanted more coffee. ''Please,'' she said, pushing her empty cup closer to the edge of the table. ''I've got a lot to think about.''

''Don't we all, honey.''

17

"Rise and shine, Cordelia. It's no use trying to hide. I know you're under there." Jane opened the mini blinds next to Cordelia's bed, allowing the bright morning sunlight to flood into the room.

Cordelia, sensing a threat, quickly jammed a pillow down over her head and let out an angry groan. "If it's not approaching noon, I suggest you leave now, while you can still walk." Her voice was muffled.

Not to be intimidated, Jane picked up the tray she had brought with her and set it down on the nightstand. Cordelia lifted up one corner of the pillow to monitor what Jane was up to. The aroma of something marvelous tickled her nose.

"What's that?" she said, one eye peeking out at the tray.

"A gooseberry tart and a boysenberry tart. Your favorites. I brought them home from the restaurant last night especially for you."

Down went the pillow. "You think I'm so easily bribed!" Jane could barely hear the voice. She waited.

"What did you say?" snapped Cordelia, flinging the pillow aside.

"I didn't say anything."

"Yes, you did. I heard you." She eyed the tarts suspiciously. "What kind of tea is that?"

"Earl Grey. Freshly brewed."

"I prefer Irish Breakfast tea." She hoisted herself up as Jane propped a pillow behind her back.

"I'll make a note of it."

Cordelia reached for the gooseberry tart even before the

tray had been lifted onto the bed next to her. She bit into the warm, chewy confection, closing her eyes in ecstasy. "Why do I get the feeling I'm not going to like the reason for which you've awakened me at this, no doubt, hideous hour of the morning?"

Jane poured the tea. "It's a very simple request. Nothing particularly taxing. I just want you to accompany me when I pay a little visit to Mitchel Page's uncle this morning. I'd like to talk to him for a few minutes. Nothing extended. The whole trip shouldn't take over an hour."

Cordelia groaned. "It's not enough that I've let you stay at my house with those two beasts who wake me up every morning with their charming little burping noises. And my cat! Blanche will need years of therapy after they're done with her."

"It's only temporary, and you know it. Just until I find out who was responsible for breaking into my house. Remember how many times you've stayed with me?" She began to count on the fingers of her right hand. "There was the recent bat incident, which I doubt you've forgotten. Before that, there was the night you broke up with Carol Lindenberg and you couldn't bear to be alone. You spent almost a week at my house hiding after the reviews came out for that Pinter play you did last spring. Then there was the time . . ."

"Okay, okay. You've made your point." She finished the gooseberry tart, licking her fingers before picking up the boysenberry. "You said Mitch's uncle. I suppose he lives some place close. Like Chicago."

"No, he lives over by the Veteran's Hospital. I got the address from Detective Trevelyan."

"Ah yes, Orville. What's the uncle's name? God forbid I should know the man."

"Samuel W. Page. I looked him up in the phone book. He has both a business and home phone at that address."

"Uncle Sam. How precious." She sipped her tea.

"We're supposed to be over to his place by ten. I called just to make sure he'd be there. We better get a move on, since it's already after nine."

"Nine! On a Monday morning? The birds aren't even up yet."

Jane shook her head. "I'm going to have to get you a good science textbook for your birthday."

"If I live to see it." She finished the tart and leaned her head back against the pillow.

"Cordelia, lots of people are up at this time of day."

"Sure. Milkmen and farmers. Children who deliver newspapers. Street sweepers. Mothers with infants. Maybe even a cab driver or two. But do I look like any of those?"

Jane shrugged. "I don't know. A milkman maybe."

"Spare me the insults. I'll get up. But don't expect cheerfulness, or physical perfection." She handed Jane the tray and swung her feet out of bed.

Jane smiled. "All I expect is to see you downstairs, ready to go, in fifteen minutes."

Cordelia fell backward onto the bed, covering her face with the pillow.

"Do you know how to get there?" asked Cordelia as they walked out into the bright sunlight.

"I think so. I'm pretty familiar with that area of town."

"What's that on your windshield?" Cordelia pointed to a white envelope under the windshield wiper as she walked around the other side of the car. "It looks like a letter of some sort. An annoyed creditor perhaps?"

"It's probably an ad. I get those all the time when I'm at your place. It's because you live so close to Powderhorn Park. People are always trying to advertise something."

"It's December first, dear. Nothing happens at the park in the winter." She snatched the envelope and opened it, taking out a thin sheet of common typing paper. "It's just two typed lines," she said, reading it quickly. She looked up, handing it across to Jane. "You're not going to like this."

Jane took it and read silently:

I know what you are.
You will be punished.

She looked away, crumpling the paper in her hand.

"Are you okay?" asked Cordelia, somewhat unnerved herself.

Jane nodded. "I'm fine. I'm glad this happened. Now I'm absolutely positive whoever is behind all of this will make some kind of move on me. And that's what I want."

"Are you crazy!"

"No. We have to flush him out, and I don't see any other way."

"Him?"

"I know what you're thinking. Whoever it is, man or woman, I want them to have their chance to punish me, but I'm going to control the *where* and *when*. They'll get their chance. I'll see to it. But on my terms."

"Like hell they will!" Cordelia's voice was sharp. "I'll lock you in my basement for the next year if I have to!"

"Just wait until you hear my plan. I think you'll change your mind." She checked her watch. "We better get going or we'll be late. I'll explain on the way."

"Does this little plan of yours, by any chance, include me?"

Sam Page sat uncomfortably in his living room, puffing nervously on a particularly foul smelling cigar. Cordelia waved the smoke away with a porno magazine she had found lying on the coffee table. It seemed to be the only makeshift fan available. She picked it off a stack of magazines, realizing only too late that the cover boasted a vivid pictorial entitled *Pussies on Parade*.

"You think I'm some kind of a monster, don't you?" said Sam, rolling the cigar around in his wet mouth. A small muscle twitched in his neck.

Yes, thought Cordelia.

"I didn't come here to blame you for anything," Jane assured him. "I just thought you might know something about Mitchel's future plans. For instance, did he ever discuss Allison Lord with you?"

"Never heard of her." He blew smoke out the right side

of his mouth. "Mitch never told me anything. I don't think I've seen him more than twice in the last three years. I'm on the road a lot. I'm a salesman for Turner Broom and Mop." He nodded toward a group of new plastic brooms leaning against the door to the front hall closet. "Have been for the last ten years. I been selling things ever since I can remember."

"But you *did* say you saw Mitch a couple of times. Can I ask if he told you anything at all about his future plans?"

Sam eased back into the plaid couch and blew smoke high into the air. "Sure, you can ask. It was the same as always. He'd come over and sit in the living room here, trying to make small talk. Maybe he'd pick up one of the magazines like your friend over there."

Cordelia stiffened.

"Maybe he'd ask me how I was. Maybe he wouldn't. But sooner or later he always got around to the point. It never varied. He wanted money. Sometimes he'd ask me outright, and sometimes he'd call it a loan. But it always came down to the same thing."

Jane nodded but said nothing.

"He always had his hand out. Just like his mother. My brother, God rest his soul, married himself a bloodsucker. If they hadn't both died in that car crash, she would have sent him to the poorhouse for sure. I took Mitchie in when he was nine years old, but I could see his mother in him right away. He not only looked like her, he acted like her. Always with his hand in my pocket. If it wasn't a baseball mitt it was a pair of new sneakers. He must have thought I was made of money. We did go to a few pro-wrestling tournaments. I've always liked those. The kid didn't care, as long as he got to spend some of my money."

Jane felt more sorry for Mitch than she had ever thought possible.

A haze of acrid smoke filled the small living room, sending Cordelia into an indelicate coughing fit. She asked, gaspingly, if she might have a cup of water.

Sam pointed to the kitchen.

"Thank you," she said regally, rising through layers of smoke.

"So, you're his friend, huh?" Sam pulled the cigar out of his mouth and carefully examined the tip.

"Yes," said Jane, "that's right."

"Funny, but you don't look like the type he would pick for a friend." He shrugged. "But then, I don't suppose I knew the kid very well." He got up and walked over to the TV set, picked up a brown paper sack, and deposited it in Jane's lap. "You might as well have that," he said, sitting back down on the couch.

"What is it?" Jane picked it up and looked inside. Cordelia returned, limply carrying a glass of water.

"The police came by earlier this morning and gave it to me." He tapped his cigar above a large metal ashtray next to the stack of magazines. "It's his watch and ring—both cheap shit I should point out—and his wallet. There was about thirty dollars in it that I already took. I figured he owed me for all the years I took care of him. He's also got a motorcycle I'm going to sell. I should get four, maybe even five hundred for it. You know anyone who might want to buy one?"

Jane shook her head.

He looked at Cordelia.

"You've got to be kidding," she choked, waving the smoke away with her hand.

"Too bad. I could have made one of you a great deal."

Jane never doubted it for a moment.

Sam stood up, scratching the back of his neck. "Well, that's about it, I guess. I don't mean to throw you girls out . . ."

Cordelia rolled her eyes. She wondered how he ever sold *anybody anything*.

". . . but I've got to make some calls on a couple of accounts this morning. My life hasn't stopped, even though my nephew's has." He walked around the coffee table, ignoring his guests, and headed for the front door. They were being dismissed. Jane managed a brief thank you at the front door, while Cordelia sailed past without so much as a nod. She was already inside the car, maintaining a dignified silence, when Jane joined her.

"Christ, you could have smoked a turkey in that room." Cordelia rolled down the window, fanning cold air into her face.

"He was just about what I expected," said Jane, putting on her seat belt, "but worse." She opened the brown paper sack and emptied the contents onto her lap. She pulled all the papers out of the wallet pocket and began to examine them.

"What's all that?" asked Cordelia.

"Well, this looks like a book list for some engineering class. And here's an American Express Card receipt for something he bought at Lundstrom's Men's Store."

"That's a little rich for his pocketbook, wouldn't you say?"

"Look at this," said Jane, handing the receipt over to Cordelia. "It's for over eight hundred dollars. The credit card belonged to Adam Lord. It appears he bought Mitch a suit. I wonder if it was the one he was wearing the day of the memorial service? It did look expensive."

"It would appear so. It's dated the twelfth of November."

Jane unfolded another slip. "This must be one of his pay stubs from the sorority. And here's something strange." She unfolded a larger sheet of paper. "My god, this is Emily Anderson's address and phone number! How did he get that! She was absolutely terrified he'd find out where she was living."

"You're sure it's her address?"

"Positive." She flipped over the paper and read the print on the back. "It's written on one of Adolph's Bible study advertisements. Mitch has torn it in half and written the address and phone on the back. This one is pretty recent I think. I just saw Adolph tacking it up." She read it out loud: "REVELATION IS THE KEY. Have you ever wondered what the Bible has to say about today's events? Does Bible prophecy . . ."

"That's quite enough, thank you. Reminds me of the stuff my grandmother sends me."

"These flyers always get used for scratch paper. Adolph puts a big stack right next to the phone."

"Well," said Cordelia impatiently, "what do you think it means?"

"I don't know." She turned the paper over in her hand. "I think I better try to call Emily's parents. Trevelyan said the police had tried to get in touch with her last Friday—the day they found Mitch's body. She lives above this old rundown drugstore in Hudson. Apparently, no one there has seen her in quite a while."

"I may not have all of this business straight in my mind, but her parents I do remember. The memory of the pleasant morning we spent shooting the breeze with those lovely, lovely people still lingers. If Emily's old fart of a father had only had a gun, I'm sure we'd be in the hospital right now. I remember the look in his friendly little eyes when he ordered us out. You know, I think I've learned something important. After this, when I join you on one of these little excursions, I not only need to wear a bulletproof vest, but this morning's episode has taught me I should also bring along a gas mask. Not that I mind, Janey. I'm not complaining. I mean, you always introduce me to the most *charming* people . . ."

Jane started the car and pulled away from the curb as Cordelia continued to rant.

"I want to make this absolutely clear," said Sigrid, speaking before the entire sorority later that same night. "Gladys is not our personal maid, she is our housekeeper. She attempts to keep this house relatively clean, but it is *not* her responsibility to pick up after each of us. From now on, anyone who sets their dirty dishes outside their rooms for Gladys to take down to the kitchen, will be fined ten dollars *per incident*. Do I make myself clear?"

The assembled group grumbled audibly. No one raised a hand in protest. Sigrid continued, "Now, on to the matter of the bath towels we just purchased last month." She looked down at her notes. "Maggie spoke to all of us about this two weeks ago and we're still having problems. If, for some reason, you happen to overimbibe some evening, and you end up coming back to the house and throwing up, *don't*, repeat *don't* think you can just go get one of the new towels and merely toss it over the mess, leaving it for Gladys to clean up the next morning. Go to the kitchen, find some soap and paper towels, and clean it up yourself! I don't think it takes a rocket scientist to figure out Gladys doesn't want to clean up your puke.'' Sigrid looked down at Edith. ''Sorry, Mrs. Holms.''

Edith nodded weakly.

''I don't mind telling you that Gladys is pretty upset about this. She does not like being treated as our servant. She also tells me some of the new towels have been found in the garbage. It seems some people are cutting circles out of the center and then just tossing them. I don't exactly know why so many of you feel you need these cloth circles, but I should remind you that these new towels were very expensive and don't belong to any one of us individually. They are for our general use. We need to stick to the budget, and that means no new towels. At this rate we'll be drying ourselves with facecloths before the quarter is over. If I find out who is responsible, they'll be up before the executive board at our next session.''

The room had become silent. Sigrid always knew when she crossed that very real, but arbitrary line. The murmuring stopped, and the silent withering stares began.

Gladys, who had been standing just outside the dining room door, took another sip of coffee. She studied the still unwaxed front entry.

''Tonight, before we have our dessert, Jane Lawless has a short announcement she'd like to make.'' Sigrid nodded to Jane and then sat down.

Jane stood and smiled at the assembled group. It was now or never. ''As many of you may know, one week from today will be the start of our winter retreat. This year it will be held at my family's lodge on Blackberry Lake. I will be driving up there this coming Friday to prepare the main lodge for your arrival on Sunday night. I just want to make sure everyone knows how to get up there.''

Jane noticed Susan Julian pull out a small pad and pencil from her purse. She smiled up at Jane beatifically.

"If everyone has found a pencil and something to write on . . ." She waited another moment. "Okay. Take Highway 49 up to Repentance River. It's a small town about forty miles northwest of the cities. Follow 139 out of town until you see a small sign off to your right that says Kettle Creek Road. Turn right and follow it about another three miles until you get down to the lake. When you see it, you'll need to turn left at the first fork in the road. Follow that down to the clearing. You'll be able to see the lodge from there. It's the largest log building and the closest to the lake. Let's hope the cold weather moderates a bit before the retreat begins. I'm looking forward to having you all up there for the week. On Friday and Saturday I'm hoping to get in a little rest and relaxation myself. I've always enjoyed being alone up there. It's very beautiful, as you'll see for yourself when you arrive. If you have any questions you can see me after the meeting tonight. Thank you. Let's make it a great winter retreat!''

Jane sat down while Maggie clanged the gong announcing dessert. Adolph and Elliot immediately circulated with trays of chocolate pudding.

"It's lovely up there, isn't it?" said Susan, her eyes popping with enthusiasm. She leaned back, allowing Adolph to set the pudding down in front of her. "And you're going up there all alone! How adventuresome. But aren't you afraid of having car trouble or being attacked by bears?"

Jane tasted her pudding. It was dreadful. "Not really. I like being alone. And there's a good mechanic in Repentance River. It's really not a problem."

"I wish I could get out of this madhouse for a weekend," mumbled Sigrid, pushing the pudding away in disgust.

"Aren't you going to eat that?" asked Maggie, nodding toward the dish.

Elaborately, Sigrid handed it over. "By all means, be my guest. Bon appetit." She stood and excused herself.

* * *

"I'm going to bed," announced Lilly Sandvik. "You two can sit and watch this crap all night if you want, but I'm too tired." She stood, stretching her long body. "I didn't think that meeting tonight was ever going to end."

Maggie, Lilly, and Jimmy O'Brian had been lying on the couch for the last hour, watching a late-night horror movie. No one else was in the green room this late on a Monday night. Channel Six had started running old horror films at midnight, and since neither Maggie nor Jimmy had a class until one on Tuesday, they had made a standing date to watch the ants eat Detroit. Maggie would make a huge bowl of popcorn and Jimmy would bring over a six-pack of pop.

"Okay, Lilly, I understand." Maggie turned down the volume with the remote. "We'll let you know what happens."

"Don't bother," said Lilly, trying to find her other shoe. "I've been asleep for the last hour anyway. I don't have a clue what's going on, and I don't care." She crawled under the coffee table, spying her shoe next to the empty bowl of popcorn.

Jimmy grunted and nudged Maggie to turn up the sound.

"Night," murmured Lilly as she stumbled out of the room.

"Night," called Maggie. It wasn't long before Maggie's own eyes grew heavy. She desperately wanted to know what the glowing green slugs were going to become once they mutated, but she no longer had control of her eyelids. Jimmy looked down a few minutes later and was surprised to find Maggie sound asleep. He smiled and gently lifted the remote out of her hand, laying it on the coffee table. Shortly after the next ad, he fell asleep himself.

Half an hour later the movie credits appeared on the screen, followed by the National Anthem. Maggie's head had fallen over onto Jimmy's shoulder. Both were sleeping soundly when a hand picked up the remote and turned off the test pattern. The room was plunged into darkness. Quickly the figure moved around the back of the couch next to Maggie.

A hand accidentally bumped the lamp, causing Maggie to stir in her sleep and finally lift her head off Jimmy's shoulder. She opened her eyes and tried to orient herself in the dark. The figure stood motionless in back of her. She reached around to turn on the light and instead of metal, her hand brushed along someone's skin. She turned around and thought she could make out someone standing behind the couch. "Jimmy?" she said, reaching over and feeling him still next to her. "Mrs. Holms? Is that you?" A moment passed before she became aware of someone's odd breathing. The hairs on the back of her neck stood up straight. "Say something please! I know you're there."

"Slut," whispered a cold voice she did not recognize. She felt a rush of adrenaline and at the same time knew she must not move.

"Whore," said the voice again.

Maggie couldn't bring herself to speak. She nudged Jimmy as hard as she dared.

"What's going on?" mumbled Jimmy, pulling himself up on the couch. "Who turned off the TV? Fuck." He reached behind the couch for the light and ended up falling on top of Maggie. "Why are we sitting in the dark?" He tried to right himself and in the process knocked over the lamp.

Maggie grabbed hold of his arm and whispered, "Someone else is in the room."

"Is that a joke?" he said sleepily. He stood and felt his way along the table until he found the lamp. A moment later the light came on. Maggie looked furtively around the room but couldn't see anyone. "I'm telling you someone was standing right where you are now. I heard them whisper something."

"Someone was in here, huh," said Jimmy yawning. "What did they whisper?" He made a mock effort to look around the room, ending with the game closet.

"I thought I heard someone whisper the word *slut*."

Jimmy laughed. "Yeah. People tell me I talk in my sleep now and then. But I assure you, if I did say something like that, I wasn't talking about you." He moved over to the coffee table. "Where's the remote for the TV? I set it down right here after you fell asleep."

"I don't know," said Maggie. If he wasn't going to take her seriously, she wasn't interested in his problems either. "Maybe you just think you put it there."

"I set it right here," said Jimmy, getting down on his hands and knees and crawling around on the floor. "What the hell is going on? You're sure you didn't take it?"

"No," said Maggie. "I'm positive. *You* turned off the TV."

"No I didn't," said Jimmy. "Last I remember the green slugs had just crawled into a phone booth. I fell asleep, too."

"Then how did the TV get turned off?"

Jimmy was losing his patience. He walked to the back of the room and out into the hallway. "What the fuck," he said loudly. "Here it is!" He came back carrying the remote in front of him and handed it to Maggie. "How did it get out there?" He fell back down on the couch. "Is this some kind of joke, or what?"

"I wish it were," said Maggie, shivering inside.

18

"You really think this is going to work?" asked Cordelia as she watched Jane adjust the controls on an old space heater. "I will not survive in this wilderness if the cabin's temperature falls below seventy-two degrees. And you'll probably tell me it's my imagination, but that mattress over there looks like it has a lump in it."

"It's just your imagination."

Cordelia unwrapped a bar of candy, mimicking a smile.

"There," said Jane standing back. "That should do it."

"What about the lump?"

"What about it?"

"You expect me to sleep on that?"

"The princess and the pea," said Jane, grabbing the candy bar out of Cordelia's hand and taking a bite.

"No, the commoner and the lump."

"Get a grip. Remember this is all in a good cause."

Cordelia snatched the candy bar back. "Don't forget, you have to show me how to work that." She pointed to the intercom that sat on a stand next to the desk.

"It's all very simple, Cordelia. Thank goodness my brother is not *only* a great cameraman and photographer, but a tech freak as well. He had this whole lodge wired up before he was fifteen years old. All you have to do is keep this button pushed down. You can hear everything that happens in the main lodge. This dial," she pointed to a round knob underneath the speaker, "will adjust the loudness. If you have to go to the bathroom, turn it up. And remember, when you go to sleep, put on the headphones. That way you'll be sure to hear any screams or gunshots.''

"Very funny."

"I was kidding. But remember, if someone should show up, be sure to hit the record button on that.'' She pointed to an old reel-to-reel tape recorder on the desk. "Then everything that's said will be on tape.''

"Right. And the rest I already understand.''

"Repeat it to me anyway. We can't make any mistakes.''

"Okay, these are my official instructions. When the maniac finally shows, first I turn on the tape recorder, and then I make a quick call to the police station in Repentance River. The phone number is taped next to the telephone. I explain briefly the situation and ask them to come immediately. Then I take the gun—which I should point out once again that I am thoroughly trained to use thanks to my two-year liaison with a member of St. Paul's finest—and enter the lodge through the locked back door. I have the key hanging around my neck. You will tell me which room you are in as you try to engage the person in a discussion, attempting to get them to admit what they have done. I will approach unobserved and most likely move into the room quickly, taking them by surprise. If you are correct, and the suspect does not use a weapon, then he or she will be a sitting duck. As they say.''

"That sounds good. I have a hunch that neither Ally's nor Mitch's death was planned. This person doesn't come in with guns blazing. He likes to take advantage of whatever is around to get rid of people. It's kind of a strange way to eliminate someone, but it leaves people thinking it could have been an accident or a suicide. Creating that doubt is half the battle. This person is either terribly clever or crazy—or both.''

"You do think it was murder, then?''

"Without a doubt. This individual relies on the immediate circumstance to provide them with a murder weapon. With Ally it was the lake, and with Mitch it was alcohol mixed with sub-zero temperatures.''

"Well, if we're lucky, no one will show up at all. That's the scenario that gets my vote.''

"I think someone's going to pay us a little visit. I'd bet on it."

"I've got a birthday coming up in a couple of weeks, and I'd like to be around to celebrate it. So don't go doing anything stupid. What am I saying! I already think what we're doing is crazy!"

"Give me one other way we can flush this person out?"

"I don't know why *we* should have to do anything. Let the police do it."

"Right. You mean I should let them protect me the way they protected Ally and Mitch? No thanks. If someone wants to punish me, I can at least control the circumstances." Jane sat down wearily in a old armchair next to the window. "I can't help but feel a little ill at ease about Emily. I called her parents the other night and told her mother I'd be up at the cabin all weekend if Emily should call. I left the lodge phone number and address. Her mother sounded pretty upset. The police had called the day before trying to locate her. If I can believe her, she said she hadn't seen Emily in two weeks. Apparently Emily had made some comment about coming over for Thanksgiving dinner. It wasn't for sure, but when she didn't show, both her Mom and Dad got pretty upset."

"Wasn't Ally's brother going to go see her that weekend he came down? Remember, the night he stopped at your house you gave him Emily's address."

"He may have been the last person to see her, that is, if he actually did succeed in finding her that weekend. I suppose I should have asked him about it when he called yesterday."

"He called you? The avowed ascetic who likes fine crystal and fast sports cars called little old you?"

"Be nice, Cordelia. I don't know that he ever said he was an ascetic. I realize he's a bit enigmatic. He was coming down this weekend and asked if I'd like to get together for lunch. I told him I'd be up here all weekend. He said he might stop by to see me on the way into town, so I gave him directions. He won't stay long. I'll see to that."

"Wonderful," said Cordelia, closing her eyes. "We could have a veritable flotilla of potential crazies around here."

"You aren't saying I should consider Edwin a legitimate suspect?"

"If the shoe fits. God, I hate it when people speak in cliché."

"How can I suspect him? He has absolutely no motive. He loved his sister and liked Emily. He had no problem with her lesbianism, and he's rarely even *in* Minneapolis, so how could he be behind any blackmail attempts?"

"You only have his word for all of that. After all, Ally's diary did have whole sections torn out. And he had ample chance to do that. You never really got a chance to read much of it before it was stolen. I don't know. I think you better reevaluate your position on brother Edwin."

"And I thought *I* suspected everyone. I suppose you think even Edith Holms had a motive."

"Is she the one you introduced me to a couple of weeks ago when I picked you up at the sorority? The one with blue hair?"

Jane nodded, smiling at the description.

"No. I generally trust people with blue hair. I think we can scratch her off the list."

Cordelia put on the headphones and waited for Jane to get back to the main lodge. It was now almost midnight.

"I'm in the living room," said Jane's voice over the loud-speaker. "Can you hear me?"

"Right," said Cordelia into the microphone. "I can see lights going on in your bedroom."

"Good," said Jane. "I'm just coming into the room." Jane could hear a slight static when Cordelia spoke. It was usually nothing to worry about. The system was old, but reliable. "Okay, I'm going to leave the light on in the living room all night. I think it's about time for bed. I'm ex-hausted."

"This cabin gives me the creeps," hissed Cordelia's voice through the speaker next to Jane's bed. "Something is dripping on the roof. You *know* what a light sleeper I am. Instead of looking thirty-six on my next birthday, I'm going to look fifty, and it's all your fault.''

"I'm counting on your being a light sleeper," said Jane, stretching out on the bed. "Put those headphones on before you get in bed."

"They're already on. I don't know if I'm *going* to get in bed with that lump. I may just sit up and be miserable in the chair all night.''

"Suit yourself," said Jane, pulling a quilt over her. "But it seems to me that you've slept with a lot of lumps in your lifetime.''

Jane awoke stiff and cold on Saturday morning. She had been so concerned about getting Cordelia's heater working she had forgotten to turn on the space heater in her own bedroom. She pulled the quilt up tightly around her neck and looked around. Her father's family had owned Blackberry Lodge since the early twenties. She had first picked out this room when she was only eight years old. She had liked the large window that looked out onto the pine woods just south of the main lodge. A dull ache grew inside her as she recalled those last few days before Christine had entered the hospital. They had driven up to the lake to be alone. To be together. They knew Chris had little time left. The cancer had gone too far before it was diagnosed. Nothing could be done. They had spent most of those last days just sitting in the lodge, holding each other. Even now Jane could feel Christine's soft, sweet hair against her shoulder. God, but it still hurt so much. She closed her eyes against the pain of remembering and turned her head, burying it in the covers.

"This is Cordelia speaking," came a voice through the speaker next to the bed. "Are you up, Janey? I thought I heard you stirring." The static seemed to have cleared itself overnight.

"I'm here," said Jane from under the blanket. "Are *you* awake?''

"Of course. I've been up for hours. I'm having *so* much

fun, I just have to tell you all about it. Some darling little furry creature jumped on the roof about six A.M. and nearly gave me a coronary. I saw him crawl down the screen, and if I ever see him again, I'm going to take this gun and teach him some manners. May I say, with all due respect to nature lovers like yourself, that this nature crap is highly overrated.''

Jane began to laugh.

"You think it's funny, do you?"

"No," said Jane. "But I think you're saving me from a morning of memories I can't afford to dwell on right now."

"Do I get any breakfast out here? I'm starving. That squirrel is in more danger of being eaten than shot."

"Give me fifteen minutes, and I'll be out with a basket of goodies. It's going to have to last you all day, so go easy on it. I don't want to be making trips out to the cabin. If someone is watching, it might look suspicious."

"I understand that, birdbrain. Just don't forget the paté, french bread, brie, and chocolate chip cookies. If I'm going to rough it inside this rustic paradise, at least I intend to be well fed."

About one-thirty, Jane heard the sound of a car motor. She put down her book and walked over to the window that looked out onto the plowed drive between the lodge and the tool barn.

"Cordelia, wake up. We've got visitors."

"Who is it?" asked Cordelia's voice apprehensively over the loudspeaker.

"It looks like Susan Julian's car. Yes, I can see her now."

"Call out the Marines. We're under attack! I mean it, Janey. It's time to be careful."

"We're *being* careful," said Jane. "Keep quiet and listen carefully."

She closed her book and walked over to the door, opening it just in time to see Susan climb to the top of the stairs.

"Good afternoon," said Susan, gliding into the room and removing her leather gloves. "My, this is a lovely log cabin.

And so big! This will be a perfect spot for the retreat.'' She walked around examining the rafters.

"I didn't expect any company this weekend," said Jane taking Susan's fur coat and draping it over one of the old chairs. "But I can always put on the tea kettle if you'd like to stay a few minutes."

"That sounds wonderful." Susan's bulging eyes and little girl voice seemed even more affected in the rustic atmosphere. "My cabin is about thirty miles from here. It's on New Prairie Lake, over by Hammerville. Actually," she said, sitting down at the oilcloth-covered dining room table, "I own the entire lake." She gave a little giggle. "And it's not really just a cabin, but I like to refer to it that way."

"How nice for you," said Jane, adjusting the fire under the kettle. "Are you out for an afternoon drive?"

"My no. I drove here on purpose. I thought it might be a good opportunity to get away from my place for a while. My brother arrived this morning with a friend of his. I thought . . ." Her voice trailed off as she looked out through the picture window at the lake.

"You thought what?" asked Jane, fixing a tray with cups, cream and lots of sugar. She remembered Susan's sweet tooth.

Susan appeared to be in some internal confusion. "I guess I was going to say that I thought this would be a good time to see what your lodge was like." Her smile was thin. "How many can comfortably sleep in here?" She picked up the largest chocolate chip cookie from the plate Jane had just set down in front of her.

"There are five bedrooms that easily sleep six people each. More if we want to use the sleeping bags. The living room can sleep another ten. I doubt we'll have over thirty-five, so it's really no problem." Jane could detect a certain tension under Susan's studied calm.

"These are wonderful cookies," said Susan eagerly. "That was awful news about Mitchel Page."

Jane sat down at the table waiting for the water to boil. "Yes. I spoke to his uncle on Monday."

Susan looked startled, jerking the half-eaten cookie out of her mouth. "You did? Why on earth would you want to do that?"

"I don't know. I guess I just wanted to see what he was like."

"And?" said Susan, still holding the cookie away from her mouth.

"I didn't like him."

"Did he give you any idea how Mitch's death might have happened?"

Jane got up to turn off the kettle. "A few ideas," she said, pouring the water over two tea bags she'd placed inside the tea pot. "And I've got a few ideas of my own."

Susan stuffed the rest of the cookie into her mouth. "Have you told any of your suspicions to the police?"

"No. Not until I can prove them."

The sound of a second car motor sent Jane again to the window. She pulled back the curtains and looked out onto the clearing. "It looks like Elliot Kratager's Jeep."

"Elliot?" said Susan, finishing another cookie before rising. "What would he be doing coming up here?"

"I don't know, but we'll soon find out." Jane moved over to the door and opened it. She stepped out onto the deck and was surprised to find Maggie heading up the walk. "What are you doing here?" She tried to hide the frustration in her voice.

"Hi Jane. I just didn't think you should be up here alone with that crazy person on the loose." She squeezed Jane's arm as she walked past her into the lodge. "I mean, you could be in some real danger up here all by yourself. Brook is just terrified that something's going to happen to you. I volunteered to come up. I promise I won't get in the way. I brought up a bunch of homework."

Jane cleared her throat and nodded toward Susan. Maggie turned and smiled weakly. "Susan. What a surprise." She looked back at Jane.

"Did you tell anyone you were coming up here?" asked Susan casually.

"Well, just Elliot. Do I smell tea? Have you got an extra cup?" She stepped into the kitchen and pulled the cover off the teapot, sniffing it audibly. "I asked Elliot if he'd mind if I borrowed his Jeep until Monday. It's got four-wheel drive. I figured I might need it because of the forecast. It's supposed to start snowing any time. I guess we could get several inches, that is if the weatherman is correct, which he usually isn't. I don't know why we even have forecasts sometimes. They're always wrong."

Was Maggie nervous, or what! Had she recently developed this need to talk nonstop, or was Jane just now noticing it? She decided it was nerves. She followed Maggie into the kitchen and took down another cup. Maggie's unexpected appearance was going to complicate matters.

"You might be snowed in here for the evening, Susan, if you don't leave pretty soon. There were a few flurries in the air as I drove out of Repentance River."

Jane brought the tea tray into the living room and set it on the coffee table. Maggie threw herself onto an old recliner, and Susan and Jane sat down on the sofa.

"I don't think I've got anything to worry about," said Susan, pouring the tea. "The weather looks fine. Besides," she added cheerfully, "there are worse places one could get stranded." She smiled and reached for another cookie.

Saturday afternoons were always the pits for Sigrid. She had made a deal with herself early in her college career that this was the time she would clean her room and do the laundry. It was boring, but it had to be done. After a late lunch at the Campus Grill with Peter, she trudged back upstairs to get her basket of dirty laundry. She lay down on the bed just for a moment and closed her eyes. It was good to rest a bit after lunch. Hadn't Grandma always said that? Two hours later she awoke wondering where she was. Afternoon naps were so disorienting. She checked her watch and found that it was nearly four. Outside, the light was beginning to fade. With something less than profound enthusiasm, she jumped off the bed and grabbed her laundry basket. As she breezed into the first-floor level foyer she happened to glance into the living room. There in the darkened room stood the Christmas tree draped in colored lights. It fairly glowed in the darkness. It was magical the way a lighted tree could dominate everything around it. She set down the basket and walked into the room. Ever since childhood, she had been awed by the sight of a lighted Christmas tree. She breathed in the smell of pine and only then noticed Brook sitting on the floor around the other side.

"It's wonderful, isn't it?" said Sigrid. She looked back up at the tree. "I'm sorry you couldn't be here when we decorated it. I think that's something I look forward to all year." She sat down in the wing chair by the fireplace.

"I feel the same way," said Brook. She looked worried.

"I know something's been wrong lately. Is there anything I can do? You seem so upset about something."

Brook was upset. Elliot had just called to tell her that Maggie had borrowed his Jeep and gone up to Blackberry Lake. Brook could hear the clanging sound of a prison door closing. She was sure something terrible was going to happen. "Sigrid, if I tell you something, will you promise to keep it a secret?"

"Sure," said Sigrid. "I'm good at keeping secrets."

Brook looked up at the colored lights. "Someone has been blackmailing me. For months."

"What?" said Sigrid. "What do you mean?"

"It's a long story, but I've been getting these notes. I told Ally, and she said she'd take care of it. She died the same night. And Mitch. He overheard Maggie telling Jane about it, and a couple of nights later he was dead." She began to sob. "I'm terrified that something is going to happen to one of them. Maggie took Elliot's Jeep and drove up to Blackberry Lodge this afternoon. I don't know what to do or where to turn."

"It's all right, Brook. Everything will be fine." Sigrid turned away and thought for a moment. "How long has Jane known about the blackmail?"

"I don't know, maybe a week and a half."

"If you had told me before things could have been a lot simpler. Let's see. It only takes an hour or so to get up there."

"What are you going to do?" asked Brook anxiously.

Sigrid stood up, trying to think. "Don't worry," she said, looking down at Brook. "I'll take care of everything."

Maggie looked out through the front window as the snow continued to fall in great swirls. "It's beautiful, isn't it?" she said, glancing at her watch. It was nearly five, and the light was completely gone. Jane had turned on the floodlight between the lodge and the barn, allowing Maggie to watch the snow pile up on the cars and walkways.

"I should have left hours ago," said Susan, finishing off the last of the chocolate chip cookies. It was a good thing Cordelia didn't know that Susan had eaten them *all*. If she had, she would have raced in and drop-kicked Susan through the picture window. Thankfully, Cordelia could only hear what was going on. Susan did not chew loudly. "I don't think I dare drive thirty miles in this." She nodded toward the window.

"The snow is really light and fluffy," said Maggie, allowing the curtains to fall back over the window. "Elliot's Jeep would make it like nothing, but I don't think he'd want me to let you borrow it. I was very surprised he let *me* take it. It's not like him to be so accommodating."

Jane stared at the empty plate of cookies. This was not turning out the way she had thought. It seemed less likely that someone would try something with so many people around.

"Does that fireplace work?" asked Maggie, moving over and removing the front grate.

"Yes," said Jane absently. "There's dry wood out in the tool barn."

"You mean that big building next to where the cars are parked?"

Jane nodded, watching Susan fidget with a paperweight. She had been fidgeting all afternoon.

"Let's go get some," said Maggie, walking over and poking Susan on the arm.

Susan shrugged. "I don't know."

"Come on. The fresh air will do us good. Jane, you could stay here and make some sandwiches, and we can eat them in front of the fire once we get it going."

"Sounds fine to me," said Jane, rising and going into the kitchen in search of a flashlight. "Just as you enter the barn, turn to your right. You'll see a workbench full of tools. Right next to that, on the same wall, is the wood pile. You might also want to bring in some kindling. I think there are some old newspapers out there, too. You'll have to look around." Jane handed Maggie the flashlight. "I hope you don't mind peanut butter. I don't have a very big selection."

"That's great," said Maggie, handing Susan her fur.

"Here, put this on," said Jane, reaching into the closet and pulling out one of Peter's wool hunting jackets. "That way you won't have to worry about getting your coat full of wood splinters."

"No, we can't have that," said Susan seriously. She put it on and followed Maggie out into the snowy dark.

"It may take us awhile," called Maggie over her shoulder. "So don't worry if we aren't back right away."

Jane closed the door and sat down at the desk by the intercom. "Cordelia, are you there?"

"Where else would I be? I don't know how you can listen to that woman babble on and on and on. Several times I almost came in there to tie her up and gag her."

"Yeah," said Jane. "Both she and Maggie have been pretty talkative all afternoon."

"But Susan never says anything! It's hard to believe anyone that stupid could be behind something that took even a modicum of brains. But I hope you're still being careful. She's still my number-one suspect."

"Thanks," said Jane. "I'll be careful." She got up and walked into the kitchen, taking down the tea kettle from its spot on the shelf. A cup of tea might help her to think. She filled the kettle with water and then lit a match to the gas.

The English thought tea could solve any problem. Maybe they were right. As she stood waiting for the water to boil, she stared thoughtfully into the living room. What *was* it she was missing? There was something she wasn't seeing. The whistle of the tea kettle broke her concentration and brought her back to the moment. She warmed the teapot, filled it with water, and dipped the tea bag inside. Then she put a mug on a tray, lifted the pot down next to it, and returned to her seat by the intercom.

Leaning back comfortably in her chair, she opened the desk drawer. Inside, she had put several folders of work she'd brought with her in case she had either the time or the inclination to work. On top of it all lay Mitchel Page's wallet. She took it out and flipped it open. Something continued to bother her about that piece of paper with Emily's phone number and address on it. Why did Mitch want to talk to Emily? Where had he gotten the address? Could it really be possible that Emily was right and Mitch was behind Ally's death? Except that now Mitch was dead, too. Jane flipped over the scrap of paper and read the printed message about the book of Revelation. She remembered reading it over Adolph's shoulder that day at the house. REVELATION IS THE KEY! said the announcement. She turned it back to Mitch's note and then back again to the printed side. Oh my God, she thought to herself. That's it! Why didn't I see it before? The Book of Revelation *is* the key! She got up, grabbing her coat and running to the door. "I've got it, Cordelia. No time to explain right now. I'm going out to the barn, and I want you to take your gun and follow me. Stay out of sight. I'll explain everything when we get back inside." In her haste, Jane failed to notice that there was no response from the intercom. Not even static.

"Susan, where are you? Maggie?" The electricity in the barn had been turned off since early October. It took her eyes a moment to adjust to the blackness. She wished she'd thought to bring the other flashlight. "Come out, I need to talk to you." She could barely make out the wood pile in the darkness. Neither seemed to be anywhere around. This is all wrong, thought Jane. A chill crawled slowly down her back. She pulled her coat more tightly around herself and turned to walk back outside. Before she reached the door, a dark figure stepped in front of her, blocking her exit. The stranger had on a hunting jacket and a black ski mask. Jane froze at the sight of a gun pointing directly at her.

"I know who you are," she said, stepping backward.

"I don't doubt that," came the familiar voice. "I suppose I can dispense with this. It was only a matter of time before you figured everything out. I've known that ever since I read your diary." The ski mask fell to the ground.

As frightened as she was, Jane found a certain satisfaction in having finally put enough things together to come to the correct conclusion. She looked around quickly to see if there was some way of escape.

"Don't try anything, Miss Lawless. I don't want to use this gun, but I will if I have to." Adolph motioned for her to move further into the barn. "Maggie and Mrs. Julian are tied up in the same cabin with your other friend. That was clever of you." He noticed her look of fright and added, "I haven't hurt them."

Jane groped behind her for the old tractor. It would be something solid to hold her up. "Why, Adolph? Why the blackmail?" Instinctively she knew she had to stall for time. Maybe if she got lucky, someone else would show up. Or she might get the chance to get away from him somehow. As long as she kept him talking she still had a chance.

"Blackmail? Is that what you think?" He smiled his shy smile. "No, no. It was nothing like that. I told Brook in the notes. Didn't she tell you?"

"Tell me what?" asked Jane, trying to look at his eyes but fixating on the gun.

"It was a chance for her to show that she had repented of all her wickedness. My personal ministry is an important one. Ordained by God. I guess that's something I should explain to you. Before long, the whole world will know about my ministry!"

"I suppose Ally also gave you money for the same reason. That's why she knew who was behind those notes Brook was receiving."

"Yes, that's right," he said eagerly. "Only I didn't use notes last year. I talked to people openly and asked them for donations."

"If they gave money to you, then in turn you would keep certain things quiet."

"Yes, that's it exactly! That would give them time to repent and seek God's forgiveness! I told them that. Everyone seemed to understand perfectly. Ally donated twice after I caught her with that Emily. She knew what she was doing was sinful. That's why she supported my ministry so well. When I came to her again this year, I couldn't believe that she would refuse me! Me! I could tell the Devil himself had been at work on her. She threatened to expose me if she ever heard that I asked anyone for another dime. God wouldn't allow my ministry to suffer because of her! He showed me another way. A quieter way. And anyway, I came to understand that my ministry needed to be secret until everything is revealed."

"Except that Ally found out about the notes to Brook, didn't she? And she came to you and demanded you to stop."

"Yes," said Adolph, leaning against the tool bench next to the door. He let the gun dip slightly. "She called me that night of the big homecoming party. Demanded to see me. Demanded! I thought we should meet away from the sorority. I live close to Lake of the Isles, so I suggested the bridge. God was leading me to suggest that particular place, but I didn't know it at the time. We talked for quite some time, but she refused to see how important my ministry is. She said blasphemous things! I had written a statement to Edith Holms, detailing what I had done, and explaining exactly what Allison and Brook were guilty of. I could even quote from Allison's diary since I had torn out several small sections during the first week of fall term. It was clear to me that neither she nor Brook had repented! I stated that precisely in the letter. Well, Ally was furious! She grabbed for the letter, lost her balance, and fell into the water. I took off running as fast as I could. I was frightened by her. But God showed me how powerful *He* was that night. I tell you truthfully, I did not know Allison couldn't swim. God knew, but I did not. He decided that night to punish her for her sins. I didn't know until the next day that she had died. I was saved by the power of the Lord! I could begin to see more clearly just how He was going to protect me.''

"And Mitch?'' said Jane.

"Yes, Mitchel. I never liked him. That was another sign from the Lord that He was watching over my ministry. Ally had told him last year about the donations she'd made, although I doubt she told him about the reasons why. Somehow, he found out about the notes I'd recently written to Brook. It's my suspicion that Gladys Bailey told him. She's a meddling old fool. Always listening outside doors. God will punish her someday, mark my words. Anyway, Mitch called one night and was very agitated. It was the night before Thanksgiving. He wanted to speak with me. I told him to come by my house on Thanksgiving evening. I remember the night well.

"He came in and accused me of Allison's murder! Can you believe that! I told him what had happened. I explained it very carefully. After we'd talked for some time and he'd calmed down a bit, I even offered to let him read Ally's diary, which I had taken from your home. He could then see for himself just what kind of person she really was. I think he must have sat in my parlor for over an hour quietly reading it and drinking from a bottle of whiskey he said his girlfriend had given to him. He became more and more depressed as he sat there. Allison had said some nasty things about him. When he was done, he said he hated Emily. He'd been wanting to get in touch with her, so I offered to give him her telephone number and address. You had written them under her name inside the cover of your diary, Miss Lawless. Oh, you wanted me to call you Jane, didn't you? I'm sorry.

"He took the information down on a scrap of paper. When he was done, I offered to take him home. He was pretty drunk by then, but still he threatened me. He said I would lose my job when everyone found out what I had done. I decided to let God decide once again. Mitch got into the front seat of my car and fell asleep. We drove to a lonely spot I know down by the river. If God was for him, he would have lived. But God was once again for me. You saw the results the next day.'' His voice had trailed off to a whisper.

Jane looked around for anything heavy or sharp she could use as a weapon. In the dimness, she could make out a pitch-fork hanging on the side wall, about ten feet away. It might as well have been in the next county for all the good it would do her. She looked back at Adolph. ''How did you find out about Brook?''

Adolph smiled. ''I know what you're doing, Jane. You're stalling for time. But you must see there's nothing you can do. My ministry, small as it is right now, is becoming more holy every day. People like you have no idea because you worship the beast. God has sent me to warn people to come out of this corruption before the end comes. In Hosea, God said, His people were destroyed for lack of knowledge. I've been trying to impart that holy knowledge to those who will listen at the sorority. It's been a training ground. I didn't realize that at first, but it became clearer as I saw the corruption going on around me.'' He shook his head sadly. ''I can see what you're thinking. You think I'm crazy, don't you? But God's holy men have always appeared to the world as wild beings! If God can speak out of a burning bush, does it seem so odd that He would speak to me out of my TV set? We must become a pure people! The sexual mysteries we have all learned in Babylon must be rejected! Our bodies must be washed clean! Purified before the second coming. God has revealed to me that I am that angel spoken of in the Book of Revelation. He spoke to me last night on the ten o'clock news. I am the one who cries out for the people of the world to *come out* from all the false churches. God has spoken to me and shown me an even greater mystery! He is going to select a new Adam and Eve from among those I have brought to repentance. He will create a new Eden! Praise the Lord in the highest!'' He raised his hands to the ceiling, closing his eyes.

Jane jerked toward him, but before she took more than a couple of steps, he brought the gun back down, pointing it at her head.

''*You* could be among the purified,'' he said, still enraptured by his own words, ''and so could Brook. You could all be among the holy group from which the Lord will select the new Eve. How can you reject that! You *have* to repent of your wickedness! And God has shown me a way.''

Jane held on very tightly to the tractor, watching Adolph continue to thunder. He had an almost volcanic belief in his own ideas. And yet, it was almost as if he needed to explain it again and again to himself. Jane's presence was somehow extraneous. ''Did God tell you about Brook?'' She knew the question was patronizing but doubted he'd notice.

''God?'' He smiled triumphantly. ''Yes. In a way. He has led me to your sorority to begin the process. I didn't understand it myself at first. At the beginning, He called me to wait and watch. That much was clear. My eyes have been everywhere. Nothing has escaped me.''

Of course, thought Jane. *His* was the face outside Kari's window, and his was the presence everyone had felt so strongly, watching them day and night. And because he had a key, he had access to the house at all hours.

''During rush this year,'' said Adolph eagerly, ''Elliot and Mitch were in the kitchen one evening, sitting and talking after they had finished the evening dishes. I had come up from the storage room in the basement, but instead of coming directly into the kitchen, I waited and listened outside the door. Elliot was explaining about a new girl named Brook who wanted to pledge Kappa Alpha Sigma. He told a filthy story of sexual license and drugs. I felt God was showing me someone to bring to repentance. And of course, it would be another way to provide money for my ministry.'' He stopped and listened for a moment.

''And when you found out I was trying to get to the bottom

of things, you broke into my home. You also left that threatening note on my car.''

''Yes,'' said Adolph, stepping back a few paces and looking toward the cabin where Cordelia and the others were locked up. ''But you put such an odd slant on everything. God told me to find out more about you. I should have known you were a lesbian. God led me to find out about your secret sin. Homosexuality is part of the doctrine of Babylon. I realize it holds a temporary thrill. I can almost understand that. I am convinced it develops partly because of the sexless food we eat today. Animals are castrated! That is a Godless thing to do. It produces men that aren't manly, and women that aren't feminine. I don't mean just outwardly. You look pretty normal. Men must realize they need to *take charge*, and women must be submissive. Wives *submit* ye unto your husbands!

''I know Susan Julian thought she was doing something good by conducting those Bible studies in the green room, but I refused to support them. The Apostle Paul tells us that women are supposed to be quiet, submissive. They are not to preach! If they have questions, they are not even supposed to raise their voices in church, but ask their husbands quietly, at home. God has called us to come out of that confusion!'' He held his hands up again, but this time brought the gun back down more quickly. ''You probably don't understand why I have this gun, but it's all very logical, really. I am part of God's army! 'From victory unto victory/His army He shall lead/Til every foe is vanquished/And Christ is Lord indeed.' '' He sang the words in a deep baritone, marching in place.

No wonder she had found it impossible to make sense out of anything. Nothing made any sense because ultimately, there wasn't any.

''Now,'' said Adolph, lowering the gun slightly, ''God has shown me another test, much like Allison's. I'll explain it to you briefly. You are going to take Elliot's Jeep and drive it across the lake to the cabins on the other side. I've checked them out. They're all empty right now. I broke into one and left a light on for you. You can follow it through the snow.'' He looked outside for a moment. ''You're lucky, Jane. The snow has almost stopped.''

''But the ice,'' said Jane, taking a step forward. ''It's not safe! They haven't even allowed fish houses out there yet. Driving a car on the ice would be suicide!''

''That's the test,'' said Adolph. ''If you make it across, it will be a sign from God that you have indeed repented and been forgiven. In that case, I'll be only too delighted to let your friends go. If you have truly repented, you will then understand the importance of my ministry and I will have nothing to fear from you.''

''And if I don't make it,'' said Jane, holding her breath in anticipation of the answer she feared most.

''Then I'm afraid that means God has chosen to punish you. He may even consider this some kind of *sacrifice*. It has occurred to me lately that maybe He may want sacrifice reinstituted! If you think about it, it makes perfect sense.''

''What are you going to do to my friends?'' asked Jane, her voice trembling for the first time.

''You must leave that in God's hands. Now, come on. I took the keys to the Jeep from Maggie after I tied her up.'' He motioned for Jane to walk in front of him.

This can't be happening, thought Jane. She took one last look at the pitchfork before moving outside. What would a pitchfork have meant against a gun anyway? Her mind raced. The ice was not safe, she knew that for sure. But perhaps the cold spell they'd had for several weeks would be enough to freeze the more shallow parts of the lake. The problem was, the lake was fed by springs near the shore. If she hit one of those she'd sink for sure. Even a few yards out, the lake was deep, but if she kept her head, she might be able to get out of the water and perhaps even make it back to shore without being seen. If she got too wet, the danger would then be hypothermia. And of all the rotten luck, the ice was now covered by several inches of new snow. It would be impossible to see open water and avoid it. She would just have to make her way slowly and hope the ice would hold. Maybe she could position the Jeep in such a way that she could get out of it without being seen. She could crawl through the snow if she had to until she made it up the shore aways. She might even be able to double back and take him by surprise.

They walked across the clearing and down to the cars. The floodlights gave everything an eerie pink glow. Adolph opened the door and motioned for Jane to get in and start the engine. He then ordered her out to clean the snow off the windows and windshield. "You'll want to be able to see as well as possible. I want you to keep the lights on at all times. I'll be watching from the shore with these binoculars. They're quite powerful." He pulled them out of his jacket. Damn, thought Jane. This would make it harder to do anything without being seen.

"Now, get in." He held open the door. The snow had completely stopped, and the wind had died down. It would make it even easier for him to follow the Jeep with binoculars. "Put your hands on the bottom of the steering wheel."

"Why?" said Jane, looking up at him, but before she knew what had happened, he had handcuffed her to the wheel. "What are you doing! I won't have any chance like this!"

"Your chance is with the Lord. I mean that, Jane. I suggest you start praying. Talk to Him. He can be forgiving if He sees true purity of heart." He hung the keys to the cuffs over the rearview mirror. "If you make it to the other side, I'll let your friends go. One of them will eventually be able to unlock them." He reached into the car and pulled it into gear and then slammed the door. "Now go!" he said, stepping back and hitting the hood with his fist.

The words broke inside Jane's head like a clap of thunder. She drove carefully over the snow until she was fairly certain she had reached the edge of the lake. It was hard to tell where the edge was because of all the new snow. She was pretty sure one of the springs that fed the lake was just south of the summer dock. If she headed in the opposite direction, even though it would take more time, she hoped the ice would be thicker. She would simply have to weave her way and hope she wouldn't hit any open water.

The Jeep inched onto the ice. Jane could hear only the crunch of the new snow under the wheels. That was a good sign. She had seen cars drive out onto the lake in the winter many times, but never before early January. Once she had seen the ice cleave and shoot out in a straight line from the front tires. She remembered her father saying something about this being dangerous. It was a crack like that which might later break under pressure. She looked into the rear-view mirror at Adolph standing on shore, his binoculars raised. This was no time to become reflective, but it did seem he had thought of everything. The handcuffs, the binoculars, even hanging the keys inches out of reach just to torment her.

Back on shore, Adolph hummed an old gospel hymn as he watched the car's slow progress. It would be quite awhile before he really needed the binoculars. He sat down in the snow and pulled out a sandwich he'd made for himself before leaving Minneapolis. Munching thoughtfully, he considered her chances of survival. He knew he hadn't fully achieved oneness with God's mind just yet, but he felt certain she had little or no chance to make it across the lake. It was only a matter of time until she hit thin ice. Her body would never be found. It would remain cuffed to the Jeep at the bottom of the lake forever.

Jane continued to inch along, unable to see Adolph any longer. The wheels crunched over the bumpy snow causing the keys to jingle and bringing her attention back to them again and again. Maybe she *could* reach them if she moved all the way over in the seat and stretched her neck as far as it would go. It was worth a try. She would have to be careful not to let them fall to the floor. If they did, that was it. There wouldn't be another chance. A loud snap reverberated inside the car, causing Jane to hit the brakes. It was the sound of cracking ice. She moved over in the seat, placing her foot on the brake and trying to stretch far enough to be able to grab the keys in her teeth. If only her arms were just a little longer. One more inch and she'd be there. Another loud crack sent the car rocking backward as the left rear tire sank into the icy water. Immediately, she moved back into the driver's seat and tried to drive out of the hole. It was no use. She was stuck. And why hadn't she thought to turn on the defroster! The windows were almost completely covered with fog. Even if she was able to get the car moving again, she would never be able to see the small lighted cabin in the distance. I'm going to die, she thought coldly, and there's nothing I can do about it. Another crack sent the right rear tire into the water. Her only hope now was hanging over the rearview mirror.

Adolph finished his sandwich, noticing the back of the Jeep seemed to be lower than the front. He stood and looked through the binoculars. Yes! The rear tires were submerged below the ice. It wouldn't be long now. He began to sing loudly, surprised at the melody that came to mind. It was an old lullaby his grandmother had taught him when he was a child. She had been the only truly righteous woman he had ever known.

He shook his head trying to get rid of an annoying buzz inside his ears. It had started a few minutes ago and seemed to be growing more intense. He closed his eyes and tried to listen to the sound. God is speaking to me! That's it! I must not resist. I have been a good soldier, and there is nothing to fear. He began to quote out loud from the Bible. "The sun shall be no more light, neither the moon, but the Lord shall give unto thee everlasting light." He shouted the words into the night sky. The buzz continued to grow louder. He ripped off his glasses and let them fall into the snow as he raised his arms, throwing back his head in worship. "And I heard as it were the voice of a great multitude, the voice of mighty thunderings saying alleluia. Alleluia! Lord, I am here. Your humble servant, Adolph!" He sank to his knees, covering his ears with his bare hands as the noise continued to intensify. "And I will kill her children with death, and all the churches shall know that I am He which searcheth the reins and the hearts. For the Lord loveth judgement, and forsaketh not His saints. But the seed of the wicked shall be cut off!"

A helicopter hovered almost directly over him now, beaming its floodlight directly down into his eyes. "And I saw the

angel standing in the *sun*! And I saw thrones! And who was
not found written in the book was cast into the lake that
burneth with everlasting fire. I have done your work, Lord!
I have been faithful unto the end.'' The helicopter dropped
lower, its deafening noise engulfing Adolph in a rapture of
light and sound. Two people jumped out a few feet from
him, both glancing at him quickly as they ran past. "And
the *stars* of heaven fell to earth, even as a fig tree casteth her
untimely figs . . . And heaven departed as a scroll, for the
great day of His wrath is come, and who shall be able to
stand!'' Adolph folded his hands reverently in front of his
chest. "I have been faithful! I have only done your will! Be
merciful to me! I did what you commanded. . . .'' He
grabbed at his coat, feeling an odd pain inside his chest.
"And the temple of God was opened in heaven and there
were lightnings and thunderings and an earthquake. And the
earth shall help me, it shall open up its mouth and swallow
the flood which the dragon cast from his mouth.'' The pain
began to crush out his breath and still, he reached one arm
heavenward. "I gave her space to repent of her fornication,
and she repented not. And the angel lifted up his hands to
heaven and swore by Him that liveth forever and ever that
there should be time no longer. I have spoken your message
to the heathen, oh Lord, your righteous, your *hallowed* servant!'' He leaned forward and fell into the soft snow.

The WTWN weather helicopter lifted up and set itself
down in a clearing about one hundred yards from the edge
of the lake. Sigrid and Peter had already made it out to the
Jeep. Peter tore open the door and tried to pull Jane out by
her arm.

"No,'' she said quickly. "I'm handcuffed to the wheel.
The keys are hanging over the mirror.'' The Jeep was already
partially submerged in water.

"Let me do it,'' said Sigrid. "I'm lighter than you. We
don't want to add any weight to the Jeep.'' She leaned across
and grabbed the keys roughly, fumbling with them as she
unlocked Jane's hands. Jane jumped out of the front seat just
as the right front tire sank into the water.

"Hurry," shouted Peter. "We've got to get away from here. When it goes, this whole area will break up."

"Let's head for that tree," shouted Sigrid. "We know it's on solid ground."

They waded and jumped through the deep snow until they found themselves at the base of the tree. A second later, the Jeep disappeared into the water with a loud crack.

"God, that was close," said Peter, putting his arms around Jane and holding her tightly to him. "Too close."

"How did you get here?" gasped Jane. "How did you know to come?"

"You can thank Sigrid," said Peter, pulling off his gloves and handing them to her. "Are you wet?"

"I don't think so. The water never reached me." She looked at Sigrid as she tried to catch her breath. "How did you know?"

"Brook finally confided in me about being blackmailed. I don't have all the details, but I knew Adolph had tried to blackmail Allison last year. I called his house and his landlady said he had left several hours ago carrying some snowshoes. I knew you were up here all alone, so I called Peter right away. I was positive you were in real danger."

"Right," said Peter. "I called the police in Repentance River, but they said Kettle Creek Road was almost impassable. They were going to send out a plow as soon as they could get one off the main highway. I knew someone had to get here faster than that, so I called Red Summerville. He's the guy who flies the weather chopper for WTWN. I knew it was a little unorthodox to borrow it for the evening, but then Red's kind of an unorthodox guy." Peter smiled at Jane and hugged her again. "God, am I glad you're okay. Come on. Red's back at the chopper waiting for us."

"What about Adolph?" said Jane stopping him. "He's got a gun."

"We saw him," said Sigrid, "when we jumped out of the chopper. I don't think we've got much to worry about. He looked like he was freaking out. Red's got a gun, too. He'll probably have taken care of him by the time we get back."

They walked slowly through the deep snow until they reached the far side of the lodge. Jane could see Cordelia sitting on the deck steps, rubbing her ankle. She must have bruised it somehow. Susan Julian was silently pacing back and forth in front of her. Maggie was standing over by Red Summerville. Thank goodness they were all okay. She didn't see Adolph anywhere.

"Jane," shouted Maggie, spotting them coming down the path. "You're alive! I knew you would be!" She ran over and threw her arms around her. "But Adolph," she said, taking a step back. "It's all so awful. He's dead. We found him lying over there in the snow." She pointed to a slumped figure on the ground next to Red. "The man who flew the helicopter thinks it was a heart attack."

Sigrid walked over to the lifeless figure, frowning. "I think maybe he finally ate some of his own food." Everyone began to laugh a little too hysterically. Sigrid clearly had no pity.

"What's going on over here?" said Cordelia, limping through the snow. "I know he was a detestable man, but sidesplitting laughter *does* look a bit ruthless." She approached and leaned on Jane's shoulder, nodding toward Susan Julian who stood alone by one of the cars. "Don't ask. You don't want to know. If you think Adolph's heart attack was funny, you're going to die laughing when you hear what *I* just found out."

Jane slipped her arm around Cordelia's waist and looked gratefully at Sigrid. "You know, don't you, that you saved all our lives?"

"I prefer to think of it as a group effort," said Sigrid, her eyes twinkling at Peter. "It was only a matter of time before Adolph would have caught your brother and me engaged in something indecent. Let's say we all saved one another."

Everyone took a moment to look down at the lifeless body cradled in the soft snow.

"Boy," said Maggie, looking up and gazing out at the dark hole in the lake. "Is Elliot going to be pissed!"

19

After the theatre on Monday night, Cordelia arrived home exhausted and ready for a nice long soak in a hot tub. Her ankle had begun throbbing again during the third act. As a matter of fact, it seemed to be empathizing with the female lead. Every time the woman would wring her hands and snivel, the ankle would respond by throbbing more intensely. It was a welcome relief when she was finally put out of her misery and Cordelia could go home. The box office had been overwhelming for the first three repertory productions of the season. Even Duncan Smith, the board chairman, had come over this evening to congratulate her on the inspired artistic direction. It did feel good to finally achieve a certain amount of recognition for her talents.

Cordelia was about to turn off the kitchen light and head up to her bath when the front doorbell chimed. Now what? she thought, limping into the front hall and pulling open the door. "Jane! I thought you were going to be staying up at the lodge at least through tomorrow. Come on in!"

"I was," said Jane, squeezing past her carrying a large box. She hoisted it into the dining room and set it down on the lace-covered dining room table. "But something came up at the restaurant so I drove back early this afternoon." She took off her coat and muffler and threw them over a chair.

"What have you got there?" asked Cordelia, limping closer and eyeing a pale blue bow placed decoratively on top of the box. "It's a little early for my birthday." She picked it up and began shaking it.

Jane grabbed for it, taking it away from her before she

223

could do any more damage. "Let's wait before we open this, just for a couple of minutes." She set it down gently. "Come into the living room and talk to me. I haven't seen you since all that mess on Saturday night. How did you like riding back to Minneapolis in a helicopter?"

Cordelia draped herself casually over the living room sofa. "I don't really know. I had my eyes closed the entire time. You know how I feel about flying."

"You didn't have to go back in the chopper, you know. Susan would gladly have driven you."

"Right. My choices were to stay there with you and the corpse until the police arrived, drive home with Susan at the risk of my own sanity, or get in the helicopter and pray. I think I made the healthiest choice under the circumstances."

Jane laughed as she dumped a stack of scripts out of her favorite easy chair and sat down. "So. Aren't you going to tell me?"

"Tell you what?"

"Don't be coy. I've been dying to know what you found out about Susan the other night. I suppose being tied up by a lunatic in a small cabin and then being left there for over an hour might lend itself to some pretty interesting truth telling."

"It did," said Cordelia, kicking off her shoes and stretching out. "Believe me, it did. Prepare yourself. First, Susan started by asking me if I remembered her brother, Brian. I mean, of course I remember him. He was student body president. I think he was a few years older than us. Then, out of the blue she changed the subject. I mean, I was terrified this Adolph was going to come back and commit triple murder, and she starts to rave about homosexuals, pansies as she called them. How they were ruining the country. How AIDS was God's revenge on their sinful life-style. How they were destroying the family. Buggering our youth. Causing earthquakes. Spreading humanism over the countryside like mayonnaise on a sandwich. Infiltrating the FBI. Selling secrets to the Russians. I thought I was going to lose my mind if I had to listen to this for another minute. I mean, there was no point in trying to talk to her rationally. I think your friend Maggie felt the same way. But then, strangely, the conversation turned back to her brother. I should have guessed immediately. Brother Brian, the apple of her eye, appeared on her doorstep one night a couple of weeks ago, and told her he was getting a divorce. You can probably guess the rest. He announced that he was going to move in with his lover, a man named Donald. Bear in mind, this is the brother she's always been so close to.''

Jane let her head sink back against the chair. "Poor Brian. I can just imagine how she took the news.''

"Damn right, poor Brian. You remember I told you she nearly drove over a friend of mine coming out of her condo on the night Ally died? I thought it was clear proof she had something to do with Ally's death because she lied to you and said she'd been home all night. Well, turns out she was on her way to the police station. Brother Brian and a friend of his had been downtown at a gay bar and there was a fight. Neither of them had anything to do with it, but the police hauled them in anyway. She was in such a state that night because he had called her to come right away and bail them out. This was a couple of nights before he told her about leaving his wife. I think she said she wondered at the time why he was at a gay bar, but apparently he made up some story about liking it there because of the cheap drinks. I don't think she bought it. Then a couple nights later he came over and told her the truth. They sat up all night talking. I think she just about disowned him. That's what she was so upset about the morning she came to visit you. It sounded like they had had a terribly intense discussion. Brian tried his best to tell her how he had felt his whole life trying to deny something so fundamental, and Susan responded by quoting the Bible and repeating her church's party line. I mean, I think she almost made the sign of the cross and forced him out the door. She gives the term *homophobia* new meaning. It sounded hideous.''

Jane shook her head. "Has she mellowed at all since the night he told her?''

"It doesn't sound like it. But the problem is, she really does love him. He's not some slimy, satanic, homosexual, child-molesting communist generality. He's a real human being she knows and admires. It's quite a problem for her. After that night, she was afraid she'd lost him forever. And yet she felt she couldn't apologize, since everything she'd said was the gospel truth. It's really eating her. *I* even felt sorry for her. Except that she kept talking about it. On and on. Back and forth between her rigid righteousness and the reality of a brother she loves very much. I thought she was going to drive me nuts. I mean, is there some reason why a grown woman should sound like a twelve-year-old? That woman needs a speech therapist! I even wondered at one point if this wasn't old Adolph's plan all along. Confine normal humans in a room with a bigot who sounds like a sixth grader, and what do you get? Brain death."

Jane sighed and smiled sadly. "So that's what she's been so preoccupied about. That's quite a story. I can still remember the night I told my dad."

Cordelia was sure she heard a sound coming from the other room. She pulled herself up and peered into the dining room. Nothing seemed to be amiss. "It must be the cat we're hearing," she said, lying back down.

"I expect you're probably right," said Jane reassuringly. She looked entirely too amused.

"What's so funny?" Cordelia looked down at herself, thinking she might have spilled something on her clothing. "I'm just going to ignore your tasteless behavior. I have some questions of my own, you know, about what happened on Saturday night. For instance. You said you knew Adolph was behind everything *before* you went out to the barn to get Maggie and Susan. How did you figure that out?"

"Simple reasoning," said Jane, brushing a piece of cat hair off her slacks. "I really only had one concrete clue, but it was enough. Except that I overlooked it until it was too late." She lifted her feet up onto the coffee table. "Remember that slip of paper we found in Mitch's wallet?"

"The one with Emily's address and phone number on it?"

"Right. If you remember, it was written on the back of one of Adolph's Bible study announcements."

"Yes, I remember you saying he always left a bunch of them next to the phone at the sorority and everyone used them for scratch paper. That's why you weren't surprised to find it in Mitch's wallet used for exactly that."

"But that was the key I almost missed! I remember the day Adolph tacked that up. It was the Friday *after* Thanksgiving. I read it over his shoulder as he was centering it under the menu. It was all about the Book of Revelation. The thing is, he was one day late putting it up that week because of the holiday. He usually posted it on Thursday morning, but he couldn't that week since the sorority was closed for Thanksgiving. He always picked up the flyers at the Bible study he attends on Wednesday night. So he no doubt had them on Thursday, he just couldn't post one until Friday. That's the clue I almost missed. Think about it. Mitch died Thursday night. Adolph didn't post it and leave the stack next to the phone until Friday morning. But Mitch was already dead by then. The only way he would have had access to them was—"

"He must have gone to Adolph's house on Thursday night! Brilliant. That was the only way he would have ever seen one. Adolph gave him Emily's address, and he grabbed what he was probably most used to using for scratch paper."

"Exactly. That was the proof I needed to tie someone to Mitch's murder. And I already had suspected Adolph. I felt certain that whoever was doing the blackmailing had to have been around last year."

"Why is that?"

"Because Allison knew who had done it. That meant she had either been blackmailed herself or knew someone who had. My guess was that *she* had been a victim. And I was right. Remember, we were only a little ways into fall term when she died. Almost certainly her experience with the blackmailer would have to have been last year. And that, I'm sorry to say, eliminated Susan Julian, since both she and I were new this year. So was Elliot."

"Who else did you suspect?"

"Really, I had so little to go on. Only my feelings. Gladys, the housekeeper, seemed unusually snoopy to me. Maggie even said she knew everything that happened in the house. Under the circumstances, I felt that was pretty suspicious. We only had her word about what went on that evening at the house after Brook went up to her room. I think there would have been time for Gladys to have done it. But what would have been her motivation to do the blackmailing in the first place? Maybe money. But that didn't seem enough."

"Revenge."

"What do you mean?"

"Revenge on all the snotty, spoiled little rich girls." Cordelia smiled a little too gleefully.

"I must say, I did think of that. I suppose people have been murdered for a lot less. I'm sure her frustration has built up over the years."

"Who else? This is fascinating."

"Well, of course Adolph. He also seemed unusually interested in everything that went on around the house. And he had a key that gave him access to the house at all hours. But once again, I didn't have any real motive. I never believed money was the main issue. Too many other crazy things were happening at the same time. And of course, then there was Mitch and Jamie. I thought they were strong possibilities, for obvious reasons, at least for Ally's death. But I didn't think the blackmail was a separate issue. I thought everything had to tie together."

"And Emily?"

"No. I guess I never really considered her. I couldn't believe she would want to hurt Allison."

"Maybe she was jealous?"

"If she was, and also happened to be the murdering type, she would have gotten rid of Mitch, not Ally. Granted Mitch did finally die, and I did wonder if perhaps Emily had not had something to do with that, but ultimately I felt it all must hang together. And more to the point, I don't think she *was* jealous. Frustrated maybe, even angry, but I think it was pretty clear that she and Ally loved each other and were planning a future together.''

"Who's left?"

"Well, one person I suspected quite strongly was Sigrid, believe it or not. She was smart, clever, had access to the house and I'm sure lots of secrets, and most importantly, I never felt I had a grip on what her real relationship with Allison was. And I couldn't read her very well. She's a hard person to figure.''

"Lucky Peter."

Jane looked away and made no comment.

"What about Brook?"

"Yes, I thought about that, too. I mean, we only had her word about the notes. It could have all been a lie to put us off the track. But her story did seem to be legitimate. I talked to Elliot about it privately, and he gave me the names of people who could confirm it.''

"You've forgotten one person. Brother Edwin."

Jane shook her head and smiled. "I suppose it was possible. I must say, I did have it in the back of my mind when I gave him directions to the lodge. But I don't think I ever seriously considered it. He had no real motive that I could see, and I guess I always had a sense that he was honest. He called me yesterday, by the way. First thing he said was that his father had finally cut him off financially.''

"Score one for Daddy," said Cordelia snidely.

"Actually, he sounded almost relieved. Apparently his December check had not arrived so he called his father's accountant. The man rather curtly suggested that Edwin look for a job.''

Cordelia began to laugh.

"Be nice, will you? Edwin will do just fine for himself. Oh, and it appears he did find Emily that weekend he was down. He talked her into returning with him up to a friend's house near St. Victor's. He said she seemed so tense and frightened he couldn't just leave her there all alone. She's been up north for several weeks, and he said she's just now beginning to talk through some of her feelings. He said he'd be bringing her back down for Christmas. She wants to spend it with her family if they can come to some sort of truce. If not, she may go back with him. I think they've become quite close, and I have no doubt he's helped her a great deal, if nothing else, then by listening. He and Ally were more alike than even *they* knew. I'm sure it must be like having a little part of Allison back again.''

They both sat silently listening to the grandfather clock strike twelve.

"The witching hour," said Jane. She rose and walked into the dining room, picking up the box and bringing it back with her into the living room. Very carefully she set it down on the coffee table in front of Cordelia.

"What have you got in there?" asked Cordelia, trying not to sound too curious.

"I stopped by Adolph's house earlier this afternoon."

"Oh great! This is some kind of joke, right? What is it? The collected works of Charles Manson? No, it feels too light for that. Maybe it's his private collection of fifteenth-century torture instruments used during the Spanish Inquisition for the glory of God."

"Just listen for a moment, will you? I wanted to see if I could get my diary back. I figured it must be somewhere among his things. Maybe I could even find Allison's diary to give to Emily."

Something began scratching at the sides of the box. Cordelia looked startled. "It's alive!" She moved a little further down the couch.

"Well, actually, yes it is."

"It's not some kind of rodent, is it?" She clutched her chest.

"No. No rodents. I guess I should just take it out and show you." She lifted off the cover. "Do you want to close your eyes?"

"Do I look like I've lost my mind? No. They will remain open, thank you." She glared at the box.

Jane reached inside and lifted out the largest striped tabby cat Cordelia had ever seen. She set it down on the floor stroking it for a moment before sitting back down. They both watched as the cat peered appraisingly around the room, stretching its long, rather rotund body. It turned its head slowly until it found Cordelia. Then, padding over to the couch, it leapt up and began a slow examination.

"He belonged to Adolph. Isn't he wonderful? His landlady was going to have him put to sleep. But, I mean, we can't have such a beautiful animal put to sleep, can we? I thought it might be a wonderful opportunity for Blanche to have a companion."

Cordelia leaned back farther and farther.

"See, I even think he likes you."

Out of the corner of her mouth Cordelia said stiffly, "Isn't it highly probable that a deranged man would have a deranged cat?"

"Oh, I don't think so," said Jane reassuringly.

"What's his name?" Cordelia and the cat were now nose to nose.

"You're going to love the name. I mean, maybe Adolph had a sense of humor after all."

Cordelia narrowed one eye as the cat stared down at her.

"I don't think he'll be any trouble. His name is Lucifer."

Coming soon to bookstores,

VITAL LIES

by Ellen Hart

The second book in the Jane Lawless series.
Published in paperback by Ballantine Books.
Read on for the opening chapters of VITAL LIES. . . .

1

Monday Morning, December 21, Winter Solstice

"Twin Cities Weekly," said a young man sitting behind a grimy reception desk. He held the phone precariously between his shoulder and ear as he unwrapped a sticky caramel roll.

"I'd like to speak with one of your staff reporters," said a soft voice.

"Just a minute." The sound of computers whirred in the background as the call was routed up to the third floor.

"Editorial. Can I help you?"

"Hello," said the caller. "I understand you're doing a feature article on The Fothergill Inn in Repentance River."

"Yes, that's right. We've heard it's a great place for a vacation."

"Yes, it is," agreed the voice. "But I have some information I doubt you were given. It's something you might want to include in your article."

"Oh? And what would that be?" The reporter leaned forward in her chair and looked out the window. From her vantage on the fifth floor she could see traffic backed up for blocks along Hennepin Avenue. It was all that new construction on the basketball arena. Just what Minneapolis needed. Another sports facility.

"Do you have a pencil?" asked the caller.

"I do."

"I assume you'll be telling your readership what a wonderful place the inn is for a little rest and relaxation. That will not be entirely true. Has anyone told you about the bomb scare that occurred there in early November?"

The reporter flipped open a notebook. "When was that? Can you give me an exact date?"

"The night of November the fourth. The entire house had to be evacuated. The police were called but found nothing. It was a highly distressing experience for the guests. I'm sure you can appreciate that."

"I can. Anything else?"

"Many things." The voice grew confidential. "A dead raccoon was found in a guest's bedroom. It was rotting. I'm sure I don't have to paint you a picture. Broken glass was scattered in the parking lot and caused a fair amount of damage to some tires. Several pieces of expensive leather luggage were slashed. And three days ago, cow manure fertilizer was scattered over the dining room floor before breakfast. All of this and much more is documented in the police reports if you want to check."

The reporter wrote quickly.

"If you care to follow the events of the next few days, you may have even more to add."

"How do you know that?"

The caller was silent.

"Who are you, anyway?"

"Let's just say I'm someone who doesn't want to see any of the guests hurt."

"Is that right?"

"If you don't believe what I've said, call Leigh Elstad. Or talk to Dale Freeman. He's the chief of police in Repentance River."

"I need your name," said the reporter. "Where can I contact you if we have more questions?"

"No names. Just this information. It's up to you to report the truth. I'm sure it will make an interesting addition to your story."

Damn straight, thought the reporter. "But what's behind it all? Who's doing it?"

236

"I don't know. I just know being at that inn right now isn't safe. Warn your readers."

The line clicked.

2

"What am I going to do with you?" asked Leigh, smiling down affectionately at her aunt.

"What do you mean?" said Violet. She knelt next to the Christmas tree and draped tinsel on the lower boughs.

"You have tinsel stuck to your sweater, in your hair, on your shoes. . . ."

Violet examined herself briefly, her smile sheepish. "Well, I guess you could say I take my work seriously. You better get busy yourself. We've got to finish decorating the parlor pronto. If we don't, we'll never be able to get everything done before the solstice gathering tonight."

For a moment, Leigh let her eyes travel around the large, richly decorated room. She loved looking at what she had created out of a huge, run-down Victorian house. She'd even received an award from The Minnesota Trust for Historic Preservation. It had come as a complete surprise and added to her sense of accomplishment.

"Get going," prodded Violet. "You need to straighten that star on top of the tree."

Leigh climbed a rickety stepladder she'd brought over from the barn. The stately Fothergill home had been rental property since the late thirties. Back in the fifties, her grandfather had rented it after his retirement from teaching. As a child, the lofty ceilings, spacious rooms, majestic fireplace, and intricate carvings had made a big impression. When she came up to look at it three years ago—shortly after her mother had died and left her a sizable inheritance—she knew exactly what she wanted to do. She'd been working in hotel management for seventeen years, learning the business from the bottom up. At the age of thirty-eight, opening this inn was a dream come true.

"I remember spending Christmas here once," said Leigh, cocking her head at the star. "I must have been about five. That was before Uncle Daniel quit college. I guess I always thought it was really great of Grandpa to let his son move back in. Especially with an infant daughter."

"Your grandfather loved children. Ruthie was his pride and joy."

"I know," groaned Leigh. "Ruthie keeps telling me that."

"Be nice to your cousin," frowned Violet. "Her life has not been easy. Now that she's living here at the inn, she really wants to be your friend."

Leigh didn't feel like another lecture on Cousin Ruthie. She decided to change the subject. "How long did Grandpa live here before he died? I can never remember."

"Almost ten years." Violet's voice grew wistful.

While they were speaking, a middle-aged man had entered the parlor, hastily stuffing papers into a briefcase. Physically, he was slight, with thin, clipped features and a small, shrewd mouth.

"Stephen! I thought you'd already left for work." Leigh climbed down the ladder and stopped as the man brushed a kiss across her cheek.

"Not yet." He approached the carved oak mantel and tossed his cigarette into the fire. "I wanted to remind you to have someone pick up the station wagon at the garage in town today. I'll be needing it tomorrow."

Stephen Laporte was dressed expensively in a black pinstripe suit. At his side was a hand-stitched Italian leather briefcase. His hair was slicked back, revealing a wide, intelligent forehead and piercing blue eyes. Turning from Leigh, he glanced at Violet, who was still kneeling next to the tree.

"Shall we wrap you in red ribbons and tell everyone you're part of the decorations?" He grinned, a mischievous glint in his eye. "Perhaps you could hang some of that tinsel over your ears. It's the only part of your anatomy that isn't covered."

Violet attempted a hurt look. "Just because I throw myself into my work, I've become the target of abuse."

Stephen laughed, turning back to Leigh. "Try to take it a little easy today, sweetheart."

"I'm fine," said Leigh. "Really. By the way, the solstice festivities officially begin at seven. I hope you won't have to work late."

Stephen's smile dimmed. "Don't worry. I won't be late." Turning briskly, he left the room.

Leigh felt like a nag. Yet it had been a pattern lately. Promises broken again and again. Stephen seemed angry and preoccupied about something. At times, it was almost as if he tried to pick fights. No doubt it had to do with his pending divorce, yet he never seemed to want to talk about it. He was under a lot of stress right now, and Leigh knew she had to be patient. If only they could get away for a few days. Spend some time alone together. But around the holidays, there was never enough time. Perhaps after Christmas they could drive up to the North Shore. Relax and unwind in front of a roaring fire with a bottle of Stephen's favorite . . .

Violet cleared her throat.

Leigh realized she had been staring into space.

"Work, remember? Plenty of time for pondering later."

Leigh nodded. "Yes ma'am."

Violet pulled a box of gold Christmas ornaments across the floor and began hooking them onto the lower branches. "Stephen doesn't seem very excited about the solstice gathering tonight."

Leigh sighed. "Unfortunately, that's pretty accurate. He's also not thrilled to have Winifred's coven here again. But since I'm so irresistible, he puts up with my quirks. Even my quirky friends."

"Is that right?" Violet arched an eyebrow.

"Is what right?" asked a plump, white-haired woman standing in the archway. Slowly, she jingled across the floor holding a small brown paper parcel in one hand. Her clothing, makeup and jewelry—gold and silver chains, bracelets, hand-made rings and other assorted pins—as well as her general aura, were more rococo than the parlor's ornate furnishings.

"Aunt Inga!" said Leigh, her voice delighted. "You have to see what we've done to the tree! Isn't it beautiful?" She put her arm around her aunt and drew her close.

Inga put a finger to her cheek and pretended serious consideration. "Yes. Definitely a masterpiece *à la* . . . who shall I say . . . Jackson Pollock?"

"Pollock?" Violet winced. "Surely not. What's that in your hand?" She pointed at the parcel her sister was holding.

Inga handed Leigh the package. "This just came in the mail, dear. I thought you might want to look at it right away."

"I'm such a sucker for presents," grinned Leigh. "Do you think I have to wait for Christmas Eve to open it?" Without waiting for a response, she began to unwrap the small parcel, slipping out a brightly colored red and gold paper box. Lifting it to her ear, she shook it gently.

"There's a note," said Inga, pointing to a small card inside the brown wrapping.

Leigh unfolded it and read out loud:

> "For a joyous solstice celebration!
> A traditional herb tea. Try some
> right now and see if you like it. If
> You do, perhaps you'll want to prepare
> it for your guests on Monday evening.
> See you soon.
>
> Jane Lawless

"How lovely," exclaimed Leigh, opening the box. Inside were dried leaves and roots, orange peel, and lemon verbena. It smelled wonderful. "Isn't that sweet of Jane? This is such a nice idea. What do you say we try a cup right now?" She handed the box to Inga. "Would you mind asking one of the kitchen staff to brew us a pot?"

Inga took the box and left, delicately sniffing the contents.

"You know," said Leigh after she had gone, "I don't

know what I'd do without you two. I'm so glad you agreed to move out here to the island.''

Violet plunked down on the floor and brushed off her sweater. ''Tempting us with that beautifully renovated gate-house didn't hurt. Inga and I have lived quietly in our little cottage in Repentance River for over forty years. It was time for a change.''

''What kind of joke is this!'' boomed a deep voice from the doorway. A short, stocky man with mounds of curly brown hair and a thick mustache entered the parlor. He was wearing a white chef's uniform and holding the box of herbs in front of him like an accusation. ''This is sick! Who gave you this?' he demanded, shaking the little box under Leigh's nose.

Leigh blinked uncomprehendingly. ''What's wrong, Burton?'' She offered him the note.

He grabbed it and studied it for a moment. ''Preposterous,'' he grunted, flinging it into a chair. ''Jane would never have sent you this.''

''What do you mean? Why?''

''It's pokeweed!''

''What?''

Burton brushed past her and tossed the entire box into the fire. Flames licked the fragile contents, turning it quickly to smoke and ash. ''I'm doing you a favor, Leigh. That is, unless you want everyone around here to have a bellyache the size of the Grand Canyon!''

Coming in '94
STAGE FRIGHT
by Ellen Hart
The third book in the Jane Lawless series.
Published in paperback by Ballantine Books.